The Patriot Game

GEORGE V. HIGGINS

The Patriot Game

 Alfred A. Knopf   New York   1982

THIS IS A BORZOI BOOK
PUBLISHED BY ALFRED A. KNOPF, INC.

Copyright © 1982 by George V. Higgins

All rights reserved under International and Pan-American
Copyright Conventions. Published in the United States by
Alfred A. Knopf, Inc., New York, and simultaneously in
Canada by Random House of Canada Limited, Toronto.
Distributed by Random House, Inc., New York.

Library of Congress Cataloging in Publication Data

Higgins, George V. [date]
The patriot game.
I. Title.
PS3558.I356P36   1982   813'.54   81-18655
ISBN 0-394-51672-9   AACR2

Manufactured in the United States of America
FIRST EDITION
BD 5-10-82 12.95 8.42

THE PATRIOT GAME

Come all you young rebels and list while I sing,
For the love of one's country is a terrible thing.
It banishes fear with the speed of a flame,
And it makes us all part of the Patriot Game.

My name is O'Hanlon and I'm just gone sixteen,
My home is in Monaghan where I was weaned.
I have learned all my life cruel England to blame,
And so I'm part of the Patriot Game

It's barely two years since I wandered away,
With a local battalion of the bold I.R.A.
I've read of our heros and wanted the same,
To play my own part in the Patriot Game.

This island of ours has for long been half-free,
Six counties are under John Bull's tyranny,
So I give up my boyhood to drill and to train,
To play my own part in the Patriot Game.

And now as I lie here my body all holes,
I think of those traitors who bargained and sold,
I wish that my rifle had given the same,
To those quislings who sold out the Patriot Game.

Irish Folk Song

The Patriot Game

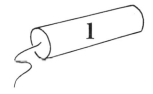

1

THREE CADDIES sat on the steps under the portico at the front entrance of the Nipmunk Country Club in Weston, Massachusetts, and watched the long, curving driveway bake in the late morning sun. There were fairways on both sides of the drive. Two women played on the fairway to the west and three women played on the fairway to the east. There were three Cadillac Sevilles—maroon, beige, black—in the parking lot adequate for two hundred cars in front of the brick steps and the pillared portico, and two Volvo station wagons, both green, next to them.

One of the caddies, thirteen years old, dug a crushproof box of Winstons, crushed, out of his right jeans pocket and lighted a badly bent cigarette with a Bic lighter. He was still in the process of learning to smoke, and did everything very elaborately. He released the first drag of smoke through his nose.

The caddie in the middle wore a Boston Red Sox cap and a bored expression. "Junior," he said to the caddie who was smoking, "you're an asshole." The third caddie received this information thoughtfully, remaining silent under his Caterpillar Tractor hat. He seemed to be thinking about it.

"I *have* an asshole," Junior said. "That's why I'm not full of shit like you, pugpuller." The third caddie accepted that information silently as well. He moved his feet up from the second step to the top step on the entrance and rested his forearms on his knees.

"You couldn't pull it if you wanted to, Junior," the caddie in the middle said. "It's so little that you couldn't get a grip on it."

"You got it all mixed up, Howard," the caddie said between drags and ostentatious expulsions of smoke. "The way it works is, you either got a big prick or a big mouth. We all know what you got, Howard. We can hear you all the time."

"You're the one that's got it all mixed up," Howard said. "I got brains enough, I don't smoke. You ever hear of lung cancer or something?"

"Yeah," Junior said, "I heard of it. I also heard about a guy that was caddying for Mrs. Blake on Monday, and she thought he was in the woods looking for her ball and she went looking for him because he was gone a long time and he was in the bushes looking for his balls and playing with himself. I heard she said something to Walter down the pro shop when she came in, and Walter hadda tell the kid he couldn't beat his meat when he was supposed to be working for Mrs. Blake. You hear that, Cody?" He leaned away from the pillar to look at the third caddie.

"No," the third caddie said. "I wasn't here this week." He did not shift his gaze.

"No," Junior said. "Yeah, that's right. I didn't see you."

"I was visiting my father," Cody said.

"Howard did it," Junior said. "Mrs. Blake caught him jerking off Monday and she told Walter. He tried to pretend it wasn't her or Howard, but it was just something he wanted to tell us about. We all knew it was Howard though. Right, Howard? We all knew it was you."

"Shut up, Junior," Howard said.

"Mrs. Blake," Junior said with relish, "Mrs. Blake was so pissed off about it she was still mad when she got in the clubhouse and she told Mrs. Tobin, and then Bishop Doherty comes in for lunch and Mrs. Tobin was having lunch with him and she told Bishop Doherty."

"I told you, Junior, shut up," Howard said.

"And Bishop Doherty got this look on his face like he does when he's out onna course with her or Mister Tobin or Father Clancy and somebody says *fuck* and then gets all embarrassed like he didn't know what the word means, and Bishop Doherty starts laughing and pretty soon Mrs. Tobin was, too, and Mrs. Blake heard them from where she was having her *lemonade* out on the patio and she knew what they were laughing about and she got all mad again and came in and started reading out Mrs. Tobin, and Bishop Doherty told her to shut up, there was no need to make a big deal out of a small matter. Which is how everybody knows, Howard, that you got a small one, because Mrs. Blake started laughing too and she said if it was what she thought it was, it wasn't big enough to do any damage with anyway."

Cody started laughing, very quietly.

"You shut up too, Cody," Howard said. His face was red. "I can beat up Junior and I can beat you up too if I have to."

"No," Cody said, looking at him and grinning, "no, you can't. You used to be able to beat me up, but I'm bigger now. And besides, you can't beat anybody up now, can you? Because if somebody gets mad at you now, Howard, all they got to do is say something about Mrs. Blake and you'll get all embarrassed like you are now."

"My parents aren't divorced," Howard said.

A light green Ford sedan entered the driveway and started toward the clubhouse. Junior raked the coal of the cigarette against the brick steps and threw the butt into the shrubbery.

"Mine," he said. "Saw it first."

"I know," Cody said to Howard. "Mine are, though."

"You didn't see it first," Howard said.

"I said it first," Junior said.

"Come on, you guys," Cody said, "Walter's got the list. He decides."

The Ford pulled into the parking lot and stopped next to the maroon Seville. All the windows were closed in the car.

"Doesn't matter," Howard said. "Cheap car. He'll have a cart. Too hot to play anyway."

The door opened on the Ford and the driver got out. He weighed about two hundred and forty pounds and there was no noticeable fat on him. He was about six feet four inches tall. He had black hair which was long, greasy and cut unevenly. He had thick black sideburns and an ill-kept Zapata mustache. He wore a tan twill shirt with epaulets and flapped pockets; it had long sleeves and he had rolled them back at the cuffs, exposing a stainless steel Rolex Submariner watch on his left wrist and a broad white scar that began on the back of his right hand and disappeared under the shirt midway up his forearm. He wore oversized Ray-Ban sunglasses. His pants were gray twill, held up with heavy green suspenders and a heavy brown belt. He wore Survivor boots, tan, with lug soles. On the left side of his body there was a holster snapped onto the belt. It carried, in the cross-draw position, a .357 Magnum Colt Python revolver. He reached into the car and brought out a gray Harris tweed jacket. He put it on and closed the door, locking it. He started toward the steps.

"*Jesus,*" Junior said. "Did you see that thing?"

"*Yeah,*" Howard said.

"This guy," Cody said thoughtfully, "didn't come out here for no golf, is what I think."

The driver walked with a slight lameness of his right knee, which required him to swivel his foot away from his body when he took a step. He reached the bottom of the steps where the boys sat and swung the right foot onto the first step. He got his left foot onto the step, planted it, and swung the

right foot again. There was sweat running down his face and
he needed a shave.

"Caddie, mister?" Junior said, somewhat insolently.

The driver looked at him from behind the sunglasses. "I
don't think so," he said. "I got it out of bed this morning, into
and out of the shower. I think I can make it up the stairs here,
things work right."

"Club's private," Junior said.

"So what?" the driver said.

"Members only," Junior said. "Just members."

"And their guests," Cody said, a trifle anxiously. "Guests
can play too."

"I didn't come to play," the driver said.

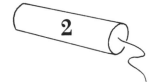

2

PETE RIORDAN, still wearing his sunglasses, walked through the foyer and down the main hall of the Nipmunk Country Club toward the French doors that opened onto the eighteenth green. He took a right at the doors and went into the bar, which was empty. He walked through the bar to the sliding glass doors that opened onto the patio shaded in part by the green-and-white-striped awning over the white, circular metal tables. Beyond the shade there were women in golf clothes drinking iced tea and iced coffee. They wore pink Lacoste shirts and Lily Pulitzer flowered skirts in lemon and lime colors. They wore lime Lacoste shirts and yellow divided skirts. They wore white sun visors with green plastic inserts over the eyes, and under those they wore blue sunglasses. Beyond them were low green boxes containing low green hedge plants, and beyond the boxes was the swimming pool where seven or eight children were pretending to have diving skills that they had not mastered. The children shouted a lot and jumped off the diving board feet first. They swam furiously for a while before getting out to stand at the edge of the pool and blow their noses with their fingers. Now and then a lucky one would catch one of the others clearing his nasal passages and elbow him into the pool. The women ignored all of this.

Pete Riordan sat down at a table near the sliding doors, under the awning, and folded his hands in his lap.

After several minutes, a young man in a white jacket and black trousers, carrying an oval aluminum tray, came through the glass doors. As he left the bar area he picked up a folding table and carried it in his right hand, balancing the tray aloft on his left. He went to the table farthest from Riordan and set up the tray table with one hand. He put the tray on it and started serving salads to the four ladies who were talking at the table. Riordan could not hear what they were saying, but they laughed a lot and he could hear that.

The waiter completed serving the women and started back toward the bar, leaving the table behind but carrying the tray in his left hand, like a discus. He saw Riordan when he got out of the sun. He stopped in his tracks. "Sir?" he said.

Riordan nodded.

"Can I help you with something, sir?" the waiter said.

"Screwdriver," Riordan said.

"I'm sorry, sir," the waiter said.

"Screwdriver," Riordan said pleasantly. "I'd like a screwdriver. On the rocks."

"Excuse me, sir," the waiter said. "Are you a member here?"

"No," Riordan said.

"Because," the waiter explained, "I've never seen you before." Riordan did not say anything. "I thought maybe you might've just joined," the waiter said.

"No," Riordan said.

The waiter cleared his throat. "Well, ah, you see, ah, sir, unless you're a member or a guest of a member, I can't serve you."

"I'm a guest of a member," Riordan said.

The waiter shifted his weight and held the oval aluminum tray with both hands in front of him like a large metal fig leaf.

"I'm sorry, sir," he said, firmly, "but I have to have the name of the guest."

"I'm the guest," Pete Riordan said. "You don't need my name. I'm right here."

"I mean the member," the waiter said, shifting his weight again and slapping the tray against his knees.

"Don't do that," Riordan said.

"What?" the waiter said.

"I'm sorry," Riordan said. "*Please* don't do that with the tray. I've got a headache."

"Oh," the waiter said. He stopped banging the tray.

"Doherty," Riordan said.

"Yessir," the waiter said. "See, that's just our rule here, Mister Doherty. They make us ask. Who's the member, please?"

"Look," Riordan said, "I had a bad night. You ever had a bad night, son? I had one. You want a bad night some time, you just call me up. You can have my next one, no charge. A screwdriver is a simple thing, right? It is some vodka and some orange juice and some ice cubes. A baby could make one. I could make one myself, probably, even in this condition, if it wasn't for the clanking of the ice cubes and I don't know where they are in this place anyway.

"Now," Riordan said, "I am not Doherty. I am the guest. Doherty is the member. I am meeting Doherty here. He doesn't know I'm meeting him here, but I'm meeting him here."

"Doherty," the waiter said, thinking.

"*Paul* Doherty?" Riordan said. "That ring a bell, maybe?"

The waiter shook his head and looked puzzled. "No, sir," he said, "and I've been here almost three years now. I think I know all the members."

"He's a priest," Riordan said.

"Ohh," the waiter said. "You mean Bishop Doherty?"

"Yeah," Riordan said. "Him. Paul Doherty. That's the guy. I'm meeting him here and he doesn't know it."

"Are you sure?" the waiter said.

"Oh, yeah," Riordan said, "I'm sure. I mean, I never saw the papers or anything, but he's a truth-telling man. Known him for years, never led me astray once. Told me himself, right to my face. Told me the Pope made him a bishop. I'm a skeptical sort of fellow, myself, but Paul Doherty's a trustworthy man. He says he's a bishop, you can bank on it. Why, it would've insulted him, I'd've said to him, 'Ah, come on, Paul, you aren't no bishop. You're just funnin' with me, huh? Tryin', bamboozle me?' Nah, Paul wouldn't do a thing like that, lie to an old friend like me."

"No," the waiter said, "it's not that. It's . . . you're not the sort of . . . Bishop Doherty meets lots of people here, but I never saw . . . I *know* he's a bishop and everything, but what I mean is . . ."

"*Aw* right," Riordan said. He unclasped his hands and put them on the arms of the chair. He extended his right leg straight out in front of him until there was a muffled grinding sound and a louder click. After the click he stood up, keeping the knee locked. He unbuttoned the Harris tweed sports coat, exposing the butt of the magnum.

"*Jesus*," the waiter said.

"Sand wedge," Riordan said, resting his weight on his left leg. "Very useful when you get yourself in a trap." He used his right hand to fish in his left inside jacket pocket. He brought out several airline ticket folders and slapped the collection down on the table. Keeping his right leg straight, he bent at the waist and shuffled through it until he found a black morocco credential case. He swept all the airline ticket folders into a pile and, using the stiff right leg as a pivot, spun to face the waiter. He flipped open the credential case as he did so. On the lower half there was a seal embossed in gold;

pinned next to it there was a small gold badge with blue lettering. In the upper half there was a picture of a clean-shaven man with a short haircut and no expression on his face, glued to a card that gave his name and department. "Justice," Riordan said. "Inspector General. Riordan. Okay?" He snapped the case shut.

The waiter immediately resumed looking at the gun. "What is that?" he said.

"My credentials," Riordan said. "Now can I have the screwdriver?"

"No," the waiter said, "*that.*" He released his right hand from the tray and pointed at the gun.

"Magnum," Riordan said. "Now, here is what you tell the guy to do. Take two shots vodka, six ounces juice, large glass, lots of ice, and pour them together, they play 'Stormy Weather,' and lightning shoots out of your ass." Riordan scooped up the airline folders, slapped the credentials on top, stuffed the whole collection into his jacket pocket, buttoned the jacket, ran his right hand down his right leg to the inside of the knee, bent at the knee, shoved against the inside of the knee joint, made the grinding and the clicking sound repeat, and sat down in the chair. He clasped his hands in his lap.

"Screwdriver," the waiter said.

"Screwdriver," Riordan said. "The way I told you. And if Bishop Doherty comes in the back door, like he never does, tell him Riordan's on the porch."

"Yessir," the waiter said.

"Oh," Riordan said, "and a pack of Luckies. Regular, old-fashioned, good-time Luckies."

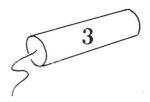

PAUL DOHERTY in a white Lacoste shirt, light blue cotton trousers and a floppy white hat over Foster Grant sunglasses drove a white golf cart up the eighteenth fairway at Nipmunk. About one hundred and eighty yards from the hole, he stopped the cart and got out. There was a clump of rhododendron bushes behind him, and he swatted flying ants away from his head as he took a three-iron out of the bag in the back of the cart. He looked toward the green and the patio, where Riordan sat, hidden from his view in the shade. He addressed the ball without settling himself into an easy position or wriggling his buttocks. He swung the club through and watched the ball's flight, using his right hand to provide additional sunshade. The ball landed and rolled to a stop about fifteen yards from the edge of the green. Doherty stuck the club into the bag, climbed into the cart and headed for the green.

He had a year to go before he turned fifty. His face was drawn under the golfing tan, and he had lost a lot of weight. There were slack folds of skin on his lower jaw. The collar of the golf shirt stood away from his shoulders and neck, exposing his scapula bones. There was a slack roll of flesh at his middle, and his pants were baggy on him. When he reached the ball, he stopped the cart, got out, took a pitching wedge from the bag and used it to slap the ball onto the green. The ball rolled well beyond the flag. He climbed back into the cart, stuck the club back into the bag, and drove around the green to the back. He got out of the cart, picked up the ball, dropped that into the bag with the clubs, got back into the cart and drove around the clubhouse to the right, down the hill toward the pro shop. He did not look at the patio. He parked the cart in the row outside the small white-shingled building that was the pro shop and lifted the bag of clubs out of it. The pro was standing in the doorway, leaning against the frame.

"Good round, Paul?" he said.

"No," Doherty said, "lousy round. It's a good thing a snake didn't come out of the woods and challenge me. I couldn't hit anything that was standing still today. I don't know how the hell I could've hit anything that was moving."

"They come, they go," the pro said. "It's still a nice outing."

"I guess so," Doherty said. "I keep telling myself that, anyway."

"You keep telling yourself to keep your head down?" the pro said.

"Oh," Doherty said, "sure. That, and lock the elbow. I know all the recipes. I tried to take up skiing about fifteen years ago, and to this very day I remember what the instructor said about bending the knees. I couldn't ski either."

"You've had some good rounds," the pro said.

"Walter," Doherty said, "when you're my age, any round you come back from's a good round." The pro began to laugh. "None of your damned hilarity, Walter," Doherty said. "You're in your thirties now, and you're like everybody else in that category. You shoot in the high seventies, the low eighties, and you make an honest dollar telling people how to do something that they're never going to be able to do because they haven't got your talent. If Nicklaus came along tomorrow afternoon and told you how to win the Masters, you wouldn't be able to do it even if he was telling you the God's honest truth. It's the same with your customers and it's the same with me. The bones're getting older and they weren't that obedient to begin with. You still think that you're immortal. You'll learn, my son, you'll learn. Some day, somebody like me'll be sprinkling Holy Water on a long metal box on canvas swings over a hole in the ground, and you will be in that box, headed for the hole. And up in Heaven every poor clumsy bastard like me'll be standing around yelling: 'Don't three-putt the hole, Walter, you dumb son of a bitch. Hole out, Walter, like we did. You gotta gimme there, Walter. You blow this one and the fat guys'll never play Nassau with you again.' Ashes and ashes, Walter, no matter how good you are at getting out of the rough. Remember, you heard it here first."

"You going to have a sandwich?" Walter said.

"Sure," Doherty said. "The choice's between having a bad cheeseburger here and going back to the rectory and having a bad cheeseburger there, with Mrs. Herlihy hovering around and complaining about her arthritis and then all the parishioners calling up to tell me they've got personal problems. Which always means they want me to get them a retroactive annulment, and also make sure it doesn't get into the paper, when they got four kids, minimum, and they just found out hubby's chasing ladies in some joint in Boston. Which cheeseburger would you take?"

"I would eat here," Walter said.

"Sure you would," Doherty said.

"See?" Walter said. "There're some things that're hopeless. Your swing. Nothing you can do about it. Go have your horseburger, Father, and God bless."

"Thanks," Doherty said.

"No thanks necessary," Walter said, turning back into the office. "Doesn't make any difference. You've still got a slice and there's not a damned thing in the world that I can do about it. You're a lousy golfer. I probably wouldn't be a very good priest. As long as you enjoy it, do it."

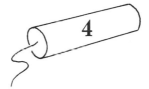

4

"PAUL," RIORDAN SAID from the shade as Bishop Doherty walked out into the sunlight of the patio, "if you don't mind me saying so, you looked like hell out there on the course." Doherty turned from the ladies who were trilling at him to join them, and squinted at Riordan's table. "Peter," he said, when his eyes adjusted to the light, "of course I don't mind. It wouldn't make any difference if I *did* mind. What in blazes are you doing here?"

"I am having a screwdriver," Riordan said. "At least I assume I am having a screwdriver. I *ordered* a screwdriver—I am sure of that. I'm not sure I convinced the guard dog in the white jacket that I should really be permitted to *have* a screwdriver, but when he gets through talking to his superiors, maybe it'll be all right. Siddown, all right? You look even worse up close in the shade than you did when you were out in the sun playing golf. Have you been sick or something?"

"You're enough to frighten small children yourself," Doherty said, sitting down. "If you don't mind me saying so, of course."

Riordan waved his left hand. "Don't mind at all," he said. "I knew that. I've been on the redeye special all night from LA, and before that I was having my usual preflight checkout in the bar. God, I hate flying. I hate all kinds of flying. I hated it when I was flying in little planes and jumping out of them

17

into the damned jungle, and I hated it when I was flying in helicopters and jumping out into the damned jungle. And I hate it now when there isn't even anybody where we land that's hiding in the bushes hoping to get a clean shot at my ass and all I have to worry about is whether they're going to let me keep my baggage with me or send it on to Omaha so I don't get too confident." Doherty had started laughing. "It's true, Paul," Riordan said. "Dammit all, it's true. There're just some things that any given human being cannot do and pretend he likes it, and flying is mine. I have to do it. I know I have to do it. But I still hate doing it. Every damned minute that I'm doing it, I hate it."

"What for this time?" Doherty said, still laughing. "My Lord, but it's a tonic to see you." The waiter brought a very large screwdriver and a pack of Luckies and set them before Riordan. "Ray," Doherty said to him, "this is my friend, Peter Riordan." He took the waiter by the right elbow. "Old and dear friend, Peter Riordan. Any time he comes here, the courtesy of the house. I know he doesn't look like much, but he is a friend of mine. And not only that, he is, as I'm sure you have noticed, *big*. Doesn't do to cross him."

The waiter was uncomfortable. "Yes, Your Excellency."

"*Excellency*," Riordan said, having consumed about a third of the drink, "my goodness. We are moving up in the world, aren't we?"

"Also," Doherty said to the waiter, "pay no attention to anything he says except when he orders a drink. He's very disrespectful and he's often insulting. I tolerate it because I'm charitable. You needn't. Okay?"

"Okay," the waiter said.

"You can bring me a vodka tonic," Doherty said, releasing the waiter.

"And another one of these little buggers for me," Riordan said, swallowing another third of the screwdriver. He said, "Ahh."

"Wow," Doherty said. "When did you start doing that?"

"Nothing to it," Riordan said. He belched softly. "Got the hang of it from an old buddy of mine in school when I was a freshman and he was instructing me in the sacred mysteries of bourbon."

"That must be where I went wrong," Doherty said. "All my school chums ever taught me were the sacred mysteries of the Sacred Mysteries."

"Probably is," Riordan said. He belched again. "No fun in that at all. Anyway, guy told me the way you avoid hangovers is by not stopping drinking, and I've followed his advice faithfully ever since. Especially when I've been flying all night, which means I have to get tanked up before I get on the plane and I can't sleep after I get on the plane, so I keep drinking on the plane and by the time I get on the ground again I feel like I had a dead cat in my mouth all night and somebody's fixing locomotives in my head. In addition to which, your beloved government makes me fly coach like all the other obstructionist bureaucrats, and I will tell you something, Paul: I am too big for coach. My legs're too long and there's too much of the rest of me, too. So by the time I get off, no matter how many times I stood up and walked around while we were in the air, I've got stiffness in the legs to go along with the stiffness in the head that I brought on myself because I hate flying."

"What were you doing in LA?" Doherty said as the waiter delivered the drinks he had ordered. Riordan finished his first and seized the second gratefully. "Run the tab," Doherty said to the waiter. "This could take awhile." The waiter nodded and left.

Riordan sipped from the second screwdriver. "Marvelous restorative," he said, setting the glass down. "IRA," he said.

"In Los Angeles?" Doherty said. "Did they move Ulster or something?"

"Oh, hell," Riordan said, "I don't know. They've been

getting very nervous about the thing all over the damned country and as soon as they get jittery they send for me. That kid from Listowel that I grabbed . . . You know how you can tell you're getting old?"

"I certainly do," Doherty said. "It's when you finally wake up and you've got a hose in your nose that you notice first. Then it's the tubes in your arms that draw your attention. Also the fact that you don't seem to be in your own bed, although of course I suspect that's a familiar discovery for the likes of you."

"No comment," Riordan said, "but you answered my first question anyway. I appreciate the courtesy. Tardy, but appreciated."

"Yeah," Doherty said. He toyed with his glass, making wet rings on the white metal table. "Well, I was sick." He looked up at Riordan. "When I woke up I couldn't remember anything. Where I was? Well of course I didn't know where I was. The last place I'd been where I knew where I was was on the seventeenth at Boca Palm, lying two on the fairway with about a hundred-and-twenty-five yarder to the pin on a par-five hole. I was playing the best round of golf I've probably ever played in my life. There was a very good chance that I could birdie the eighteenth and come in with a seventy-nine. I've never shot anything under eighty in my whole career. There've been a lot of rounds when I would've shot myself, perhaps, but this one was different. It was special. The woods clicked and the irons were true and I was putting like Ben Hogan before he got hurt. Astonishing. I wonder if the other systems of the body get wind of something going on before it happens and decide that maybe they'd better all get together and have one last fling before the door slams and it's all over. Funny. I've never played that way before and I almost certainly will never play that way again. If I do, and I catch myself doing it, I'm going to call for the EMT wagon and demand oxygen right off.

"Anyway," he said, "not knowing what was going on, the victim always being the last to know, I stood over the ball and got ready to hit the sweetest seven-iron I'd ever hit, and the next thing I knew I was waking up, connected to all that plumbing, no back in my nightshirt which I never wear, and the nurse was beaming at me and telling me I was awake. *That* I knew. What I wanted to know was why I was awake in some bed I'd never seen before, and where the devil the bed was. They answered all my questions. Especially the one that began with why. 'Coronary insufficiency,' they said. 'You had a heart attack.' "

"My turn to say 'Wow,' " Riordan said.

"Yeah," Doherty said. He sipped his drink. "And that was the pleasantest part. They had me on this and they had me on that. I was walking on treadmills with cuffs and things strapped to me. I had tests and tests and then they thought of some other tests that they omitted in the first round of tests, and they gave me those. They kept track of what went in and they kept track of what went out and how it looked. They gave me food that reminded me of the seminary. Which is no way to treat a sick man."

Riordan started laughing. He had a raucous laugh which interrupted the conversation that the ladies were having over their lunch and caused them to peer into the shade. He did not pay any attention to them and continued to laugh.

"It's true," Doherty said. "In the seminary they would sit us down too early to eat and somebody would start in praying over the awful chow that looked like it'd been left over from some disaster feeding station and probably caused the disaster in the first place. It was lukewarm when it got to the table. It was cold by the time the fellow doing the praying had finished his speech. Long-winded people, Pete, are attracted to the priesthood."

"I knew that," Riordan said.

"I'm sure you did," Doherty said. "Your memory's probably a little hazy now, but you can probably still remember what used to happen when you went to church and had to sit there and listen to one of us. Well, we got that training in the Sem, sitting over bad food until it was really cold. I wouldn't let my dog eat that food."

"You've still got the dog," Riordan said. "I always liked Bill."

"Not that dog," Doherty said. "Bill got old. Same thing that happened to me, happened to Bill, but he wasn't as fortunate. Apparently God's decided to take up hunting birds, and decided He needed my weimaraner. I don't know why He happened to choose Gangplank Bill. Bill wasn't a field dog. The only field Bill really knew was this place, and he never really did any hunting-dog sort of work, unless you count the time he spent with me in the woods, looking for a Titleist that'd gone exactly where my slice always sends them. He was good at sniffing and he kept the robins in line on the lawn, but other than that he was pretty much of a rectory type of dog. He wasn't any good at flushing birds out of cover. God works in mysterious ways, I guess."

"You get another one?" Riordan said.

"Oh, yeah," Doherty said. "Another dog, I mean. I thought about getting another weimaraner and I went to see some pups, but that was no good. Things end, Peter. They were nice dogs, very well formed, but none of them was Bill and there isn't any use pretending about something like that. Bill became an old man's dog without Bill or the old man really noticing, and then both of us took a good poke in the brisket but Bill didn't survive his. God was calling my attention to the facts, I suppose. I got an old man's dog. He even looks something like me, since I got sick and lost weight. English bulldog. Big jowls. Teeth don't fit right. Face's a little pushed in. Bowlegged. Big folds of skin on his back and shoulders. One ear flops. He's a little overweight and he looks at the world with considerable suspicion. Good Catholic, though. He often goes to church with me. Sits down and grunts on the carpet where the brides and grooms form up, which I have often felt like doing myself, especially when the happy families start firing flashcubes in my face. He peed on the font for the Holy Water one night when I went over to lock up, but that's forgivable, I suppose. I absolved him, anyway. He reads my breviary with me when the weather's good and I walk in the garden. He's good company, and he likes his rest."

"What'd you name him?" Riordan said.

"Name him?" Doherty said. "What the devil would you name a grumpy English bulldog?"

Riordan shrugged. "*Spike,* I suppose."

"Of course," Doherty said. "I named him *Spike.* I've been sick, perhaps, but I still have some sense of the fitness of things. Those things that I can come close to controlling, anyway."

"Things are getting out of hand, Paul?" Riordan said.

"I have that feeling," Doherty said. "Priests aren't supposed to feel that way, and it isn't really a thought worthy of the name, but yeah, I have that feeling. There's been a lot of trouble."

"Your brother?" Riordan said.

"Is that what it is?" Doherty said. "You came here because of Jerry? I thought you were after the IRA, and I was going to be able to enjoy this unexpected little get-together, listening to stories about the Provos. Don't tell me Digger Doherty's signed up with the rebels."

"So far as I know," Riordan said, "the Digger is not signed up with the IRA. That was something else, the IRA. They've got one of their bigger boys in roaming around all over the country, buying guns, and we don't even have a picture of him. Hell, we don't know what name he's using. That fool in

Washington sent me because nobody in LA knows me and everybody here does, and that didn't work either. What I came here for is this: The Digger knows a man named Magro."

"I thought Mikie-mike was in Walpole," Doherty said.

"He is," Riordan said. "He's doing life for that thing and he doesn't like it. Therefore, being a reasonable man, he is trying to get out."

"He blames Jerry for that," Doherty said, quite slowly.

"That's my recollection," Riordan said. He opened the pack of Luckies, removed one cigarette, tapped it down, put it to his mouth, lit it with a Bic lighter, turned his head to the left, spat a bit of tobacco on the patio, and inhaled deeply. "Magro's right, too."

"Those things'll kill you," Doherty said.

"Another on a long list of things that bore me," Riordan said. "Something will, no matter what I do. If I ever catch up to this mick guerrilla, he'll probably do it."

"Tell me this," Doherty said, "and never mind any pretty stuff about sources and that kind of thing you always use for camouflage, just how is Magro planning to get out? A life sentence is a long time."

"It's a little under fifteen years, if you make nice and don't stir up any ruckus," Riordan said. "Which is a little longer than the life sentences you've handed out to a lot of those brides and grooms that had hearing problems when you got to the part about death being the only thing that could part them."

"We're not going to get into doctrine here, Peter," Doherty said. "We're going to deal with the law and the prophets. Prophesy to me: How is Magro getting out? He's only been in about seven years and he didn't go in for running a stop sign. Is something going on?"

Riordan took another drink from the second screwdriver. "That's what I hear," he said.

"Is some money changing hands?" Doherty said. His face had reddened under the tan and his voice was rising.

"Calmness, Paul, calmness," Riordan said. "No use in disturbing the ladies and other people who have no interest in this conversation."

"Is it?" Doherty said.

"Your Excellency," Riordan said, "with all due respect and all that shit—you have lived in this picturesque Commonwealth all of your natural life. Here I am, a poor boy that was born and raised in scenic, affluent Weston and never had a whiff of corruption in his virginal nostrils—thought all the hoods were south of Attleboro and then discovered all manner of things going on. Not in Rhode Island, right here. And that was after I spent a long vacation serving my government in the winning of hearts and minds in the Republic of South Vietnam, getting no experience with real evil at all. So, you are the expert, and you interpret the meaning of things for my benefit. I am sitting here telling you that a gentleman known to you is by way of skipping on his lease at the Massachusetts Correctional Institution at Walpole. *Eight years early*, give or take a few months. You know what he needs to pull this off. You know where he has to go to get it. You tell me whether there is something funny going on."

"More to the point," Doherty said, "what is going to happen after he does it?"

"You tell me," Riordan said.

"He's going to kill Digger," Doherty said.

"Ahh," Riordan said, "I always knew it. Great minds work in the same circles."

"My turn again," Doherty said. "Wow. He's going to go for a pardon."

"That," Riordan said, "is what I hear. Can we have that waiter back again? I'm starting to feel better."

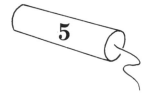

5

SEATS LOBIANCO said he was not sure that he could do what
Ticker Greenan wanted. "I know I took your call, for Chrissakes, Greenan," Seats said, hunching over the glass-topped
desk and cramming the handset of the receiver into the jowls
on the left side of his face. "You don't have to tell me that I
took the fuckin' call, for Chrissakes. I'm talking to you right
now. Why the hell wouldn't I take your goddamned call? I
don't owe you any money. Matter of fact, the only thing
outstanding between us is, you owe me lunch. When're we
gonna have lunch, Ticker, you buying and everything? You
owed me lunch since 'seventy-eight, for Chrissakes, I got you
tickets that playoff game they had with the Yankees. The fuck
you trying to do, huh? Outlive me, you can beat me out of a
lousy lunch? I know you're cheap, Ticker. I can get witnesses
that you are cheap. There're probably two or three dozen
guys right here in the building that had personal experience
with how cheap you are. You give me about an hour, for
Chrissake. I can get them all together in the Gardner Audi-
torium and we can have a fuckin' full-dress legislative hearing
on how cheap you are. No subpoenas or anything. Guys'll
show up for miles around, testify how cheap you are. 'Greenan?' they will say. 'Do I know Ticker Greenan? I sure do know
Ticker Greenan. Little shrimp of a guy he is, gets his suits

26

from the Good Will and his shoes off of guys that fell asleep
on the way to the Pine Street Inn for the fifty-cent bed but
they saw this empty doorway down on Dover Street before
they changed the name and they thought that looked pretty
comfortable. That's where Greenan gets his shoes, soon's the
warm weather starts again. Goes cruising up and down East
Berkeley Street, pretending that he's going through the
barrels, until he spots a pair he likes on some poor old bum's
feet that's sleeping, and he goes right up and takes them.
Cheap? Is Greenan cheap? He is so cheap that every year on
his anniversary he brings his wife home a loaf of bread that's
only one day old. The last time he had her out to dinner it was
when the tenement got too hot and they took their tuna fish
out and ate it in the yard under the clothesline. Yeah, Greenan
is cheap all right. He owed Seats a lunch for over two years
and he still didn't pay him and now he's back again, looking
for another favor, as usual.'

"I tell you what you do, Ticker," Seats said, "and this is it.
You meet me over the Colonnade in one hour and we will say
hello to Stradivarius there and he will give me a nice table
because he knows me and I have even given him a tip now
and then, which I tell you even though I know it is sure to
shock you, and we will sit down and have a bloody and then a
piece of fish or something, and while we are having lunch you
can try telling me again how come this fine upstanding citizen
that you know does not deserve to be in MCI Walpole and I
should do everything I can to get him out. And then I will
think about what you say in a much better frame of mind,
because I always get into a better mood when I have had my
lunch and somebody else is paying for it. Especially you,
Ticker. Especially you. Having lunch on you in my book
ranks right up there with taking that supersonic jet plane that
they got there to Paris and having lunch there at the top of the
Eiffel fuckin' Tower. One hour, Ticker. One fuckin' hour."

Seats, grinning, put the phone down. He clasped his hands behind his head and leaned far back in the blue leather chair. He put his feet on the glass-topped desk. He regarded the high shine on the Johnston & Murphy tasseled loafers with satisfaction, and beamed at the color pictures of his daughters and grandchildren beyond them. The walls of his office were painted light blue and crowded with plaques from the Holy Name Society and the Knights of Columbus. There were several pictures of him with Richard Cardinal Cushing and one personally autographed picture of John F. Kennedy. There was a long table, also glass-topped, against the wall to his right. In the center there was a photograph of his late wife. At the end nearest the desk, there was a Bearcat Scanner radio, its lights flashing sequentially but the volume turned down to the limit. Seats had received the radio in appreciation for his fundraising efforts on behalf of the drum and bugle corps of the Church of the Holy Sepulchre, which he had completely outfitted and sent to march in the inaugural parade of Lyndon B. Johnson. He did not listen to the radio.

"I can't stand the fuckin' noise," he explained. "Who the hell wants to listen to a buncha fuckin' cops yakking? It's the lights I like. All us wops love colored lights flashin' on and off like that. Fascinates us. You guys think we came over here to make money? You're crazy. It was all the lights. The Statue of Liberty? The first thing you see, you come here onna boat, is the Statue Liberty. Got lights on it. Right behind that you got New York, huh? *Millions* of lights. Some colored lights, some regular white lights, some lights that come on and just stay on, some that blink and some that flash. You think we're sending all that money back to Naples, we want all our gumbahs come over and get rich? Nah. 'Colored lights, Giovanni, you should see the colored lights. They got more lights here'n they know what the hell to do with. Save the money and come and see them. You save up enough, you come here and you work, pretty soon the two of us can open a restaurant and have our own sign with colored lights on it.' I never listen the fuckin' radio. I just turn it on. Makes me feel like my family made good in America and I got my very own restaurant with a buncha spades 'n' spics out back throwing food on the floor and robbing all my booze and not turning in the money from the checks. I want to hear a lot of goddamned *talk*, all I got to do is come the office inna morning. I don't have no choice about talk then. At least it's about something. Anybody comes in to see Seats, it's not four choice for the Celtics or six onna first base line for the Red Sox, it's about a judge or something, not just some dumb mick down on A Street had his car catch on fire or something.

"Alice," Seats said. He did not change his position at the desk. Alice did not move from her desk outside his office. "Yeah?" she said. "Alice," he asked, "what is going on that I don't know about that will stand up all of a sudden and whack me on the nose when I least expect it?"

Alice Vickery continued to read the *Herald American* while she answered. She had finished reading the *Globe* and had a Rona Jaffe novel which she had started reading the day before, as a backup to the papers. Alice did a lot of reading outside Lobianco's office in the summer. "I wasn't here," she said.

"Alice," Seats said, "you have been here for almost thirty years and you have never been here. You must have something wrong with your bowels or something."

"I was in the Ladies'," she said. "Diane was answering the phone."

"That's what I asked you," Lobianco said. "What is going on? Did Diane maybe tell you if anything was going on, while you were in there taking a goddamned bath or something?"

"No," Alice said.

"There was one message," Diane said from the room where

she sat with the other three secretaries, each of whom was reading a novel.

"Ahh," Lobianco said, "a bulletin from the fuckin' library. Don't tell me one of you broads actually went and picked up a telephone and wrote something down for a change."

"It was a guy named Riordan," Diane said.

"Good," Lobianco said. "Riordan. That tells me a lot. Was it Ways and Means Reardon from the House, maybe? Or Public Health Riordon from the Senate? Or Political Corruption Reardon from the DA? There's a hell of a lot of Ree-or-dans around, Diane. Which Riordan was it?"

"Dunno," Diane said. She snapped her gum. "He didn't say."

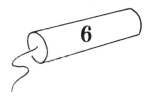

6

AT THE FOOT of the sloping driveway, behind the Cyclone fence with the reverse-curve top ten feet off the ground, the low white building with the main entrance sat flanked by guard towers. The exercise yard and the cellblocks were concealed behind it, but six more guard towers were visible, concrete buildings with mansard roofs and plate-glass windows and balconies near the top. Riordan pulled the green Ford up to the main gate and opened the window. The guard in a gray uniform came out of his house. "Yessir?" he said.

Riordan produced his credentials again. "Your business, sir?" the guard said.

"Superintendent," Riordan said.

"Is he expecting you, sir?" the guard said. He was a young man and a thin one. He had a discouraged expression.

"Yup," Riordan said, "called him this morning."

The guard stood in the sun and thought about that. He looked at the credentials again. "Something to do with a prisoner, sir?" he said.

"Yes," Riordan said, "something to do with a prisoner. Why the hell else would anybody come here, if it didn't have something to do with a prisoner, can you tell me?"

The guard looked thoughtful. "I'll call the office, sir," he said. The guard went back into his cubicle and shut the door behind him. Through the tinted glass, Riordan could see him pick up the phone and push buttons. The guard talked. He nodded. He put the phone back in its cradle and nodded at Riordan. He pushed a button. The main gate rolled open.

Riordan drove down the slope and parked in the visitors' lot, deserted except for his car in the afternoon sun. He got out of the car, removed the sports coat, took the credentials from his pocket, put the coat in the car and locked the doors. Swiveling the right leg, he walked up to the main entrance and opened it.

Inside it was cooler. There were two wooden benches to his left. In front of him there was a green barred door. Behind it there was a second, identical door. There was a desk behind a glass window to his right. It had a steel counter under it. There were three signs: ALL WEAPONS MUST BE CHECKED; VISITORS MUST IDENTIFY THEMSELVES; STATE NAME AND PURPOSE OF VISIT TO ATTENDANT. There was a sliding drawer under the glass and a speaking port about five feet off the brown linoleum floor in the center of the glass. Two guards sat on stools behind the glass, arguing about something. Riordan could not hear what they were saying. He rested his hands on the counter and rapped on the glass. The guard on the left interrupted the conversation and leaned forward. He spoke into a microphone. "Name, sir?" His voice was amplified, and carried through the room and the barred doors to Riordan's left.

Riordan spoke through the port. "Open the drawer," he said.

"Name, sir?" the guard said.

"Open the drawer," Riordan said. "My name's on this." He displayed the black morocco case. "I'll put this in there."

"I have to have your name, sir," the guard said.

"You're about to get it, if you'll open the drawer," Riordan said. "You think I'm going to climb into it, ride in and bite you?"

The guard glared through the glass. "Come on, come on," Riordan said, "open the drawer. I don't know if you've got all day, but I haven't." The drawer slid open. Riordan put the credentials into it. The drawer slid shut. The guard removed the credentials on the other side of the glass and looked at them. He leaned toward the microphone. "Shut up," Riordan said at once into the port. "I don't want my visit announced to the whole damned prison population. That's who I am. No damned need to treat me like the Duchess of Windsor at a goddamned cotillion. Put that back in the drawer and slide it back to me. I'll take it out and put something else in it that you'll want to keep until I come out."

The guard on the left looked puzzled. The guard on the right got off his stool abruptly. "Do what I tell you," Riordan said. "Have your partner call the Superintendent." The second guard told the guard at the mike that he was calling the Superintendent. "I read lips," Riordan said. "Glad to hear it. Now open the damned drawer and be quick about it." The drawer slid open with the credentials in it. Riordan took them and removed the magnum from its holster. He opened the cylinder and pushed the ejection rod to clear the chambers of the bullets. From his right front pocket he removed a trigger guard lock and snapped it onto the gun. He put the revolver, cylinder open, and the bullets, into the drawer. He spoke into the port. "You be damned careful with that thing," he said. "It was balanced when I came in here and it'd better be balanced when I get it back."

The guard at the mike opened the drawer and removed the magnum. He tagged it. He took a small brown envelope from a drawer under his desk and put the bullets in it. He put the magnum and the bullets in a pigeonhole behind him. The guard on the telephone hung up and nodded to the guard on the stool. The guard on the stool pushed a button.

The barred door to Riordan's left began to slide open. The guard who had used the telephone left the booth. Riordan walked toward the door. The guard came out of the booth as Riordan waited at the barred door. When it was open, Riordan went in and the guard patted him down. The barred door slid shut behind Riordan. The guard who had conducted the frisk opened the door to the booth and backed in. When it was shut, the second barred door in front of Riordan opened slowly.

The floor beyond the second door was steel. Riordan turned right, his boots making a clanking sound, and went to the Superintendent's office. He went in to the receptionist's area and shut the door behind him. He grinned at the short, dark-haired woman behind the desk. "Ruthie" he said, "does the boss really think I came to see *him*?"

She grinned back at him. "Oh, no, you don't, you fickle bastard," she said. "You start that line of stuff on me, and this time I really *will* tell my husband."

"Ruthie, Ruthie," Riordan said, "you hurt my feelings. Besides, Ben knows my intentions're honorable."

"I don't think he does, actually," she said. "*I* do, because you haven't got anything in your holster. But Ben's a suspicious man, and a crack shot, too. I don't think he trusts you."

"Jeez, Ruthie," Riordan said, "he did the night we had those guys holed up in the cellar in Uxbridge and I got this scar saving his life." He rolled up his right sleeve. "I did more for Ben that night'n I did for other guys the whole time I was in Nam."

"That's not the way Ben tells it," she said. "Ben says if it weren't for him and the other Staties, you wouldn't be drawing breath now, and it'd probably be just as well. You okay, Riordan? We haven't seen you since the Japs bombed Pearl Harbor, seems like."

"Well," Riordan said, "yeah, I guess so. I'm doing all right."

"You got a girl?" she said.

"Broads," Riordan said. "Broads always ask the same question. There's one thing you can't stand, it's the thought of some guy walking around with no responsibilities and no nagging."

"Well," Ruthie said, "there're some good things about responsibilities and nagging. You had a girl, you probably would've taken a bath today. And the chances are you would've gotten a decent haircut. Or you wouldn't've gotten yourself into the condition that you're obviously in."

"Now, now, Ruthie," Riordan said, "I'm in no condition to listen to stuff about the condition I'm in. Which I would have to do if I had a girl, I bet. Besides, you and I and the fellow behind the door've got work to do. Can't stand here all the day long, flirting. He in there?"

"He's in there," Ruthie said. "But, fair warning: he's got another guy with him."

"Dietz?" Riordan said. "I'm used to Dietz."

"Oh, sure," she said, "everybody is, now. Dietz's just like that, is all. All Assistant Superintendents're like that. No, this is a new one. Dietz brought him in here, about six months ago, and they go everywhere together, like Flopsy and Mopsy. If Dietz gets hungry, this guy Mayes eats a hot dog. God help us all if they ever find Cottontail and Peter."

"What the hell is Mayes?" Riordan said.

"Good question," Ruthie said. "Truth of the matter is, he was invented by the legislature, I think. He's a robot. Oh, Peter, you are going to *love* Mayes. He's the new man that's here to rehabilitate these seven-hundred-plus animals we've got waiting around for a chance to do something worse'n they did before. He's a piece of work, Peter. A day without him is like steak for breakfast and wine with dinner by candlelight."

"Uh-huh," Riordan said. "Counselor?"

"The very best," she said. "Just ask him. He'll make it plain to you, because he's not sure anybody else is bright enough to park a car straight. Even if you don't ask him, he will tell you. You know why a man commits rape and then kills and mutilates the victim?"

"No, as a matter of fact," Riordan said. "Unless it's because he's a madman and so she can't identify him later."

"See?" Ruthie said. "You don't know anything either. Nobody knows anything about anything except Mayes, and he knows everything about everything. Everything has deep-seated roots in the psyche, see? It's all very complicated. Mayes is the only one in the world who understands it."

"Grand," Riordan said. "What is he doing at this little gathering? I haven't raped and mutilated anybody lately. All I do is ask politely, and if I get turned down, well, you can't win 'em all. I don't take it personally."

"Maybe if you took a bath and got your hair cut, and that sort of thing," she said, "you wouldn't get turned down so often."

"No," he said, "I want my chums to love me for my mind, not my body. Can I see Walker now that you've prepped for this nitwit in there with him?"

"Sure," she said. "But I warn you, I'm going to go get a clean glass and listen through the wall." She pushed the intercom button.

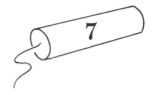

SEATS LOBIANCO left his office in the State House and walked through the cool, dimly lit corridors on the ground level. He exchanged greetings with Capitol police and men in mussed suits and his heels rapped smartly on the tiled floors. He went out through the door leading into the arcade and walked toward the parking lot. There was a guard sitting on a wooden stool in the shade at the end of the arcade. The guard wore a long-sleeved white shirt, dark blue uniform pants, a black tie and a uniform hat. He was smoking a Tiparillo and he was reading *Sports Illustrated.* "Donald," Seats said cheerfully, "a hot day like this and you got a necktie on still? Guys inna building took their fuckin' neckties off, for Christ sake, and we're supposed to have fuckin' air conditioning in there. What're you doing, for Christ sake?"

The guard lowered the magazine and looked at Seats. "Salvatore," he said, having inspected him, "you are a fine figure of a man, I must say. You got some whore lined up for nooners I assume, and then after the bump it's back to the grind, am I right?"

"Donald," Seats said, "there you are, movin' your lips, mostly lookin' at the pictures, it's summertime and the baseball teams got no cheerleaders, and so you go around accusing people like me of immoral behavior, and fucking, and things like that. Is this any way for a good family man like yourself to be acting, going around and impugning the integrity of all us public-spirited citizens? I assume you stole the magazine."

"Ways and Means Reardon left it in his car this morning," Donald said. "Gave me so much shit, I took it. Son of a bitch. Drives up here like he's some kind of goddamned emperor or something, stops inna middle of the street, goin' the wrong way, sits inna car with the ice goin' full blast and the windows up, waits till I get up and come down. He can see the lot's full, for Christ sake. This is a secret? The lot's full at eight-thirty? No shit, Ways and Means. You ever got here at eight-thirty, maybe you'd know, the lot's full at eight-fifteen, you guys start fucking around with everything. Park onna street and walk up, you fat shit. Might even lose some weight, which he could afford. Sits there in his fuckin' white Murr-kedees with the windows up, lookin' at all the citizens walkin' around, sweatin' their asses off, he's blockin' the driveway. Does that matter to him? Not him.

"I get through with the Governor and the Lieutenant Governor and the AG and the Auditor and the Treasurer and everything else," Donald said, "and then I come down here and I got cars backed up Somerset Street, cars backed up here, cars backed up on Cambridge Street? Shit, I probably had cars backed up in Fall River, all I know, and I see the white fuckin' Murrkedees and I go up to it and there is Ways and Means Reardon, readin' his fuckin' magazine. Like he's the only guy onna face the fuckin' earth. And I rap on the window, you know? It was anybody else, I use a brick, but this guy's a heavy hitter. He oughta get a punch inna mouth. He gets a polite question, all right?

"He don't even appreciate that," Donald said, his voice rising. "The son of a bitch. He looks up at me, like I woke him up when he was sleeping or something. I tell him," Donald said, rolling his right hand in a circular pattern, "roll downa fuckin' window. He looks at me. Through the tinted glass of course. Fuckin' car looks like a whorehouse with a wheel on each corner. I yell at him. 'Rolla fuckin' window down, Mister Chairman,' I say. You know what he does? He looks around and then he finally finds a button. This is *his* fuckin' car and he's inside it and I'm out here inna fuckin' *heat* and he's in there where it's nice and cool and he dunno where the fuckin' button is? Bullshit.

"He gets the fuckin' window down," Donald said, "and the son of a bitch looks at me. And he says, 'Yeah?' Like I was Cinderella and the glass fuckin' slipper didn't fit. The hell's he think I came from, for Christ sake? He lost a tooth and the fairy left me under his fuckin' *pillow*, for Christ sake?

"I don't get mad," Donald said. "I am mad, but I do not get mad. I could kill the fuckin' son of a bitch on less'n a minute's notice, but I don't get mad. I say to him, I say: 'Uh, Mister Chairman. You know, I hate to bother you and everything, but the traffic's pretty well screwed up here and, well, you're gonna have to move your car and everything. Okay?' And he looks at me. He looks at me like I was something he seen floatin' inna flush or something. 'I'm the chairman,' he says. 'There's a guy in my place.'

"Hey, Salvatore, all right?" Donald said. "How many chairmen I got? How many chairs are there inna Commonwealth? That's how many chairmen I got. Every asshole that can get his asshole onto a chair, he's a chairman and I am supposed to get him a parking space, inna lot. Where there is room enough for maybe two hundred fifty cars." He gestured toward the lot. "If I pack 'em in the aisles and also put maybe two or three in my pocket and the rest onna street and tell the cop, leave them alone. All right? I am a nice guy."

"You are a nice guy, Donald," Lobianco said.

"Exactly," the guard said.

"I know lots of guys who would say that," Lobianco said.

"Shove it up your ass, all right?" the guard said. "I know you, you fat guinea son of a bitch. Just because I save your place every day and make a whole bunch of fat-ass committee chairmen park onna street and walk up the hill and get all sweaty, you think you can give me a lotta goddamned shit and make me believe it? You think I'm stupid, you dumb fuckin' wop?"

Lobianco started laughing.

"Motherfucker," Donald said. "Anyway, the cocksucker looks at me like I was pigeon shit and I look at him and I say: 'Excuse me, Mister Chairman, but there isn't anybody who's got a space in this here yard. We take as many as we can. That's all.' And he starts to climb all over me. Called me a son of a bitch."

"*No*," Lobianco said. He did not bother to conceal his laughter.

"*Yes*," Donald said. "Ways and Means Reardon, that filthy little fat fucker that never bought a goddamned beer for anybody in his whole life, calling *me* a son of a bitch." He started laughing.

"Outrageous," Seats said.

"It is," Donald said, still laughing. "Here I am out here, sweating my ass off, and that miserable cocksucker comes around in his Murrkedees and starts giving me a whole lot of shit? It's not right."

"You're right, Donald," Seats said, "it is definitely not right."

"No," Donald said.

"What'd you do to him?" Seats said.

Donald recoiled on the stool. "Do? I am a public servant."

"Sorry," Seats said, "I forgot."

"I exist to serve the elected officials of the public in the Great and General Court," Donald said.

"Of course," Seats said.

"The Chairman of the Ways and Means Committee gave me a direct order to park his car and get things off his mind. So, I did. And I stole his magazine."

"What else did you do, if I may ask," Lobianco said.

"I didn't do anything else," Donald said. "I parked his car like he said."

"How does it look?" Lobianco said.

"Hey," Donald said, "this is a crowded lot."

"Taillights, huh?" Seats said.

"There was some problem with them," Donald said.

"Both of them?" Seats said.

"Hey," Donald said, "it's a crowded lot."

"Yup," Seats said. "Reardon got foglights on the Mercedes?"

"He did," Donald said. He laughed very loudly.

"Donald," Seats said, "I'm not sure I want to hear the answer, but how is my car?"

"The Electra?" Donald said. He stood up. "Very fine, sir. Right down in the usual spot. Shall I keep it open for you? Little lunch and so forth?"

"Yes," Lobianco said.

"Fine," Donald said. "Have the space waiting for you."

"Appreciate it," Lobianco said. "Hearing this after."

"I know," Donald said.

"Yup," Lobianco said. "Two more judges. Just a snap."

"Better you'n me," Donald said.

"Nope," Lobianco said. "Need some cash?"

"Tigers," Donald said.

"Not Sunday," Seats said. "Sunday's tough."

"Sunday," Donald said.

"Oh, Jesus," Seats said.

"Taillights?" Donald said.

"Sunday," Lobianco said.

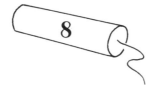

8

TICKER GREENAN bummed a ride to Copley Square with Lorraine Bedell from the Suffolk Franklin Savings Bank branch in Roslindale Square. Lorraine was the branch manager. She was a capable woman of forty-three who had been widowed four years earlier when her husband, Eugene, reached the age of forty-six and discovered once and for all that the doctors were not kidding about hypertension. Lorraine wore silk blouses which had more buttons on the front than she thought necessary, tailored suits which consisted of no more material than was absolutely necessary, and shoes that showed off her legs. Lorraine had many friends and several firm opinions, among them the certitude that Mel Parnell was a great left-handed pitcher for the Red Sox only when the game did not mean much.

"No, Ticker," she said when he called, "I do not happen to be driving in to the Colonnade Hotel today. I happen to be *riding* in to the Copley Plaza Hotel, where a friend of mine is taking me to lunch. He is sending his car for me. It's a very nice car, Ticker. It's a Lincoln Town Car, and it comes complete with a little man who wears a hat and sits up front and takes you where you want to go. Wonderful. He parks it, too. He does something with it, anyway. He goes away after he lets you off, and then he comes back when you have finished what you are doing and you want to go somewhere else. Everyone should have one.

"Yes, Ticker," she said, "as a matter of fact it is quite a large car. Very comfortable. It's bigger'n my house, as a matter of fact. But it's just a delightful way of going to the ballgame. I enjoy it.

"No, Ticker," she said, "I will not have the driver drop you off at the Colonnade on the way to the ballpark. In the first place, I am not going directly to the ballpark. In the second place, if I were going directly to the ballpark, I wouldn't be going anywhere near the Colonnade, you cheap bastard. I am going to the Copley Plaza. If you want to scrounge a ride with me, in exchange for a favor, I will drop you off at the hotel on my way to lunch. You're on your own when it comes to getting home. You could thumb, maybe.

"Now, Ticker," she said as the rose colored Lincoln pulled up at the Copley Plaza, "here is the bag." Greenan looked miserable. He wore a Haspel double-knit glen plaid suit and a white shirt and a clip-on bow tie, red. "Filene's Basement," he said.

"Wrong, Ticker," she said. "My gentleman friends don't give me marked-down crap from Eff-Bee. This is intimate apparel from Lord and Taylor, and it's on your way to the hotel. All you have to do is drop it off and get a merchandise credit for me. You can give it to me the next time you need a ride someplace."

"I wish you wouldn't make me do this," he said.

"Ticker," she said, "it's good for you. This is your constituent service that you're always bragging about. You're too cheap to keep a car and too weak to do without one, so you can take my see-through nighties back to Lord and Taylor and congratulate yourself on saving all that lovely money. Who're you beating out of lunch at the Colonnade, Ticker? Some poor bastard that doesn't know you?"

"No," he said, "Charlie Lobianco. Seats. And he's beating me."

"My God," she said, "no wonder you look so down in the mouth. You poor old skinflint, you. You must want something big, you're buying lunch."

"I guess I do," he said. "Seats seems to think so."

9

SUPERINTENDENT KENNETH WALKER was in his early fifties. He had gray hair cut very short over an angular face that was pallid. He wore a dark blue suit and a blue tie with white stripes on a light blue shirt. He had the beginnings of a gut, but he had been working on keeping firm. He sat at the head of a long oak table that needed varnish. There was one file folder in front of him. He did not get up when Riordan entered the office. He did not change his expression. He said: "Peter."

"Ken," Riordan said. Walker cocked his right eyebrow as the two men seated at his left and right stood up and faced Riordan, extending their right hands. Riordan responded the same way. "You know Oscar, here," Walker said nodding to his right. Riordan took Dietz's hand and shook it. "Oscar," Riordan said, "nice to see you again." Dietz was about thirty-five, wearing a blue-and-white cord suit, half-frame glasses, an open-collared blue shirt and a serious expression. He was smoking a bulldog briar pipe, which he removed from his mouth when he spoke.

"Peter," Dietz said. He looked at Riordan critically. "You're still abusing your health, I see."

"That's a common belief," Riordan said. "I've heard it

45

from many people who're going to need the embalmer before
I do."

Walker grinned. "And this," he said, "is Fred Mayes."

"Fred," Riordan said, extending his right hand over the
table. Mayes was about thirty-two. He was stocky. He had a
short brown beard. His hairline was receding at the forehead.
He wore a blue madras sports coat over a blue-and-white-
striped button-down shirt, with a green-and-blue-striped tie.
He did not smile. "You may call me *Doctor,*" he said.

"Oh?" Riordan said. "What of? Medicine?"

"Psychology," Mayes said.

"Fine," Riordan said. "And you, *Doctor,* may call me
Doctor."

Mayes said: "What of?"

"Philosophy," Riordan said.

"I obtained my doctorate from the University of California
at Berkeley," Mayes said. "I have published in many of the
leading journals."

"I obtained my doctorate from Brown University in Provi-
dence, Rhode Island," Riordan said. "I haven't published in
any of the leading journals, or even the second-rate journals,
because I've been out chasing thugs and learning about the
real world. Now, Doctor Mayes, are we gonna fuck around
here or are we gonna talk business, huh?"

Dietz had an expression of dismay on his face. Mayes was
turning red. Walker was grinning behind their backs. "I
didn't mean any insult, Peter," Mayes said.

"Doctor Riordan, to you," Riordan said. "I've got a question pending."

"I don't see any need to use foul language," Mayes said.

"I don't see any need to put up with your fucking airs and
graces, Doctor," Riordan said. "I asked you a goddamned
question. I came here to talk about a guy. I didn't come here
to swap résumés with you, you pompous asshole. We gonna
talk business or what?"

"This man Magro is an inmate of this institution," Mayes said.

"Right," Riordan said, "and they got lions and tigers in the goddamned circus. What other news you got for me today? You think I came waltzing out here for the exercise? I came out here because Magro is an inmate of this institution. Magro is an inmate because he was convicted of killing a guy. Somebody is getting set to let him out. I have got it on good authority that when he gets out, he is going to go and kill another guy. That concerns me, Doctor."

Walker stopped grinning. "Gentlemen," he said, "shall we sit down and have our conference?"

"Sure," Riordan said. He took the chair at the other end of the table. Dietz and Mayes sat down. Riordan pulled the Luckies out of his pocket and removed one cigarette from the pack. He commenced tapping it down. He looked around the office. He said: "Ken, is there any chance of getting Ruthie to bring an ashtray in here? I haven't got any cuffs on these pants, and besides, it makes my legs hot when the coals catch fire." Walker reached around behind him and punched the intercom button. Riordan lit the cigarette. Mayes's face was still red.

"Would you mind not smoking, please?" Mayes said.

"Yes," Riordan said, "very much so."

"The smoke irritates my sinuses," Mayes said.

"Good," Riordan said. "But enough about your sinuses, Doctor. Leave us chat about Mikie-mike Magro."

The buzzer sounded on the intercom, Walker reached back and pushed the button. "Ruthie," he said, "would you bring in an ashtray for this roughneck visiting us?" Her laugh was audible over the intercom. "Thank you," Walker said. He turned back to face the people at the table. "Pete," he said, ". . . oh . . . do I have to call you Doctor?"

"Nah," Riordan said. "We've known each other a long time, Ken. Call me Pete, like always."

"Thank you," Walker said. He opened the folder in front of him. "Tell you the truth, Pete, I know about as much about Magro as I do about seven hundred other guys in this little resort."

"In other words," Riordan said, "he's a vicious beast."

"He is not a vicious beast," Dietz said. "We go through this every time you come here, Riordan. He was convicted of a crime. He was not charged with being a vicious beast and he was not convicted of being a vicious beast. He is a human being who was convicted of a crime."

"And," Mayes said, "he has shown reliable indications of being rehabilitated."

"Sure," Riordan said. "That's how he plans to get out, bamboozling guys with stars in their eyes. I didn't say he was totally stupid. He wasn't convicted of that, either. He was convicted of murder one. He wasn't smart enough, or lucky enough, to get away with it, but now he's had some time to reflect on the whole matter, and he's figured out that he's got at least one babe in the woods —" Riordan stared at Mayes —"and possibly two—" Riordan stared at Dietz—"that he can deceive."

"Magro is not deceiving anybody," Mayes said, angrily.

"Of course he isn't," Riordan said. "Man who'd commit Murder One wouldn't lie to a guy that could maybe pave the way to getting him out. Never happen. Would you play Little Boy Blue to get out eight years early, even if it meant making a good Act of Contrition to the guys that could get you out? Of course not. You'd never do such a thing. Neither would Magro. He's a prince of a fellow. Blew a guy's head off and did it for money, of course, but nobody's perfect."

"I won't stand for this," Mayes said, standing up.

"Nobody asked you to, Fred," Walker said. "You can sit down for this, just like the rest of us." Mayes glanced at Walker and sat down. To Riordan, Walker said, "What makes you interested in this particular guest of ours, Pete? He do something federal? Because he's been boarding with us for quite a few years now, and he's only had two or three brief furloughs. If he did something while he was on vacation from here, he sure must be quick."

"Not that I know about," Riordan said. "And it doesn't matter a damn if he did something before he signed your register, because he's been in for over seven years, way I understand it, and almost all our statutes of limitations run out in five. No, it's not what he did before he came in, and I haven't heard of anything that'd give us jurisdiction while he was on furlough. There probably was something, but he got away with it if he did it. It's what I figure he'll do if he gets out for good."

"Just what is that?" Mayes said.

"All in good time, Doctor Mayes," Riordan said. "I could be wrong on this and I don't want to do a lot of talking about it until I'm pretty sure I'm right."

"Would you feel more comfortable if Doctor Mayes and I stepped out?" Dietz said.

"You overestimate yourself as usual, Oscar," Riordan said. "You don't have the talent to make me uncomfortable. Not by your lonesome and not with Mayes for reinforcements." Mayes and Dietz faces flushed immediately.

"Let's get on with it, shall we?" Walker said. "Whaddaya want, Pete?"

"Information," Riordan said. "First of all, how come a convicted killer, no crime of passion, knocks off an informer, gets caught with the gun, finally admits it was a contract job, is getting out? And on a pardon yet. Early release I can understand. But a pardon? Is the Commonwealth gonna pretend Dave Holby didn't get shot twice behind the left ear because he was getting ready to put on a one-man opera for the grand jury and take out some guys that were pretty important then and that're pretty important now? Doesn't make sense to me."

Mayes cleared his throat. "This is a new program, Doctor Riordan," he said. "One of the worst problems we have in crowded penal institutions like this is with the men doing long terms with no hope of an early release date. They're a continuing disciplinary problem. They flare up into violent reaction at the slightest provocation."

"Sure they do," Riordan said. "That's how they got their tickets in here. When they were out on the street, they flared up into violence at the slightest provocation, and killed somebody. What're you doing, admitting that you can't control these birds? You can't keep order in your own institution, which was built to keep guys like this from wandering around loose and shooting people any time it crosses their minds or somebody else offers them a commission to pull a trigger on some fellow that was making himself inconvenient?"

"Of course we're admitting that, Pete," Walker said. "We've got no threat with these men except Block Ten isolation. That's it. And a lot of them'd rather be in isolation when the weather gets hot. Gets them out of the shop. So that doesn't frighten them much either. We can't beat the shit out of them the way we used to, which I'm not saying we should've been doing but it did tend to calm a fellow down when he took a good drubbing that put him in the hospital for a couple weeks. And it kept his buddies docile for a month or so afterwards. We do that now and the word takes about twenty-four hours to hit the papers. Because the same judges that said we couldn't smack the lads around a little also said the lads've got a right to chat with the reporters. So then it's in the papers, and we barely finish reading the stories before there's lawyers in battalion strength banging on the gate and starting lawsuits, and every goddamned liberal legislator between here and Hartford's yelling his guts out about official brutality and what animals we are.

"No," Walker said, leaning back in the chair, "we can't control them. Not all the time anyway. Hell's bells, we've got them stacked like cordwood in here anyway. We're about two hundred bodies over capacity on any given day, and they don't like each other any better than they like us. You know what I do this time of year: I pray for thunderstorms. We get about a week of days as hot and muggy as this one, and I can virtually guarantee you, we're going to have trouble. And somehow I don't think the taxpayers'd be all that eager to pay for air-conditioning the shops and the cellblocks. Somehow I don't think I can put that one across with the Governor."

"So you see, Doctor Riordan," Mayes said, "the best we can do is try to encourage them to rehabilitate themselves by making them see that exemplary behavior, no fights and no attacks on guards, can have some effect on what happens to them, within a time frame that means something to them, one with sufficiently limited, foreshortened parameters within their conceptual grasp."

"Does he always talk like this, Ken?" Riordan said to Walker. "Do you have to sit through this kind of a performance every time you guys have a conference?"

"Doctor Riordan . . ." Mayes said.

"No," Riordan said, "I'm gonna talk for a while now before we all gag on our circumcised parameters and lose our own conceptual grasp. In the first place, I thought this rehabilitation giddiness for maximum security prisoners was something that went out with the Hudson Superjet and the Studebaker. If you think you can rehabilitate a contract killer, he is more than likely smart enough to figure it out. And if he isn't, his hearing is probably good enough so that when one of his buddies clues him in, he will see that you've got light cream in your veins and Cool Whip in your head, mush in your belly and stars in your eyes. And he will go back and lie down on his bunk, and instead of trying to figure out how he's gonna get his horn up the ass of that cute little eighteen-year-old bank robber that just got processed in, he is going to start thinking about how he can blow smoke up your ass instead."

"You concede my point, I take it, Doctor Riordan," Mayes said, smiling. "Homosexual rape is one of our biggest concerns in this institution. Of course we want to reduce it. This program isn't intended to prevent it entirely. Nothing can do that. But it's an ameliorative palliative for a very problematical situation, and to the extent that it does that, it is at least a qualified success. That's why we implemented it, and we are very encouraged by that result as well as a good many others. It is rehabilitative."

"It's bribery," Riordan said. "Call things by their right names, will you, for Christ sake? You're telling these lifers that they'll do at least fifteen unless they kiss your ass. But, if they'll be good little boys, with good table manners, eat all their porridge, and promise never, never, to do anything naughty again, you will let them go out and play in seven years or so. You think these guys with long bits to do're calling this little song and dance 'rehabilitation'? Is that really what you think? They're calling you a pushover, which you are, and they are losing any respect they might've had for authority. Which was damned little to start with or they wouldn't be in here, and you're waltzing around in the parameters of your little dream world, pretending you're converting sinners. Hogwash."

Mayes stood up, his face red and his jaw muscles working. Dietz, hurriedly taking the bulldog pipe out of the ashtray as Riordan stubbed his butt into it, stood up a split second later. "I don't have to tolerate this, Kenneth," he said to Walker. "If this is the sort of cooperation we can expect from the federal authorities, I for one am going to recommend that we terminate their privileges."

"What're you going to do to me, Doctor Mayes," Riordan said in a whining voice, "put me back doing hard labor? Or is it that I can't have any pudding for the next week and my allowance is cut off? Please sir, please, I didn't mean no harm."

"Okay, okay," Walker said, "I'll talk to you and Oscar later. Now just let's everybody calm down."

"Kenneth . . . " Dietz said.

Walker held up his left hand. "Later, Oscar," he said, "later." Mayes and Dietz left the room. "Well," Walker said, leaning forward, "I can't say I didn't expect it, and after Oscar, I assume, warned him, I told him what'd probably happen. But you say what you want about Mayes, keeping in mind that I've already said most of it, he is still one stubborn son of a bitch. You tell him he's walking into a straight right and he hunches up his shoulders and climbs through the ropes into the ring."

"Where, I assume, he gets hit with a straight right hand," Riordan said.

"Invariably," Walker said. "The guy . . . look, the guy's job was mandated by that same group of people that you always find reforming the prisons. They've never been in a prison in their lives, most of them. They've never had any contact with the poor mistreated men and women that they want to save for Jesus, or for happy, productive lives in the community. It doesn't matter what the justification is. They are doing good, and they don't give a good goddamn what the facts might happen to be. All a guy needs to do is make two or three speeches to those groups about how he found the Lord and was reborn while he was doing time, and they start to swoon with the joy of it all. They never even stop to think about how the guy got all that time to find his Saviour. Ahhh, it makes me sick.

"You put Mayes in front of one of those groups," Walker said, "and he comes on like an admiral at the budget hearings of the House Armed Services Committee. He has got charts and he has got graphs. He has got plastic overlays and sheets of statistics. He has two or three pet trusties that he brings with him and they do everything but cartwheels and handsprings for the crowd while Mayes tells about the structural dynamic of the rehabilitative environment, and how fine and inspiring the results of his programs have been. You get him in front of sixty ladies at the Acton Town Hall, the Rotary Club in Boxborough, or some legislative committee, and those folks can barely contain themselves when they see that their tax dollars are really being used to reclaim these unfortunate men, these victims of society, from a life of crime. They think he's great."

"Does he really believe all that shit that comes pouring out of him?" Riordan said.

"Sure," Walker said, "That's why he got so mad when you started needling him. And if he didn't believe it before he started going around and wowing the innocents, the reception he's gotten from them'd be enough to've convinced him by now. He's on Channel Two and he's a *Globe* profile and he does daytime talk shows on the radio—no night shows, though, because he got some rough handling when he started giving his spiel to the guys coming off the night shift driving cabs, or working down at the shipyard. Mayes doesn't like disrespect. He's not used to it. And since he's got a statutory appointment and the Governor loves his Commissioner of Corrections that's another dreamer, he'll probably never have to get used to it."

"He'll have to stay away from me to avoid it," Riordan said. "My God, what a shithead."

Walker laughed. "Ah, Pete," he said, "the guy drives *me* nuts, but that's to be expected, because I've been at this line of work for twenty-five years. Naturally I get pissed off when somebody like him comes along and tells me I've been doing everything all wrong. But I'm an antique. You're not. Your age, you should be taking his side. You're a throwback.

"See, what I have to keep remembering," Walker said, "is that my way wasn't very successful either. We had riots when I was just starting out and the weather got hot. We had fights with shivs in the chow line—they were over moonshine then, not pills and heroin, but the result was the same: A guy we had in our custody got killed by another guy we had in our custody. When Mayes starts preaching to me, I just sit there and listen as politely as I can, because if I start arguing with him, he can always ask me why my approach got such lousy results. And I haven't got an answer for him. So when he starts all that goofy talk about giving the men something to look forward to, I just try to scrape off all the bullshit and the fancy words he picked up in school and translate what's left. Maybe he can get us through the summer without me having to holler for the State Police and the National Guard armor. Maybe he can't. Maybe this thing, maybe nobody can run it. Maybe it just can't be done, and we'll end up admitting that we're doing exactly what we have been doing all this time without admitting it—when a guy gets convicted of doing something serious, nobody's figured out how to give him the proper outlook on life. So we will lock him up for a good long time with a bunch of other rats just as vicious as he is, and see if by the time he gets out he's lost interest in raising hell. Maybe he'll be too old to have the energy to do it again. Maybe he'll never get to be old because somebody'll throttle him with a piece of steel cable in the machine shop, or stick a screwdriver in his belly. Maybe he'll throw one gob too many of his own shit at the wrong guard some night, and get pounded to death in the corridor before anyone else can come and pull the guard off him. Just admit it. Come right out and say it. 'We don't like it, and we know it's no good, but then again, you're no good and we caught you at it, so we're going to put you in and if you're lucky you'll come out. If you aren't, you won't, but it's your life and you made the decision to take the chance on wasting a good chunk of it this way. You lost your bet. In you go.' "

"Yeah," Riordan said, "but Magro's apparently coming out again."

"It looks that way, Pete," Walker said. "Lemme put it this way: Nobody won't tell me for sure that he isn't, and that usually means he is. Why's it bother you? Guy's a short-hitting hood. That guy he took out, David Holby? When I got wind of Magro getting ready to check out of my little fantasy island here, I pulled his folder. Holby wasn't much, so far as I could tell. Oh, he was taking up singing, like you said, but the only guy he had a real chance of making, far as I could see, was some fence in Millis that handled mostly hot washing machines and television sets. The only thing the fence had going for him was that he did time down Cranston with some buddy of the boss, and he called up the guy and asked him for a favor and the guy was feeling generous and got it cleared.

"Hell, it'd been a big project, they wouldn't've put Magro on it. He was a thief. If he ever did any contract business before that, nobody was sure enough to put it in his file. He stole furs, and they couldn't prove that. He was just turning an extra dollar, doing a piece of work for a guy that might be able to bail him out in the future, getting a few points. Cripes, look at the mess he made of it. The guy came home in his own car at nine-thirty at night and drove it into his own garage. Magro's car's parked a hundred yards up the street, where of course none of the victim's small-town neighbors'd ever notice a strange car parked on a dead-end street in the bushes. The town cops'd already come by once and taken down the license number, while Magro was hiding in the guy's garage and the guy's dogs're raising hell in the yard. The cops ran that registration number through the computer and they had

Magro's name and home address before he ever pulled the trigger. There he is, waiting in the garage, the dogs yelling in the yard, the neighbors looking out from behind their curtains, the cops coming right back to where the car was, and the victim drives in the garage and Magro shoots him.

"This is a professional hit man?" Walker said. "This is a guy that couldn't spell *cat* unless you spotted him the *c* and the *a*. That victim wasn't on the floor of the garage before Magro was practically running out and jumping into the cops' arms. At least he showed a little sense then, four of them with their guns out. I'm surprised he didn't try an O.K. Corral thing with them. What the hell bothers you about this guy? He takes out another cheap crook, he'll probably get caught again, and even if he's gotten a little experience, so he can do it with some finesse and get away with it, he's still doing society a favor and making a dollar that'll keep him off welfare. What's got you so lathered up?"

"I know some things that're evidently not in that file of yours," Riordan said.

"You have my undivided attention," Walker said.

"This all goes back awhile," Riordan said, "and I was occupied with winning the hearts and minds of certain peasants in the more remote villages of South Vietnam when it went down."

"And also involved, I believe you told me," Walker said, "in picking up a few pieces of good old American shrapnel in your knee, courtesy of an artillery battery that was having a little trouble with its coordinates. Or its drug habits."

"What the hell," Riordan said, "anybody can make a mistake. Short round? Happens all the time. Kind of gives a man a little twinge or two when it happens, but it's better'n charging your ticket home on your own American Express card. That's a long ride over there, back here. Expensive."

"Well," Walker said, "like you said that night, I suppose

when you get the DSC and about your fourth Silver Star, what the hell, huh? You roll with the punches."

"You ever tell anybody I told you that," Riordan said, "and I will personally get out the tools of my old trade and jump out of a tree some night and teach you how to hold your breath a lot longer'n you think you can. I was drunk the night I told you that."

"More late-breaking news," Walker said. "Tell me about Magro. I don't care if it's totem-pole hearsay. And don't make any plans about jumping out of trees on anybody. You're finished, with all that scrap iron. First move you make, the noise'll give them time enough to get out of the way."

"The part about the furs is right," Riordan said. "Magro was a thief before he took up shooting, or at least before he got caught at it. He was much better at stealing."

"Who'd he work with?" Walker said.

"There is a fellow named Jerry Doherty," Riordan said. "Runs a tavern down in Dorchester. Big fat guy."

"I know the gentleman," Walker said. "We had him as a lodger here for a while, some years ago, if memory serves me correctly. Won the Mister Congeniality Award, or would've, if we gave one. A very beneficial influence among his peer group in the inmate population, as Mayes would say. He was always laughing and having a grand time for himself, never had a harsh word to say about anybody. Of course one or two of his fellow guests insulted him, but that soon stopped. Digger Doherty. I asked him how he managed to be so cheerful under these conditions, and why it was that even very tough guys who didn't like him, liked him. He grinned at me and said, 'Walker, I reason with them.'

"I told him he must be some reasoner. 'I am,' he said 'Oh, you'll get a guy now and then who doesn't want to listen, you know? Doesn't want to hear what the other guy's got to say. But if you catch him down by the garbage dock, you can generally change his mind for him. There was one guy that I hadda reason with *four times*. Not even he thought he was a reasonable man. But I convinced him. I am very good at convincing people, and when I get a really hard case, I call in some of my reasonable friends and we all reason with him, all at once. He comes around. I always tell a man that what goes around, comes around, and I never yet run into a guy that went around and didn't come around.'

"So I said to Digger," Walker said, " 'Digger, it sounds to me like maybe some of us in the administration could perhaps learn something about negotiating from you and your friends, and I wonder if maybe you'd be kind enough to invite us to your next meeting down by the garbage dock, so we could sort of look on and get some pointers about what we might be doing wrong.' And he started laughing like hell, and he said, 'Ah, actually, no, Mister Walker, I don't think so. See, that kind of reasoning goes best when it's completely private, just the guy that's being unreasonable and the guys that think he should do the right thing and be reasonable. If there was somebody else there, everybody doing all the reasoning would just get nervous, and that would probably fuck it up.' I told him that I understood."

"Boss con," Riordan said.

"They had their place," Walker said. "They had their uses, too. We used a few tough guys to maintain order, by giving them privileges to use and distribute, and they kept the other guys in line. It wasn't very different from what Mayes's doing now, except that he's eliminating the middleman. He's become the broker."

"Which means that instead of keeping the residents in line by bribing a few of the hard guys," Riordan said, "Mayes is offering to bribe everybody."

"It's more democratic," Walker said.

"It's less intelligent," Riordan said. "I doubt very much that any of these boyos in here now are very much afraid of Mayes. If he offered to meet them down by the garbage dock, they would laugh themselves into convulsions."

"Yup," Walker said. "You ever hear the phrase 'enough rope'?"

"Yup," Riordan said. "Good point. Anyway, Magro worked with Doherty and a crook named Marty Jay, who had an unfortunate accident in his car one night just south of Nashua. Seems he came out of a joint where he'd been romancing a girl singer, and the girl singer had a boyfriend who had some horsepower. Marty got in his Coupe de Ville and there was a very loud noise when he turned the key in the ignition. The car was totaled and so was Marty."

"*Sic transit gloria mundi,*" Walker said.

"Exactly," Riordan said. "Anyway, Jay set up a little visit to a fur store at Newton Corner one fine night, and Digger and Magro ramrodded the operation. Cut through a Cyclone fence and made off with the merchandise, as the saying goes, no one the wiser. Jay sold it and for a while, everybody was fat and sassy. It was a very neat job.

"The trouble was," Riordan said, "Doherty used a new guy named Harrington, who was moonlighting from his regular job down at the Edison plant and was not experienced in the ways of Digger's world. He was just hurting for money, which is a common complaint, and he took on a simple assignment without thinking that it would make his tummy upset."

"It did make his tummy upset," Walker said.

"I guess so," Riordan said. "Now, keeping in mind that I don't know this for sure, I gather Harrington got the jitters after he took his cut. There was a lot of heat on after that little adventure. And the cops had a fairly reliable idea that Doherty was involved in it. Along with Magro. When they started out, they didn't know much about Harrington. Shit, they knew nothing about Harrington. They didn't know he was on the earth. But, like I said, he was a rookie. And he was an old rookie. And he was a good family man. But he didn't know where to keep his mouth shut and where he could talk, and pretty soon the cops found out he had a habit of having a few pops down at Digger's bar, and he was also a little richer'n he had been. So they started asking a few questions.

"Harrington panicked," Riordan said. "He got all scared and hysterical, and he went looking for reassurance. And who did he pick?"

"Not the Digger, I hope," Walker said.

"Right," Riordan said, "the Digger. Who reassured him and then went out of town in time to enjoy some sun with his lovely wife and family in the Caribbean, or someplace like that. But Harrington wasn't reassured, or else the Digger started getting the vapors, because about two days before Doherty got back, Harrington bought the ranch."

"Figures," Walker said.

" 'Course," Riordan said, "Doherty reasons with people, and they always see his point of view. They may be in no condition to talk about it, but for at least an instant, they see it. Even if it's only a muzzle flash.

"You know how we cops are," Riordan said. "We're a little dense, a lot of the time, but if you put a couple angry owls in the shower with us, we will soon figure out that something a little out of the ordinary is under way. The cops'd been investigating Harrington, and they could see that Harrington was becoming very nervous. Then the cops get a call one fine night that maybe they would like to have a look inside the trunk of this tan Chevy Caprice that'd been parked a few days down at the bus-commuter lot at the HoJo's in the Blue Hills. So they went down there and they took the pry-bar and opened up the trunk, and there was Brother Harrington inside the trunk of his own car, all cuddled up in his blankie, looking for all the world like he was having a nice nap. Except he was pretty ripe. And besides, how did he get himself locked inside his own trunk? They decided he was dead. The medical examiner thought he knew what brought this on. Had something to do with firearms.

"So now the cops're really interested in Digger, on account of they thought maybe he might've had some interest in this. Or at least he would want to know promptly about the untimely passing of his regular customer, Brother Harrington. Pay his respects to the family, you know? So they hustled a couple cars right over to the Bright Red in Dorchester and they got there just as Digger was inviting the bitter-enders to leave. They went inside and all of a sudden the Digger wasn't having a bit of trouble persuading his loyal patrons to pay up and get out—they were practically jumping out the windows, they were in such a hurry. And Digger thanks the cops very much for coming by and helping him remain a law-abiding saloonkeeper that faithfully observes the closing hours, and says if it is all right with them, he will turn off the lights and lock up and be on his way home to bed.

"They told him that could probably wait a minute or two," Riordan said. "They said they would like to have a little conversation. So he locked up all the booze and offers the cops a Coke, which they took, and they all sat down at one of the tables. The cops asked the Digger if he knew Harrington. 'Harrington?' Digger said, or words to that effect. 'I run a bar in Dorchester and you're asking me if I know Harrington? Of course I know Harrington. There is Harrington, the fish market. There is Harrington, the tire store. There is Harrington that drives the bus. There is that beezer Harrington that works the electric plant, and there is . . . ' And the cops said, 'It is Harrington the beezer at the light plant that we came to see you about. He is dead.'

"Now," Riordan said, "the cops expected Digger to be surprised. From what I understand, there is a very high mortality rate among middle-aged men that the Digger knows. Back when he was having a little trouble with some of the gentlemen down at Neponset Circle, the Digger's friends and the gentlemen from Neponset were dropping like flies. It was getting so you couldn't take a nice evening stroll down by the beach at Wollaston without meeting up with one of those guys floating face down in a tidal creek. Digger has spent a lot of time in mourning, but he is still always very surprised to hear that somebody else has gone to meet Jesus face to face.

"The thing of it is," Riordan said, "the cop who was telling me this, guy named Petrucelli, was there that night, and he said Digger looked as though he really was surprised. 'Now this guy,' Petrucelli said, 'he is better'n Barrymore, and I've seen several of his performances, but I really think when we told him about Harrington, he really was surprised. Usually when you brought him the sad news, he would look all sad and discouraged and ask you if it was a heart attack. But this time, he didn't go through that routine. He just sat there staring at us, and finally he said, "Son of a bitch." No jazz about a shock or was the guy sick a long time, or any of that razzle-dazzle ball-handling bullshit. "No shit," he said. And he was shaking his head.'

"What Petrucelli thinks," Riordan said to Walker in the warden's office, "was that Digger had every intention of knocking Harrington off. Do it himself, get somebody else to do it, but he was going to get it done. Digger knows everything that's going on, and if he doesn't know about it, it isn't usually going on. And here was obviously something that he didn't know'd been going on, and the most humiliating part of it was that he had to find it out from the cops, of all people. 'I think he was not only surprised,' Petrucelli said, 'I think he was embarrassed. And he was also worried. Digger Doherty likes to have things under control, and here was somebody taking out one of his guys without asking him. That's not neat. Means trouble. You could almost hear the gears changing in his head. But for once, just that once, I really don't think he knew who beat him to the punch and saved him the trouble with Harrington.'

"Well," Riordan said, "the cops packed up and left, and Digger was still sitting there at his table, big fat guy in a white shirt, sitting there in his own saloon at three in the morning with one light on, shaking his head. And for the next couple of weeks that neighborhood had more buzzing goin' on'n you'll generally get in a beehive. And *nothing came out of it.* Nothing. As far as anybody knew, Digger'd been Harrington's only moonlight employer. Digger couldn't find out who the hell'd knocked him off, and it was driving him nuts. The cops couldn't find out who knocked him off, but it really wasn't bothering them—they were having too much fun watching Digger go snuffling around like some big fat hog in a pen, trying to find some fresh swill, and getting more and more frustrated.

"Then after a while," Riordan said, "Digger began to lose interest, and he pretty much gave up the investigation he was conducting on his own. The cops didn't like that a bit— destroyed their entertainment. 'So,' Petrucelli said, 'we kind of let it be known on the street that we were pretty close to cracking the Harrington thing. Got everybody all stirred up again, and after they stewed in their own juice for about a week, it was picture-taking time again. Run all the boys in, new mug shots front and side, case they changed their hairdressers or grew mustaches or something. Didn't even question them or anything. Even let a couple guys go that had some small stuff in their cars when we stopped them. They'd ask us what we wanted, must've been about thirty of them, and all we'd tell them was we thought we might have a witness to something fairly big but the witness wasn't sure about the pictures in the books so we thought we'd take some new ones.'

" 'And we did something else,' Petrucelli said, 'that was really mean. I must say, even I was impressed. We grabbed

Digger and brought him in, and Magro was standing right next to Doherty when we picked him up. But we didn't pick up Magro. He was practically begging us to take him in, and we wouldn't do it. So now all the boys know that we've got a witness who doesn't recognize any of the boys on sight, which means that somebody who does recognize the boys must've tipped us to the witness, and who is the one guy that we don't haul in? Magro.' "

"Ahh," Walker said to Riordan, "that is cute. Old, but cute. Done it myself now and then, but you can't pull it too often, they catch on."

"Digger and his boys didn't," Riordan said. "So all of a sudden Magro is in the shit up to his earlobes and thinking seriously about dialing nine-eleven and asking for emergency police protection. And that is when the call came through to Magro from down south of the line there, that a fellow who was maybe in a little trouble with his buddies might think about doing a favor for the boss. Show his heart was in the right place, you know? So that's why Magro knocked off Holby in a hurry and made a mess of it. He had to do it then, or somebody was going to do something to him. Guy was desperate."

"Which leaves Harrington," Walker said. "Who did that?"

"Ahh," Riordan said, "we'll never know. Some volunteer, probably. Goes out to do Digger a favor, come back and brag about it later, be a big man with a bigger man. Probably some tough young kid we never heard of, yet. Looking to make his bones. Then the shit hit the fan, and he was smart enough to keep quiet. Thing of it is, Magro's in here doing a long bit, and he thinks it's Digger's fault. So I think I know what he's going to do when he gets out, only this time he'll plan a little better."

"What do you care?" Walker said. "Nothing but another thug."

"Kenneth," Riordan said reproachfully, "I am a government agent. I am sworn to uphold the Constitution and the laws of the United States. Jeremiah Doherty is an American citizen, and he cannot be deprived of his life or property without due process of law. I don't think Magro's going to be too keen on due process for the Digger, if he gets out."

"What's the real reason?" Walker said.

"You ever been in the Bright Red?" Riordan said.

"Can't say as I have," Walker said. "Little outside my regular rounds."

"I have," Riordan said. "I have been in there once. I got made within forty minutes. I was sitting at the bar, having a dog, onions, mustard, Labatt's ale, some chips, and I was watching the ballgame. And every so often I would sort of glance around and see all these little white fund-raising canisters. The kind you drop quarters in? For Little League and the softball team and poor Flynnie the fireman that fell off the ladder practicing on a three-decker up in Savin Hill? Now Ken, I am used to seeing quarters go into those things. Sometimes two quarters at a time, if Flynnie was a real good guy and him and Frances had about three hundred kids and she can't work on account of that mastoid thing she's got. I am used to that. But there are bills, American currency, going into those canisters, and this is not a wealthy crowd. In addition to which, there are no labels on those canisters. Not even any Magic Marker writing. So if you look at them, you don't know where your hard-earned dollars're going."

"Unless, of course," Walker said, "you do know where those hard-earned dollars're going."

"That's what I was thinking," Riordan said. "That's what I was thinking when all of a sudden I noticed a mean-looking guy across on the other side of the room and he was looking at me real hard. He said something to the guy who was having refreshments with him, and that guy said something to the next guy, and pretty soon the only voice in the saloon was the announcer on the ballgame. So I decided I was right, and I do know where those hard-earned dollars are going. I got up and I paid my money and I left."

"Gunrunning," Walker said. "A little noisemaker or two for some people up in Ulster and Connaught who resent the British soldiers in their midst."

"That is what I thought," Riordan said. "And I also think that if I get time enough, sooner or later the Digger will show me where those party favors are. Unless the guys I am running around trying to find all over the damned country because my asshole boss in Washington decided I can catch unicorns if he decides that he wants unicorns, unless those guys come out of the bushes some night and knock me off. Which could happen."

"So," Walker said, "Mister Magro's release could complicate your life."

"Indeed," Riordan said.

"Well," Walker said, "I'm not sure this'll do any good, but it's all I can do. You can put me down as opposed to commutation or pardon, on the grounds of the seriousness of Magro's offense."

"How about Frick and Frack there," Riordan said. "Any trouble with them?"

"Right now, yes," Walker said. "Next week, no. Mayes wants me to let a nasty little bastard out for this weekend, even though I know the shifty little rat's gonna run for the woods the minute he gets outside the gate. I was gonna fight it tooth and nail. Now I think I'll just record my opposition, for the record, and cite Doctor Mayes's confidence in the man's rehabilitation. That should keep Doctor Mayes's plate full for the next six months or so, when the papers get ahold of that one."

Riordan stood up. "Always a pleasure to talk to you, Kenneth," he said.

"Mine too, Peter," Walker said, "mine too. Except generally, I'm the only one I do have to talk to."

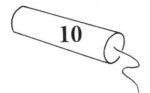

10

"So," Seats said, as Greenan walked in with the Lord & Taylor bag, "here is Greenan, late as usual. And he is carrying a bag. This is probably a large amount of money that a guy gave him in a hotel room at the Sheraton and told him he was some fuckin' A-rab or something, and Ticker would be rich if he did what the guy wanted, and the guy was from the Eff-bee-eye and somebody inna next room was probably takin' pictures the whole thing. You wanna be careful, Ticker, is what I think. Sooner, later, you're gonna find out the grand jury is mentioning your name a lot and you have got serious problems down Post Office Square there. Which is the next stop before Leavenworth."

"It's not money in this bag," Greenan said sullenly. He gripped it tightly at his side and came to the table.

"There you go again, Greenan," Seats said. "It's probably drugs or some goddamned thing you started selling. You know what they're gonna do in honor of you? They are gonna reopen Alcatraz and put you out there all by yourself with the fuckin' gooney birds and all them other animals that shit all over everything. And you will probably feel right at home, you are such an asshole."

"Quit goosing me, all right?" Greenan said.

Lobianco snatched the bag out of Greenan's hand. "I got to see what's in this, Ticker," he said. "You keep a sharp eye on things here, Francis," Seats said to the maitre d'. "Somebody comes in here with some indictments or something, I want support that I was merely doing my duty as a law-abiding citizen and everything."

"You son of a bitch," Greenan said, grabbing for the bag.

"Uh-uh," Lobianco said, holding the bag away from Greenan's grasp. "You got this here bag with the Lord and Taylor thing on it, and I wanna know what's in it, before I let you sit down at my table and end up getting the next room at Alcatraz. Man's got to look out for himself in this world, and that is all I am doing." He opened the bag. He removed a beige shorty nightgown, decorated with lace at the bodice. He held it up by the straps and admired it. "This is very *nice*, Ticker," he said. "I think it'll be quite attractive on you." He tossed the nightgown to Greenan, whose face was red. "Here you go, Ticker," Lobianco said, "why'ncha model it for us? Jesus, all these years I known you, I didn't know you liked to dress up. Lemme see what else we got in this here Lord and Taylor bag. Cripes, you shop the fancy stores, huh?" Lobianco rummaged in the bag. Greenan rolled up the nightgown and put it in his jacket pocket. "*Panties*," Lobianco said. He held up the beige panties with the decorative lace. "Bikini panties for Christ sake, Ticker. Oh, you're gonna be a knockout in these, huh?" Lobianco waved the panties around. The other patrons looked up from their lunches and grinned. He held them up to the light from the windows. He squinted at them. "Although come to think of it, Ticker, I would think these might be a little snug on you. You ain't fat, exactly, but you're carrying a little more baggage inna trunk than you used to. You sure you can get these on and feel comfy and everything?"

Greenan grabbed the panties away from Lobianco and

stuffed them in his jacket pocket with the nightgown. "They're not mine," he said.

"Oh ho," Lobianco said, tossing him the paper bag, "you got something going on the side, huh, Ticker? Wait till Mrs. Ticker finds out about this, you got a honey. Whaddaya think? Think she'll be mad?"

Greenan sat down. He put the empty Lord & Taylor bag on the floor. He took a pink napkin off the table and spread it over his lap. Francesco returned and stood over him. "A cocktail, sir?"

Greenan looked up as though he had not expected to encounter a waiter in a restaurant. "I . . . " he said.

"Of course, Francesco," Lobianco said. "Mister Greenan always has a cocktail before lunch when he's not buying. Naturally he will want one today, when he *is* paying. I'll have another one myself. A bloody for me and . . . what're you drinking these days, Ticker? Is it pink squirrels, or orange blossoms, or grasshoppers? I forgot. See, Francesco, the last time we had lunch, me and Ticker, I was buying, and he drank about thirty-five things that looked like ice cream sundaes that my grandchildren're always pestering me to buy them. Except there isn't any booze in the sundaes, I don't think. They don't act as funny afterward as Ticker does, anyway."

"Cuba libre," Greenan said.

"Pardon?" Francesco said.

"It's not a fuckin' battle cry, Francesco," Lobianco said. "What he wants is a rum and Coke."

"Yes," Greenan said, "rum and Coke."

"Rum and Coke," Francesco said. He left the table.

Seats leaned toward Greenan, who sat farther back in his chair. "Ticker," he said, "rum and Coke. You *must* have something serious on your mind. Here you are, buying lunch and actually starting off with a drink that you can almost taste the hard liquor in. What is on your mind?"

"Well," Greenan said, "first thing is: I don't think you should make fun of me like you do."

"Why not?" Lobianco said. "I make fun of everybody else. Everybody else makes fun of me and takes advantage of me all the time, and I grin and bear it. Why the hell shouldn't I have a few laughs at you? What makes you different?"

"I'm not used to it," Greenan said.

"Ticker, Ticker," Lobianco said. "You grew up in Roslindale, Ward Nineteen. You stayed in Roslindale, Ward Nineteen. You run for Mayor twice and got your ass blown off three times, twice running for Mayor and once when you first tried, get back inna Reps, because everybody was still laughing at you for running for Mayor them two times. The only reason they put you back in was that they got sick of laughing at you and decided they were ready for somebody else to have a laugh at and they hadda give you something to occupy your time so you wouldn't be around so much, making everybody laugh. You should be grateful, people're always going around and laughing at you. It gives them something to do instead of getting up a posse and going out to lynch you. Getting laughed at's your biggest strength in politics. You'd be out a fuckin' job, people decided all of a sudden Ticker Greenan isn't funny anymore."

"Seats," Greenan said.

"I mean it," Lobianco said. "Them heart attacks they always make you get inna House when the Speaker hasn't got the votes and they need adjournment quick, a recess inna middle the night? People just about bust their guts every time Ways and Means tells you, keel over, and you do it. You got the best act this side Houdini, and he really is dead. I think you must've set the record, heart attacks in the Great and General Court, and you didn't once break your teeth or even sprain an ankle or anything. This is a great talent, Ticker. You brought much joy into the lives of many people that would've otherwise've spent their entire lives on Beacon Hill without one single goddamned belly laugh, and thanks to you, they had thousands of them. I'm telling you, Ticker, you get to those pearly gates up in the sky and Saint Peter's gonna let you right in. 'Swing 'em open for Greenan,' he'll say the guy that runs the motor, 'if it wasn't for him it would've been like being in a coma in the Massachusetts Legislature, but this guy could always take a header when it really counted.' You make Buster Keaton there look like a fuckin' amateur, and you done a lot more good, the human race in general, and I don't care how many people saw his movies, I will back you any day. Except I don't think you should start wearing the dresses, there. You don't need that."

"Seats," Greenan said. The waiter brought the drinks. "I got to talk to you."

"Just a minute, Ticker," Lobianco said as the waiter set the drinks down, "you're forgetting all the things you should've learned in all these years. You never talk about anything that you've got to talk to anybody about until there is nobody else around that can hear it. You know better than this. This is a nice fellow here, but he is not part of this here discussion and there is no need burdening him with such matters." The waiter grinned and left. "Now," Seats said, "you may say what is on your mind besides flimsy things for sexy ladies, Ticker, but you have to remember to keep your voice down."

"There's a hearing on today," Greenan said.

"No shit, Ticker," Seats said. "Even I knew that, the notorious do-nothing and overpaid public servant that I am. You've been reading the papers again, haven't you, Ticker? Or having somebody read them to you. Which is it? Yeah, there's a hearing on today. You wanna come and tell the people what it is that's being heard? I can save you the trouble. It's the usual shit. We got two judges up for confirmation. There is one that is black and is stupid and is honest and a woman, and I will give you three guesses about who wants to take the oath to tell the truth, the whole truth, and nothing but the truth on that one. After which, they will inform the thoughtful people in the room that this is a black woman who got through law school with a fuckin' tour guide and a goddamned roadmap and didn't swipe anything once the bar examiners give her the license to steal anything that nobody else happened to be using at the time. This is jerk-off city because everybody in the world knows she is gonna get the fuckin' job right this very minute, and they've known it since the last election because she happens to be one of the first black women that came out and said this guy was gonna be one hell of a governor. Which proves she is a liar but nobody's perfect. I know a lot of judges that I have met personally who do not always tell the truth when it is their jobs that are involved. Small potatoes.

"Then," Seats said, "we have got the guy that saw a law book once but he isn't really sure what it looked like and he cannot describe it. It is his bad luck to be a white man getting a judgeship that a lot of other people would like to have. Some of them are women and some of them are blacks and some of them don't even happen to want the fuckin' job, but they are sure they don't want him to have it and they are therefore going to make one hell of a ruckus which will go on until the TV crews have to pack up and go home. That should be a pretty good show, actually. It won't make a fuckin' bit of difference to anything except the news and the people who like to scream and yell a lot, but it's something that you got to get through in this line of work and we sort of look at it as the temporal punishment due to sin. I figure the whole parade'll be over by four, which is good for me because I got an appointment tonight someplace else."

"There is something else on the agenda," Greenan said.

The waiter came back. "Are you gentlemen ready to order? he said.

"I haven't looked at the menu yet," Greenan said, opening it quickly.

"I have," Lobianco said. "While he's doing his studying, lemme have a dozen oysters and a stein of Heineken, please."

Greenan looked alarmed.

"Very good, sir," the waiter said.

"Then," Lobianco said, "the crabmeat cocktail. Cocktail sauce. A lot of lemon wedges. No mayonnaise."

"Very good, sir," the waiter said.

"*Hey,*" Greenan said.

"Some white wine with the crabmeat," Lobianco said, "the Muscadet, I think."

"Yes, sir," the waiter said.

"Seats," Greenan said.

"Now," Lobianco said, "for the main course, the Dover sole with the lobster sauce." He flapped the menu shut.

"Thank you, sir," the waiter said. "That will be a full bottle of the Muscadet?"

"Of course," Lobianco said. "And bring my companion a cheese sandwich and some digitalis."

"This isn't funny, Seats," Greenan said.

"I didn't say it was funny," Lobianco said. "The last time I took you to lunch, at Anthony's, you had shrimp Rockefeller, clam chowder, roast prime rib of beef, half a bottle of white wine and half a bottle of red wine, and strawberries Romanoff for the finish. You do it to me, I do it to you. You've been in politics long enough to know that."

"I'll have the fish chowder," Greenan said to the waiter.

"Also," Lobianco said to the waiter, "he will have the prime rib, cooked until it looks like anthracite, and a baked potato with sour cream and chives and all the butter you can carry, and a half-bottle of the best Cabernet Sauvignon you've got, and take no back talk from him. Okay?"

"Yes, sir," the waiter said.

"And you listen to me," Seats said to Greenan. He pointed his left index finger at him. "I know you. I've known you a long time. You've got a short memory and it doesn't help you none. You call me about seeing me, you got something on your mind. But it's temporary, Ticker, it's temporary. I helped you before, and I did what you wanted, and it was temporary. Many times. I did it many times when you asked me, and many times you forgot that I did it. *All* of the times. Now we are going to play with a little harder ball. This time you are going to remember. And this time you are going to do the right thing."

Lobianco sat back in his chair. "Now, Ticker," he said, "we are going to have a little chat. What exactly is it that you want? Because you want something, for sure. You don't care about black ladies becoming judges, unless those undies that you brought in here with you are for some chocolate dumpling that I never heard about. Which I would've, if there was one. The only judges that interest you are the ones that can get your stupid friends jobs being court clerks. You don't care about the guy that is heading for the Supreme Judicial, because you never knew a lawyer that's as smart as he is, dumb as he may be. So, what is it? There's nothing else on the list today that deserves this kind of lunch. Just a lot of pardon applications and other chickenshit that's going to get pushed under the rug with a broom by the first guy that comes into the room."

"The Mugro thing," Greenan said.

"I never heard the son of a bitch," Lobianco said. "All I know's he's in the can and he wants to get out. Lots of guys inna can feel the same way. The fuck're you interested in that one for?"

"I want him out," Greenan said, looking down.

"What put him in?" Lobianco said. "Those things're pretty routine, it wasn't too serious."

"Well," Greenan said, "it was murder."

"Ohh," Lobianco said, "murder. That does make it a little more difficult. Care to give me some details?"

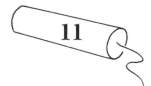

11

THE WAITER brought the oysters and the beer to the table and set them in front of Lobianco. He returned to the serving tray and brought a bowl of fish chowder which he set before Greenan. He said the chowder dish was very hot, and he left the table. Seats scooped an oyster out of its shell, dipped it in horseradish, dipped it in cocktail sauce, chewed noisily and said: "Ahh. I tell you, Ticker, you should get yourself an order of these oysters. These're really good. Nice and crisp, you know? Delicious." He took a gulp of beer. "Howsa chowder? Looks good, all that butter on the top and everything. I had it here a couple times. Very tasty."

"Seats," Greenan said, "look, now, all right?"

"Jesus Christ, Ticker," Seats said, "eat, eat. You don't wanna let it get all cold there, you know. I realize chowder's even better warmed up the day after you cook it. But you're not gonna be here tomorrow, I miss my guess. They are not gonna save it for the next two years, you know, you got another favor that you want from me and I haul you in here again, carrying a bag, looks like you brought your own lunch and the only thing you wanna order's some iced tea, to go with your peanut butter crackers."

"Seats," Greenan said, "this is serious, all right?"

"Oh," Seats said, "I'm sure it is, Ticker." He speared two

oysters on his fork, dipped them both, and put them in his mouth. "Needs some lemon," he said reflectively. He stabbed the lemon wedge with the fork and squeezed it over the remaining oysters. "Always remember this, Ticker, when you're dining in some classy joint, right? You got to puncture the lemon before you squeeze it. Otherwise you're liable, spray juice and pulp all over everybody. You were saying something?" He resumed chewing.

"I said, this's *serious*," Greenan said, desperately. The chowder steamed in front of him.

"I'm sure it is, is what I said," Seats said. "If you didn't tell me it was serious, I would know it was serious, because you are paying a lot of money for that chowder and you are letting it get old in front of you. Pretty soon them flounders in there're gonna be on Social Security and shivering in their unheated apartments." He speared two more oysters.

"Seats," Greenan said, still not eating, "will ya lemme talk?"

"Sure," Seats said, chewing. "You can talk all you want. That's why you're taking me to lunch. Only thing is, two guys go to lunch, it's impolite if one of them doesn't eat, you know? Makes the other guy feel embarrassed." He belched softly and took another drink of beer. "My God," he said, shaking his head, "there is nothing quite like a good glass of cold beer with some oysters on a warm summer day. Didn't used to be you could get oysters inna summer. You remember that, Ticker? Only time you could get oysters was in the winter, months with an *r* in them. Supposed to give you food poisoning, you ate them inna summer.

"You know why that is? You think the oysters get poisonous all of a sudden, end of April, they're not good to eat again until Labor Day? Nah. Refrigeration. They didn't have no refrigeration when they had that rule. Oysters spoiled in warm weather. That's all. Nothing else to it. My father, my father loved oysters. Right after Labor Day he would start eating them, but *bang*, right on the dot of May first, he would stop again. But that was the reason. No reason for it at all, now. Get oysters any time you want, all year round." He took another and dipped it. "Expensive though, I will say that."

"Seats," Greenan said, taking a spoonful of chowder, "will ya lemme talk about Magro, the Magro case? All right?"

"Ticker," Seats said, leaning forward, "sure I will let you talk about the Magro case. But like I said, I know you. And I know why you're in such a hurry to talk about the Magro case. You're gonna eat your chowder, and tell me what it is you wanna tell me, and then all of a sudden you're gonna remember an important appointment and you're gonna get up before the rest of the lunch comes and run out of here with your undies in your pocket, and skip on the check. I've seen you do it before, and you got to pardon me, but this was all your idea and you are not gonna pull the scoot on me. Those other guys that you stuck with the bill, they hadn't been around as long as I have. You tell me your story and you eat your fuckin' soup, and you eat your baked potato and you drink your fuckin' wine. And I will have my crab cocktail and my Dover sole and my wine, and if *I* feel like it I will have some coffee, and then my faithful Indian companion here will bring us the check and you will still be here, to pay it. I've seen lots of horses, over Suffolk Downs, couldn't get out of the gate as fast as you can get away from a table when you think the check's coming and you might have to pay it. Like you agreed. I bet on most of them horses, I am sorry to say. If my horses were as quick as you getting away from a check, I would be a millionaire."

Seats took another oyster. "So," he said, "here is your choice. As you know, I can outtalk you. I can outtalk any guy in Boston that's got an all-night call-in show, along with all the nutcakes that call him up. You wanna get cute with me, you won't get to the Magro case until the check comes, and then I will bounce outta here like I was Tinker Bell and you never will get to tell me what is on your mind. But you will still pay for lunch. Which is what I have got in mind. Eat your soup."

Greenan began to eat the chowder. "Don't eat so fast, Ticker," Seats said. "First thing you know, you'll give yourself indigestion and you'll have to find somebody, takes Maalox, and bum a couple off him, and a friendly cow that doesn't know you and will give you a glassa milk, free." Seats took two more oysters, put sauce on them and put them in his mouth.

"Look, Seats," Greenan said.

"I am looking," Seats said. "You don't have to call my attention to it." He chewed his oysters. "You oughta know better'n that, nice Irish boy like you, had a good upbringing. Don't talk with your mouth full."

"For Christ sake, Seats," Greenan said, with his mouth full, "you're doing it. You've been doing it since you got those oysters."

"Of course," Seats said. "Everybody knows I'm vulgar. You're supposed to have some class, even if you are running around with ladies' underwear in your pockets."

Greenan threw his napkin on the table. "Are you gonna listen to me or not, Seats?" he said.

Seats chewed silently. He took another oyster and put it into his mouth. He chewed. With his mouth full, he drank beer and swallowed. He took another oyster. He chewed some more. He drank more beer. He swallowed.

"Well?" Greenan said.

"I'm thinking," Seats said. "Is it all right if I think, for Christ sake? Good God, I try to do a man a favor and come to lunch with him, and all he does is yell at me. I need this? I can get yelled at without even leaving my desk."

"You keep this up," Greenan said, "and I am warning you: I will get out of here and you can pay for your own goddamned oysters and your crabmeat and your goddamned

fish that you ordered with the lobster sauce and the fancy
French wine."

"Okay," Seats said, "go ahead. You're right. I can pay for it.
Of course, on the other hand, you won't have told me
whatever the hell it is that you want me to do. But that's your
business, none of mine." He put the last oyster in his mouth.

"I assume you know your business, Ticker."

Greenan took the napkin back and tucked it into his shirt.

He sighed. He went back to the chowder. "It's a serious
thing, like I said," he said.

"I heard of very few murder cases that were all in fun,"
Seats said. "What'd he do?"

"He killed a guy," Greenan said, eating chowder rapidly.

"Well," Seats said, "no shit. You mean to tell me a guy
doing time for murder got himself convicted of *killing* somebody? Son of a bitch, Ticker, I tell you, a man learns
something different every time he runs into you. And all these
years I been thinking when they charged you with murder, it
meant you let your dog run around with no license or you
threw your beer bottles on the neighbor's lawn. Goddammit,
it's a rare day you don't find out something new in this great
land of ours."

"Seats," Greenan said, finishing his chowder and wiping
his mouth, "lemme up, all right? The guy's a convicted
murderer."

The waiter took away the oyster plate and the chowder
bowl. He brought the crab cocktail and set it before Seats.
Seats nodded. The waiter brought the Muscadet and
displayed the label to Seats. "Fine," Seats said. "Open the
bugger and pour me some." The waiter returned to his station
for a corkscrew. "Who'd he kill, Ticker?"

"He killed another hood," Greenan said, "a guy out in
Framingham."

"Another hood?" Seats said. "This means the guy's a hood
himself, and he's going for a pardon? Good luck to you and

the Red Sox, Ticker. I couldn't get that one through the
Council with a crowbar. You got any idea what happened to
the guys that let the boss out, about fifty years ago? Actually,
it was less'n that, and he wasn't the boss, not then anyway, but
there was air-conditioned hell to pay. One guy went to jail, for
Christ sake." Seats took a forkful of crabmeat and dipped it in
the cocktail sauce. "I can see, maybe, a guy killed his wife and
he's not gonna do it again, for goddamned sure, her being
dead and all. But a hood kills a hood and we let the winning
hood out and tell him not to worry, go forth and sin no more?
Christ sake, Ticker, I'd've known it was this kind of weight
you're asking me to carry, I wouldn't've asked for fuckin'
lunch, no matter how this's hurtin' your feelings." He chewed
crabmeat. "I would've told you I want a fuckin' pension, for
Christ sake, and a condo down Sea Island, Georgia, and
maybe a little motorboat, I can go fishing."

"No, look, Seats," Greenan said. "Magro hasn't got any
money."

"This's really good crabmeat, Ticker," Seats said, chewing.
"You oughta have some." The waiter brought the opened
bottle of Muscadet and poured a little. Seats tried it and
smacked his lips appreciatively. "My friend," he said, "thou
hast saved the good wine until the last. Pour me a glass there,
and bring me a bucket of ice so the rest of it doesn't get
warm." The waiter bowed, and left the table. "Okay, Ticker,"
Seats said, "what is it exactly that I am supposed to look at?"

"This guy," Greenan said, "this guy Michael Magro is
small-time stuff. No heavy hitter. He never pulled a trigger on
anybody before in his life."

"Yeah," Seats said, eating crabmeat. "How you know
that?"

"Well," Greenan said, moving around in the chair as Seats
punctured another lemon and squeezed it on the crabmeat, "I
just know it."

"Right," Seats said, taking another hunk of crabmeat, "and

I know that for every drop of rain that falls, a flower grows. How you know so much about this guy? Where you get your information? How good is it? How do I know somebody didn't blow smoke up your ass and now you're tryin', blow the same smoke up my ass? Used smoke, for Christ sake."

"Look," Greenan said, "his mother's a great friend of my mother's."

"For all I know," Seats said, "George Washington's mummy played bridge every week with Benedict Arnold's. What's that got to do with me? That doesn't mean shit. You got to come up with something better'n that."

Greenan slumped in the chair as Lobianco finished the crabmeat and drank wine. "Seats," Greenan said. "Do me one small favor, all right?"

"Right," Seats said. "One small favor, like get a killer out of the slammer so he can do it again. I changed my mind, Ticker. I'll buy lunch. You go on your way with your nighties and I'll have my fish."

"That nightgown isn't mine," Greenan said. His face was red.

"All right," Seats said, "it's somebody else's nightgown. I believe you, Ticker. I believe everything you say. This guy Magro is a poor unfortunate kid that happened to get caught dusting off another poor hood that wasn't quick enough on the draw for him, and if he gets out, he will never do it again. I believe that. You know what gullible means? Consider me gullible. Who'd he kill?"

"It was a guy named Holby," Greenan said, "and that's really all I know. Except that Holby had a record."

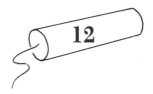

12

SEATS WAS in his office with his feet on the desk. He had loosened his tie and unbuttoned the collar of his shirt. His face was flushed. He had put on his half-glasses for reading, but he was laughing and they had slid down nearly to the end of his nose. He had the phone receiver buried in his jowls again.

"Ahh, Mattie," he said, "I tell ya, ya wouldn't fuckin' believe it. First thing the guy does is, he shows up late, right? And he's got this bag with him. It's one of those Lord and Taylor things. So I take it away from him and he's got a fuckin' nightie and some sexy little drawers in it, and I wave them all around. I thought he was gonna have some kind of a fit, everybody in the place's sittin' there laughing at him and you know how he looks. He don't look like no self-respecting Irish at all that comes from Rozzie Square and knows how to do the right thing. He looks like some hayshaker, just come down from Bangor, see his first tall buildings. There he is, all skin and bones, his ears stick out like them television antenna things and he gets his hair cut down the barber school where they do you for a quarter if you let the rookies practice on you, and he's got on this suit that I bet his grandfather liked pretty well when he got it for twelve bucks, two pairs of pants with extra-heavy knees back at Raymond's just before the war, the one that Pershing was in. And I'm wavin' these

83

undies around at everybody. And he sits down and I stick him for the whole ball of wax, the crabmeat cocktail and everything. I mean, Mattie, this's gotta be serious, right? Ticker Greenan, buying a lunch like that? I had all I could do, I didn't ask him the minute he came through the door, what the hell it was. I mean, it hadda be he wants his nephew to be appointed *Pope* or something, it's that important to him. Thing of it is, though, I know the minute he gets it offa his chest, he's gonna screw on me and beat lunch.

"So, Mattie," Seats said, "I finally let the guy talk, and you know what is bothering him? This guy Magro that wants the commutation thing there, the pardon? And it's murder, for Christ sake. No murder that matters a good goddamn to anybody, not like he tried to shoot the Governor or something. Hell, maybe even that wouldn't get anybody too excited, considering the number of guys I heard over the years say they'd like to try it. But I thought maybe he wanted the black lady knocked down that we got coming up this after the judgeship and he wants me give it his idiot nephew that's the deputy clerk in Lawrence, which there is no way on earth I can do. And the only other thing that I can think of that'd make Ticker spring for lunch is the SJC thing. Not even Ticker's got the balls to go for that one for some hacker like he's always putting up.

"But, no, what he wants is a third-rate hood that knocked off another lowlifer, and I can't figure it out. So I make it sound real difficult, you know? I say to him, I say, 'Ticker, Ticker, murder one? You been reading all that stuff in the papers, you think the Council's just a cheap pawnshop? Good Christ, Ticker. Kid makes a little mistake, like he steals a car or something, I maybe got some chance, I can do something for you. But murder one? Who is this guy Magro? He Mrs. Ticker's long-lost brother or something?' And Ticker won't tell me. I got to snake it out of him like he had the reason under one of his tooth fillings. And I finally get it out of him. At least he says I got it out of him. He is doing a favor for Monsignor Fahey down at Precious Blood. Seems like Monsignor Fahey's faithful housekeeper, some simpleminded old tad that's most likely been tiddly on the communion wine for about a hundred years, this kid Magro's her nephew and she's been so sick at heart she practically got football knees making novenas for the poor lad, and now she's gettin' ready to kick the bucket and Fahey wants this favor done her."

Seats paused and listened. "No, Mattie, no, I'm not sure of that at all. That's probably what Ticker thinks he's doing, nice little favor for the Monsignor and everything, but Ticker's so dumb you could tell him you could get by on eating nothing but wood, and he would think you gave him a surefire way to save more money. He would go out and get a truckload of used shingles and siding. That's why I'm calling you. See if you can find out what the hell is going on here, will ya? It's one thing to have somebody snorkel you, happens to the best of us, but if it's Ticker Greenan doing it, that'd be very embarrassing. Besides, if there is money changing hands here, I want to know about it. Isn't anybody going to whipsaw old Seats into settin' up a payoff, puts me in the can. I understand the food in there is lousy."

Pete Riordan entered the east wing of the main building of the State House through the back door at the portico. He climbed the marble steps with difficulty, his boot heels slipping somewhat, and turned right down the corridor toward Lobianco's office. He passed the elevator on the right where two men in short-sleeved shirts were studying a racing form, came to the door to Lobianco's office and went in. His face was streaming with sweat.

Alice Vickery looked up from her paperback copy of *Rich Man, Poor Man.*

"Can I help you?" she said. "My God, you're roasting in that." She put the book down. "Take your jacket off and sit down, wearing a heavy thing like that in weather like this. You'll have a stroke for yourself." She started to get up.

Riordan smiled at her. "No, really, it's okay, ma'am. You know how it is: Every man to his own hangover cures. I've got several, and this is one of them. When I make a fool of myself, I sweat the poison out of me the next day."

"I have a beer, myself," she said. "That always works."

"Ma'am," Riordan said, "I didn't say the sweat cure is the only one I use. I also replace the old poison with new poison, when I've got a really critical attack. Which I have today. Is Mister Lobianco in?"

"Yes," she said, "and it's a good thing for you, too, because he's got his own air conditioner in there and he keeps that office cold enough to age meat in. Who's calling, please?"

"Well," Riordan said, "I don't have any appointment or anything. If he's busy . . ."

"He isn't doing a goddamned thing," she said. "They had a short meeting today and he's on the phone the way he always is, telling lies to his buddies and getting them to tell him stories in return. What's your name?"

"Riordan," Riordan said.

"Hey, Seats," Alice yelled, "man named Riordan here to see you."

"Hey, Riordan," Lobianco said, "I haven't got your goddamned magazine. Nothing I can do about your foglights and your taillights, run around in that surgeon's car you got, impressing everybody."

Riordan looked at Alice. "Some other Riordan, I guess," she said. "Joint's crawling with them. Go on in and let him find out for himself."

Riordan opened the door to Lobianco's office. Seats continued talking until he could see Riordan. "What you got to do is duke the guy five now and then and quit acting so goddamned high and . . . Who the hell're you?"

"I'm Riordan," Riordan said.

Seats took his feet off the desk and stood up. "Sorry," he said, "I thought you were somebody else I know named Reardon."

"I guess not, huh?" Riordan said.

"No indeed," Lobianco said. "Which Riordan are you?"

Riordan took out the credentials and flopped them open as he walked toward the desk. "Inspector General's office," he said. "Department of Justice."

Lobianco sat down fast in the chair. "Jesus Christ," he said.

"Hey," Riordan said, "don't take it so hard. This's just a courtesy call." He put the credentials back into his pocket. "Can I sit down?"

"Oh, sure," Lobianco said, waving his right hand. "Courtesy call. That's what they always say, just before they come with the wagon. Sure, sit down. How long we got to wait, you figure? They get tied up in traffic? Can I call my lawyer? Shit, what am I saying? I haven't even got a lawyer. Okay, what's the beef, huh? I can take it."

"I'm awful thirsty," Riordan said. "Is there any chance somebody could get me a Coke?"

"Coke?" Lobianco said. "Coke? Sure, we can get you a Coke. Like some nice Chivas Regal instead, maybe? Little Bombay gin and tonic? You just name it and you got it, General Riordan. Always like to make a man feel comfortable, while he's waiting to take me away."

"Coke'll be fine," Riordan said. "It's Agent Riordan. Pete will do."

"Alice," Lobianco shouted, "get the nice man from Justice a nice cold Coca-Cola, all right?" To Riordan he said, "You serious? I'm not in the shit? Because I swear to God, I haven't done anything."

"Honest to God," Riordan said, laughing. "I'm here for information, and I hear you're a right guy. Okay if I take my coat off?"

"Sure, sure," Lobianco said. "Anything you want. Take your fuckin' pants off, you want, just so's I don't have to go down to the Federal Building. Jesus Christ," he said, as Riordan took the coat off.

"Relax," Riordan said, "I'm not here to take you in, and I'm not here to shoot you, either." He tossed the coat onto the table where the scanner blinked. His tan shirt was wet under the arms. "I know a guy in State Police, says you're all right." Alice came in with a can of Coke and a paper napkin, widened her eyes when she saw the gun, and left the room silently. Riordan drank from the Coke can. "Tell me all you know about Michael Magro."

"Jesus Christ," Lobianco said. "Here I was sitting here, minding my own business, and then this guy with more firepower'n the Sixth Fleet comes in and he's the third guy today that wants to talk to me about Magro. I must be losing my touch. I figure you're gonna want payoffs and kickbacks and stuff like that, information about that, and instead it's this same two-bit hood that I came back from talking about at lunch and I never even heard of the guy in my life before. And then again at the meeting. I mean it. Until today, I never even heard the guy. And now his name's on everybody's lips, like they say."

"Well," Riordan said, "his name's up before the Council."

"Ahh," Lobianco said, "that goes for lots of guys. They go away for a long time, they try every court thing they can think of to get themselves out, and then when they run out of courts, they try the Governor. Some of those things we just deny. A few of them, sure, we vote a hearing. Guy knocked off his wife or something. Won't do it again. Kid did a year for B and E when he was eighteen, got out, went in the service, good record, honorable discharge, got himself married, college nights, worked hard, law school nights, then he comes in and he wants a pardon so he can get his ticket, practice law. Sure, no hearing on that either. Don't need one. This guy Magro? He doesn't stand a chance, I figure. Why waste everybody's time on it? We haven't got as much time as he's got, and we got more things to do. Then all of a sudden, his case comes up for the first hearing today. I get a call from a Rep, he wants the thing heard. Then a Councillor, same thing. Now you. I called a guy I know, also knows everything, he doesn't know from this guy either. I was just talking to him when you came in. Because, see . . ."

"Who's the Rep?" Riordan said.

"Guy named Ticker Greenan," Lobianco said. "Edmund Greenan. D. Roslindale."

"Heavy hitter?" Riordan said.

"Standing joke'd be more like it," Lobianco said. "They keep sending him back for sentimental reasons, I guess. He's harmless enough."

"On the take?" Riordan said.

"Suppose he could be," Lobianco said. "Pretty hard to believe, though. He hasn't got enough horsepower to do anything important here. Tell you the truth, Greenan never asks me for anything that he wouldn't get anyway, without asking me or anybody else. I never told him that, and I'm not gonna, because I think he's funny.

"I get back from lunch," Lobianco said. "I go into the meeting, we do diddly-squat on one judgeship that was just a formality, and pretty soon the lady gets her robe. Then we got a first hearing on a Supreme Court judgeship, no particular problem—guy's well qualified, clean, good family man, you couldn't pick a better candidate. That gets us to the junkpile.

And one of the Councillors says, before I can even call the matter, 'This Magro case. I think we should address that. In executive session.'"

"What's the Councillor's name?" Riordan said.

"Tommy Emmett," Lobianco said. "The Right Honorable Thomas J. Emmett, of Worcester."

"And did you?" Riordan said.

"Executive session?" Lobianco said. "No. Nobody wants to throw the reporters out in order to discuss something they don't know anything about. We tabled it."

"This Greenan character," Riordan said. "He say anything else to you about Magro, why he was doing this?"

"Yeah," Lobianco said. "I don't know if it's worth a pisshole in the snow, but he said he was asking me for this Magro kid because Monsignor Fahey out at Precious Blood asked him. Precious Blood is West Roxbury."

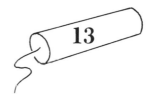

13

RIORDAN ENTERED the narrow gate in the high stucco wall surrounding the stucco rectory and Church of the Holy Sepulchre on Larkspur Street in Weston, the light green Ford sedan having inches to spare on each side. He parked in the oval in front of the rectory, nosing the Ford into the overhanging branches of the rhododendrons, and got out in the morning sunshine. He wore the sunglasses, and a long-sleeved white shirt, open at the neck, with tan chino pants and the Survivor boots. The magnum rode against his hip. He reached into the car and took a light blue linen sports coat from the front seat. He put it on, shut the door and locked it. He noticed, without distinguishing the varieties, flowers blooming along the wall, and the long green lawn extending southward from the rectory, shaded under the black maples. He went to the double door of the rectory, gated in the same wrought iron that framed the driveway gate, and rang the bell.

Mrs. Herlihy, the housekeeper, answered as promptly as she could. She was pushing seventy, but was lamed up and bent over with arthritis, and she moved slowly. When she got the door open, a smile spread across her face. "Peter Riordan," she said, "you rogue. Father told me that he saw you yesterday, and I was very angry with you for not coming here."

91

Riordan stepped into the foyer onto the Kerman runner. "Mrs. Herlihy," he said, smiling back at her, "now I ask you, would I be after doin' a thing such as that? It's but little you're thinkin' of me these days, I can see."

She began to laugh, and moving as best she could, embraced him. He hugged her in return, but she stepped back with some agility. "And that thing on your belt," she said. "Just what might that be, may I ask?"

"A mere trifle required in me job by the government of the United States of America, Mrs. Herlihy," Riordan said. "Have not a care for it; I never discharge it in friendly surroundings."

"Yes," she said, "I had me granduncles, made the same claim, I did. And when I was but a little girl I lost me two of them at the Post Office at the Rising of the Moon. I suppose you want to see Father."

"I do," Riordan said, "although I'm beginning to wonder why he stays here. At the club yesterday, they called him Your Excellency, and here he comes home and the best he can expect is Father."

"Father is what he prefers," she said. "When he was raised to the bishopric, they started to call him Your Eminence, and he asked them to continue calling him Father, so they started calling him Your Excellency. Makin' fun of the poor man as usual. I believe he should have his own preferences, in his own house, and if Father is what he chooses, then Father it shall be, as far as I'm concerned. I'll take you to him."

She turned and started down the hall, moving with difficulty, Riordan limping behind her. "And a fine pair we make, don't we, Peter," she said. "Here I am, all crippled up and long before my time, barely able to get around at all, and you, staggering along there like you spent all the night in some pub. And himself in the study there, nothing but a bag of bones as he is since he's sick, waiting for the rest of us other wrecks to come in. A fine business it is, when the meek and the merciful are punished like this for the sins of the rest." Riordan began to laugh.

"I mean it," she said with firmness. "Why, would you look at all those brave young men, so fine in their clothes and their fancy cars, escorting their families to the Holy Sacrifice of the Mass, and not one of them with the common decency to have fought for his country in her hour of need, they was all hidin' out in university or somethin'. And a fine brave fellow like yourself that goes and does his duty, comes back here exactly the same age as them, all shot up and wounded like a common criminal, with nothin' to show for it and the back of the hand from the people he was defendin'. That isn't right, you know. And then there is the poor Father here, a better man you could not hope to find, still in the prime of his life and the best of it left, and what happens to him? Struck down like a steer in for the slaughterin', and it's only by the grace of God he lived at all."

"It was that serious, then?" Riordan said.

"It was that, Peter," she said. "And here we are, always seein' these mealy-mouthed priests with not half the courage nor a third of the brains that he's got, out there paradin' with the do-nothin' lazy welfare people and raisin' their voices for this and for that, on the television every night—why, I tell you, Peter, it's enough to make you sick at heart. Why don't it happen to them, I ask you? The likes of them that care nothin' for people but only for gettin' up with a microphone there and makin' a lot of damned noise and gettin' their pictures on the television. And then what do they do? Why, they take off their collars and run off with some nun and get married. That's what they do."

They were at the open door to the study. Paul Doherty in a rose-colored golf shirt and light blue trousers, both garments too large for him, was practicing his putting on the rose-colored Oriental, aiming toward an automatic ball-return device in front of the French windows that looked out on the lawn. In the kneehole of the desk, a large, liver-and-white bulldog inspected Riordan with dignified thoughtfulness.

"Mrs. Herlihy," Paul Doherty said, bending over the ball, "if you keep on ranting like that about all of the young priests and nuns running off to get married, you'll be the next to have an attack in this house."

"Well," she said, "it's true and you know it. Breakin' their vows like that, and all. Breakin' their solemn word to God. Priests and nuns. A fine thing."

He attempted the putt, straightened up, and watched as it rolled up the slight incline of the device and back down again onto the carpet. "These things're great, Peter," he said, turning to face them. "The wonders of modern ingenuity. You get the ball in the hole and the little thing in there fires it right back down to you. The thing of it is, you have to get the ball into the hole first. And anyway, I've seen very few putting greens where the hole was at the top of a little hill."

"Some coffee, Father, Peter?" she said.

"Uhh," Riordan said, "you wouldn't have any of that breakfast tea around that I remember, would you?"

"I do," she said, "and you, Father?"

"The same, please," he said. After she had left the room, he said, "I see your memory of Mrs. Herlihy's coffee hasn't faded, Peter."

"No more'n my memory of my own cars, get the parts and supplies down at Western Auto and save a couple dollars. And the first time I ever drained a crankcase, I recognized it right off. 'So that's where they get the stuff,' I said. I didn't taste it, but then again, I didn't have to—it looked the same and it smelled about the same, so it had to taste the same. I took it on faith."

"How is your own dear mother?" Doherty said. "Your own

dear father, as far as that goes, God, it's been years since I've heard from them, seems like. Card at Christmas, and that's about it. How do they like it out there?"

"I think they don't, actually," Riordan said. Doherty rested the putter against the desk and motioned toward the red leather two-cushion couch and and two high-backed chairs at the fireplace opposite. There was a coffee table between the couch and the fireplace, and there was a large spray of daisy chrysanthemums in the grate.

"I thought they were making a mistake when they moved away from here," Riordan said. "Actually, I thought my father was making a mistake when he sold his practice and retired early. I wouldn't go for spending any part of my life doing what he did, examining squalling brats all day, giving shots, taking phone calls in the middle of the damned night from some hysterical parent whose kid coughed once in his sleep, but he loved it. My mother loved it here too. All their friends're around here, were then, and most of them still are. Every letter I get from my mother, she tells me how So-and-so's thinking about moving out there to join them, and as soon as this one gets her husband's estate settled, she's coming out. And then there's Mister Whoever-the-hell-it-is, who's moving out as soon as his wife's long illness is finally over. But they never do, I guess.

"Funny, I can't even remember half of those people," Riordan said. "Well-to-do insurance men and brokers and their wives who puttered around in real estate and had Tuesday afternoon luncheons on each other's sunporches, getting silly on a small glass of white wine and eating tomatoes stuffed with chicken salad. They bored me when they came to visit my parents, and their kids bored me when I got dragged along to visit with my parents. But it was their life, and they did love it. I don't care how much they save on oil in Sun City or Roy Rogers Villa Estates or whatever the hell they call that damned thing out in Arizona, they are *lonely*.

"That's what I think, anyway. They play golf every day, and there's a pool that all the neighbors share, but all the neighbors are old. Everybody in that town is old. My parents aren't old. Not like that. Not young, certainly, but not old either. That's why the people're in that town. They're old. They spend their nights having one cocktail on each other's terraces and talking about their pension plans and what's going to happen with Social Security.

"My mother writes to me every week. I write to them every week, and even though there's a lot of stuff I can't tell them—and a lot more I wouldn't tell them if I could, because they would be packing for the next plane east, come and save their darling boy—that still leaves me with more to write about'n she's got. The only fun any of them seem to have out there is when somebody comes to visit with grandchildren, and then I gather the poor little kids get no peace at all. God, must be awful, paraded around like prize pigs to every goddamned meeting place in town. 'And these are our grandchildren. Tom and Edith, meet young David, little Priscilla, and this is the youngest, Orville. Confidentially, Edith, they haven't said anything to us yet, but we think Orville's going to have a little brother, Wilbur, around Christmas.' Jesus."

Doherty was laughing as they sat down. "Getting a little heat from June about settling down and starting a family, Pete?"

"I have that impression," Riordan said. "Although if what I'm getting is a *little* heat, God pity the poor stokers in the Pittsburgh steel mills."

"Why don't you do it?" Doherty said.

"Ahh," Riordan said, "that's my sisters' department. Joansie and Anne grew up in organdy frocks and spent their summers on the Irish Riviera, wearing little white slacks with strawberries on them and having everybody simper at them.

Doctor Will's little daughters. Both of them married guys who're just perfect, talk with their teeth clenched and flail Volvos around the charming lanes of the better areas of New Jersey. 'Take the eight-forty into the city, you know,' because being *partners* and all, and doing so well, they don't have to be at the office at any special hour. 'Let's drop the kids off in Arizona with June and Will for our holidays,' while the couples jet off by themselves for a couple weeks à deux in Honolulu. Really zoomy people."

"You do that lockjaw pretty well, Pete," Doherty said.

"I should, goddammit," Riordan said. "I grew up in this tent cocoon for privileged caterpillars, didn't I? The fact that I hated getting my suburban credentials doesn't change the fact that they're genuine. I can't hack that stuff, Paul. I wouldn't be any good at it, and I know it. Every man's got his own deficiencies, and that's another one of mine. I hate flying and I'd be a lousy family man."

Mrs. Herlihy brought the tea in on a tray. "That isn't so, Peter," she said. "When you were senior altar boy, growing up, you were always very kind and helpful to the new boys. I heard many people remark on it, what a fine husband and father you were being brought up to be."

"Oh, nuts, Mrs. Herlihy," Riordan said, "begging your pardon and all. Brought up to be? Sure. Be any good at it now? Uh-uh. Man does well what he does best. Besides, I waited too long."

"It's never too late to start," she said, serving the tea on the coffee table. She left the room, shutting the door behind her.

"You're in better shape today," Doherty said, drinking tea.

"Compared to the shape I was in yesterday," Riordan said, "sure. Compared to the shape of any respectable citizen of the community: mediocre but showing signs of improvement. One more good night's sleep and I'll be nearly fit for human society."

"What have you got?" Doherty said.

"Not sure," Riordan said. "You got anything?"

"Nope," Doherty said. "I was afraid I'd screw everything up if I marched in and started hacking around with this thing without more information. You know your sisters after all these years, and I know my brother just as well, for just about the same reasons. I don't like my brother as well as I like your sisters. Your sisters may be stuffy, but they're nice and they haven't kept you in one dire emergency after another since the three of you got out of school. My brother didn't exactly get out of school—he was thrown out on his big fat arse, and he's nothing but a wise guy. I know it, and I most emphatically do not like it, but I know him and I know enough not to mess around in anything that involves him without having every available fact at my disposal."

"Yeah?" Riordan said. "Well, I know my sisters, and stuffy is far too mild for them. They turned on the afterburners of their life-styles while they were still at Newton College of the Sacred Heart, and they left stuffy far behind. They hit boring ten or fifteen years ago, and they're still accelerating. Or is it decelerating. Probably. God knows what they'll be ten years from now. Brain-dead, probably. Still marching around in those goddamned clothes from Talbots but you slap an EEG on their skulls and you'll get a wave as flat as a shirt cardboard. At least your brother's alive. He may be a holy terror, and he may drive you nuts, but by God, you have to admit that old Digger's never dull. I like him much better'n I like that pair."

"All right then," Doherty said, "keeping in mind that it's much easier to like Jerry if your interest is professional and you're merely trying to put him in jail, instead of your interest being familial and trying to keep him out of jail, or the morgue—which is much harder—what've you got?"

"I feel like I'm reciting the answers for Confirmation," Riordan said.

"Oh, shut up," Doherty said.

"Saw Ken Walker at the prison after I left you," Riordan said. "We were right on the peg about Magro. Walker didn't have enough information. Gave him what I had. Good guy, Walker. Saw the light immediately."

"Good," Doherty said. "Magro's not getting out, then. Means we can relax. Glad I didn't do anything. Always trust your instincts, Pete, always trust your instincts. It's your guardian angel, giving you a little nudge in the right direction."

"Always have, Paul," Riordan said, "always have. Be dead now, I didn't. Trouble is, guardian angel works a straight forty-hour week. Days, only. No nights, weekends or national holidays, and three full weeks off with pay. Those angels've got a union, I think. Doesn't do a bit of harm, do a little of your own looking out at the same time while you're waiting for him to give you your messages. Walker can't stop Magro from getting out. He agrees with me—I didn't see any need to bring your name into it—but he can't knock it down all by himself."

"Well, for the luvva Mike," Doherty said, "he's the damned warden, isn't he? Doesn't he have last say on who stays in and who gets out?"

"Used to," Riordan said. "That was before the great enlightenment. Remember all those seminars you gave me, when you still hadn't given up hope of making me into a civilized human being and maybe even doing a little gentle recruiting for Holy Mother Church? The Great Enlightenment and all? Well, they had a great enlightenment in this Commonwealth a few years back, and some of it seeped into the corrections system. If Walker wants to keep a guy in now, he has to convince a couple of airheads that the fellow is Jack the Ripper, at least. Told me he's got trouble doing that."

"So," Doherty said, "what's he going to do? Sit back, throw

up his hands, and let him loose to pull the trigger on my brother? I'm a celibate, Peter. I'm a celibate on purpose. I've got my flock. It's diminishing rapidly and it's getting old before my eyes, but it is my flock and I have to take care of it. I can't raise my brother's family for him, after he gets himself plugged."

"Gee," Riordan said, "aren't you the guy that was peddling the joys of family life to me a few minutes ago?"

"Easy, Peter," Doherty said. "There's a lot of difference between a man your age, your condition, starting a family, and a man my age, my condition, picking up where Digger Doherty never really tried to begin. I'm not saying his kids are bad, because they're not. Not yet, anyway. Not too bad. But Patricia's almost fourteen now, and a beautiful young woman. Even a celibate knows what that means, especially if the celibate's heard a few confessions.

"The boys're well into their late adolescence," Doherty said, "and they never had a great deal of discipline from their father. Hell, he never had much discipline for himself, let alone any left over for them. I'm worried about the middle boy, Andrew. He's hanging around on the street corners late at night, drinking beer and acting tough with a bunch of punks who drink beer and act tough and dammit, are tough. Andrew thinks his father's a real hero, because he plays the angles and he did time in prison, and that is not an encouraging sign to me. I'll do all I can for that family, but a lot of what needs to be done is undoing what Jerry did wrong or didn't bother to do at all. He's got a couple of real little roughneck kids coming along there, and quite honestly, I wouldn't know where to begin shaping them up."

"How about military school," Riordan said. "That's what Doctor Will always threatened me with, when it looked like I might have some ideas about getting off the reservation."

"Yeah," Doherty said, "that's a good one. Will's idea of you getting off the reservation was when you did a jackrabbit start as the light turned green. Digger's idea of his kids getting off the reservation is when they steal something he can't sell; so far, I guess, they haven't brought any of their business to him, if they have any to do. Stoning school buses with black kids in them, though—that's all right. Drinking underage? Boys will be boys. Skipping school? Jerry didn't like school much himself. It's okay to get mouthy with the cops, because Jerry knows all the cops're jerks and there's no need treating them with any sort of courtesy because that only encourages them to push you around. Little shoplifting here and there? Perfectly okay—hey, what the hell, goddamned merchants're ripping everybody else off, do them good to get a taste of their own medicine for a change. Oh, Jerry's bringing those kids up in the right way, Pete. They'll be street-smart if he's got anything to say about it. He makes Fagin look like Father Flanagan. You think I want that job? Raising the James Boys from scratch? Far from it. As a senior altar boy of mine once said: 'I'd rather pour horse liniment in my jockstrap.' "

"Sorry I mentioned it," Riordan said.

"You should be," Doherty said.

Riordan leaned forward. "Paul," he said, "mentor of my youth and builder of my character . . . "

"See?" Doherty said. "That just goes to prove it. You're blaming me for the disgraceful scoundrel you turned out to be, and you were a fairly promising candidate from a respectable family. Can you imagine how I'd screw up the job of trying to keep those outlaws out of the penitentiary? I mean it, Pete. I don't want that damned job. I had it for a while when he was in the slammer the last time, and I don't want it again."

"Okay, okay," Riordan said, settling back. "Anyway, Walker's going to do something that he figures'll screw up the do-gooders that want to let every contrite assassin loose in the

street, and that should help keep Magro right where he is for a
few more years."

"Let's hear about it," Doherty said, "what exactly is he
going to do? Just to make me feel better."

"Paul, Paul," Riordan said, "you're asking too much of me
now. Do you think if Ken Walker or anybody else asked me
what you said to me in private, I would tell? Is that really
what you think?"

"Oh oh," Doherty said, "now I think I'm the one that's in
trouble."

Riordan sighed. "You certainly are, Paul. I thought we had
it all straight, that there's a seal of the confessional in my line
of work too."

"All right," Doherty said. "More tea, Agent Riordan?"

"Is there any chance," Riordan said, "that we could maybe
persuade Mrs. Herlihy to let us have a couple beers, if we ask
politely? I assume you still stock that Amstel."

"It isn't noon yet, Pete," Doherty said.

"When I want the time, Paul," Riordan said, "I will ask for
the time."

"Just a minute," Doherty said. He went over to the desk
and pressed the intercom button. He asked Mrs. Herlihy to
serve two bottles of Amstel.

"Airs and graces," Riordan said. "Intercom and all, I see.
Go with being a bishop?"

"Goes with having a lame housekeeper," Doherty said,
returning to the couch. "I hate it myself."

"Used to be, as I remember it," Riordan said, "man could
actually get up on his hind legs in his room and walk his own
butt out to the icebox and fetch his own beer. Take care of his
own health and safety."

"At night, Pete," Doherty said, "only at night, when she's
supposed to be off duty. Hurts her pride if you do it during
the day. She thinks you're suggesting that she's too infirm to

do her job anymore. So, I put the intercom in, and I told her it was orders from my doctor, while I was recuperating from the attack. You see, Mrs. Herlihy was put on the earth first to take of the late James Herlihy, and then to take care of me. It is perfectly all right in her estimation for me to be feeble. In fact, it is only right that I be feeble, because otherwise God would never have dispatched Mrs. Herlihy to see to my care and upkeep."

"Complicated, isn't it?" Riordan said.

Doherty shook his head as he sat down. "Complicated? Good Lord, I had no idea how complicated it would become as I got older."

"So I'm discovering," Riordan said. "All right, that's Walker out of the way. I left him and I went in to the State House, where there is this fellow that may not know where Captain Kidd hid the gold, but when it comes to where the bodies are buried, he is supposed to know everything."

"Seats Lobianco," Doherty said immediately, laughing. "Salvatore Lobianco."

"You know him, then," Riordan said.

"I'm alive in the Commonwealth, am I not?" Doherty said. "If you've ever been at the intersection of Beacon and Park Streets on a sunny spring day, you know Seats Lobianco. He's been around since the statue of George Washington on horseback in the Garden, but with one important difference: No pigeon in his right mind would ever dump on Seats Lobianco. Seats would ruin his career without ever raising his voice above a whisper."

"Is he all right?" Riordan said. "My guy said he is all right. I went on that. I had to. I've been out of the state for a while, you know. Out of the States, for that matter. And since I've been back, I had very little to do with that place on the hill. I don't know much about all that back-and-forth they've got going up there."

"Nobody does," Doherty said. "A great many people think they do, and even more say they do, but very few actually know. There's too much of it. It's like watching the Marathon. There's more than twenty-six miles of it. Nobody's ever seen the whole Marathon because there's too much Marathon to see. What they see is a little bit of it, and they think they've seen the whole thing. Comforting, I suppose, but a myth. Talk about wheels within wheels. When Cushing was alive, I used to go up there now and then. Spent quite a lot of time up there for him, doing one thing and another and you're not to ask me too many questions about that, either."

"Bingo," Riordan said.

"Damned WASPs," Doherty said. "WASPs and mobsters. Pretty lethal alliance against the forces of light and truth and a solvent bourse in the parishes of the Archdiocese of Boston."

"Is Lobianco straight?" Riordan said.

"Oh, sure," Doherty said. Mrs. Herlihy hobbled in with the tray of beer. She looked suspiciously at Riordan and disapprovingly at Doherty. "You can look out for yourself, Peter," she said, "I guess you're old enough and young enough. But you, Father, you remember what the doctor told you about this sort of thing." She set the Amstels on the table.

"Call him up, Mrs. Herlihy," Doherty said, "and tell him that I'll anoint myself on the way out if one beer carries me off. And if it does, I wasn't long for this world anyway."

"Well," she said, "you just remember, that's all." She walked slowly out and shut the door.

Doherty began laughing. "Tyranny," he said, "absolute tyranny. I hear all these complaints firsthand from the kids that their parents're tyrants, and I get all the beefs secondhand from the parents that the clergy's tyrannical, but not a one of them has the faintest notion of tyranny, real absolute rule, until he's been subjugated to the will of a pedigreed rectory housekeeper.

"Yeah, Pete," Doherty said, leaning forward to pour the beer. "Seats is all right. He plays the clown, and he puts on a good act about being a plotter and a conniver. Which in a way I suppose he must be, or he never would've survived as long as he has in that place. But he is absolutely dead honest."

"He told me that he is," Riordan said. "I wasn't sure I believed him, though."

"Ah, Peter," Doherty said, after drinking beer through the head of foam, "the Holy Scriptures are right: 'Wiser in the ways of the world are the children of Mammon, than are the children of the Light.' Every one of those birds up there will tell you he's as honest as the day is long, and then he will take you aside and whisper that you better watch them other guys, though. Lobianco is one of the lot that actually means it. He is straight. What'd he tell you, or is it another sin if I ask you that?"

"Nah," Riordan said, "you have that one, free, gratis and for nothing. He said I was the third guy came at him yesterday on Mike Magro. Up till yesterday morning, Lobianco'd never heard of the guy. He was damned if he could figure it out."

"Who were the first two?" Doherty said.

"The guy right before me," Riordan said, "was one of the Councillors. Follow by the name of Thomas Emmett. Democrat out of Worcester. He was the only guy on the Council that'd apparently ever heard of Magro before the meeting, and he wanted the pardon application rammed through all at once, executive session."

Doherty furrowed his brows. "Emmett," he said, "that's odd. Tommy Emmett."

"You know him?" Riordan said.

"Little," Doherty said, "not a heck of a lot. Never draws much attention. Which of course're often the most devilish kind, because nobody notices when they pull something off. Never heard anything much about him one way or the other, though. Oh, the standard stuff—covers his district when there's a judgeship, clerkship, something like that. Any judgeships coming up?"

"Lobianco said one filled yesterday, and the other one's locked up for delivery the next meeting."

"Can't be that, then," Doherty said. "Besides, doesn't make any sense. Where the hell would a thief and killer like Magro get the weight to pull a judgeship out for somebody? Unless Emmett also wants Jerry killed, which is equally hard to imagine. I doubt they even know each other, let alone one of them carrying that kind of a grudge." He shook his head. "Nope, can't do anything with it. There's obviously something there, but I don't know what it is. Who's the other guy?"

"Rep name of Greenan," Riordan said, "from Roslindale."

"Ticker Greenan as I live and breathe," Doherty said. "One of the grand characters out of vaudeville, now continuing an extended engagement in the Massachusetts House of Representatives."

"He was in vaudeville?" Riordan said.

"I don't think so," Doherty said. "He's funny as the devil, but he doesn't mean to be and he doesn't know he's doing it when he does it. Where does he fit in?"

"Told Lobianco at lunch before the meeting," Riordan said, "he was pushing Magro's application as a favor for a priest."

Doherty leaned forward and put the beer down. "Ahh," he said, "now we are getting somewhere. The priest is a domestic prelate."

"Right," Riordan said.

"He's got a parish in West Roxbury," Doherty said.

"Right," Riordan said.

"His name is Fahey," Doherty said.

"Also right," Riordan said.

"Right Reverend Monsignor Vincent J. Fahey, to be exact," Doherty said. "Or, as we called him affectionately in the seminary, Trimmer Fahey. Ah yes, my dear Watson, it all comes clear now. Clearer, at least. Trimmer Fahey's at the root of this little adventure."

"Care to fill me in?" Riordan said.

"Not now," Doherty said. "The ball's in my court now, and I believe I'll take a little canter with it and see who chases me. When I get a reading, I will tell you. . . . Tell me, Peter, and be straight with me because we are old pals, are you telling Warden Walker everything you know, such as that you know me?"

"No," Riordan said.

"Are you telling Lobianco all you know?" Doherty said.

"No," Riordan said, "like I said. I didn't see any reason to drag your name into it."

"I appreciate your thoughtfulness," Doherty said. "Now for the hard part. Keeping in mind that what you've told me is quite bad enough, have you told me everything you know about Jerry? And why he interests you?"

"Tell you the truth," Riordan said, "no."

"Peter," Doherty said, swatting Riordan mildly on the knee, "and I mean this: I really appreciate that, both your candor and your reticence. Yes, when I have scouted around Fahey a little, I will fill you in. But I will not tell you everything. Fair?"

"Fair enough," Riordan said. "Wish all my sources were this candid."

The bulldog, which had sat, listened and watched attentively during the conversation, yawned loudly, and slid slowly to the floor into position for a nap. He was snoring when Riordan reached the door.

"Pete," Doherty said.

"Yeah," Riordan said.

"You maybe put Spike to sleep there, but you sure woke me up. Thanks." He was grinning.

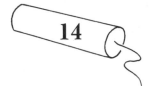

14

THE RIGHT REVEREND Monsignor Vincent Fahey, wearing black trunks he had adopted under protest when the University Club admitted women to the use of its athletic facilities, swam length after length in the indoor pool at the red brick building on Stuart Street in Boston. Every Monday, Wednesday and Friday (he arrived around 11 A.M.), he did sixty laps in the pool. He was a trained swimmer, and had competed occasionally in informal meets with other clubs in his younger days, but upon turning fifty had started to beg off.

"Getting too old to help the club, Tommy," he would reply when Thomas Emmett approached him. Emmett arranged all the meets. He resided in Worcester but he lived in an apartment on Somerset Street, next to the State House. "Still got the moves, like you on the Executive Council, but I don't have the speed anymore." Monsignor Fahey prided himself on his ability to appraise realistically any matter of earthly or heavenly concern referred to his attention. "The best I can do now, Tommy, is endurance, and keep myself in shape. Can't let yourself get into the sad condition of the fellows on the track up there."

Monsignor Fahey left very little wake as he moved through the water, doing a steady Australian crawl with great economy of motion. He wore ear plugs on a black rubber headgear. He put his left side down and dug powerfully with his right hand at the slightly steaming surface of the pool. His legs and feet kicked just below the surface; he took air through his mouth, rolled onto his right side, submerged that ear, dug the water with his left hand, reached the end of the pool, submerged, did a kick turn off the wall and broke the surface once again, working like a diesel engine. On the track suspended above around the pool, the runners labored along, Mondays, Wednesdays and Fridays, panting. Men half Fahey's age wore headbands, wristbands, sodden tee-shirts, shorts, sneakers and socks. Their faces became red and their feet sore thudding on the wooden surface.

"Running," Monsignor Fahey would scoff in the men's locker room, toweling off his flat belly and his muscular chest and legs, refusing both offers of beer and invitations to join the runners. "Can't do it. Haven't got the equipment for it. I don't like beer so I don't have the belly that it looks as though a man needs for the first lap. My face wouldn't get red fast enough. You guys'd all be sweating like horses and I'd still be comfortable. The only thing that'd get me is shin splits, and I don't want those."

Completing his laps, Monsignor Fahey climbed out of the pool and took his white towel from the hook. He removed his headgear with the ear plugs and dried his bald head and the fringe of gray hair at the base of his skull before he mopped his face and neck. From the bench beneath the hook, he took the glasses with the black frames and fitted the bows over his large ears, reddened by the water. He put his feet into slippers made of coarse brown paper and walked toward the door and the stairs to the locker room. Above him the early lunchtime joggers thumped earnestly around the wooden track. He shut the door on their noise behind him.

On the carpet before his gray-green locker, Monsignor Fahey scuffed off the disposable slippers. He removed the black nylon bathing suit and the white supporter he wore under it. Entering the same row of lockers, Daniel Minihan of the Massachusetts Turnpike Authority paused in the act of taking off his green-and-blue-striped silk tie when he saw Fahey undressing. Minihan wore a gray linen suit, with a vest, and a white broadcloth shirt. His face was well tanned. "Father Fahey, as I live and breathe," Minihan said. "And not wearin' the trunks so's you're lookin' down on the unemployed."

Fahey turned toward him. "*Monsignor* Fahey to the likes of you, Minihan," he said. "No, as a matter of fact, I try to keep it out of sight in case you might forget sometime when I'm around you which one belongs to whom, should your hand start twitching. Still shaving your palms are you, to dispose of the evidence?"

"Ahh, Father," Minihan said, "and fine talk it is, comin' from a man of the cloth like yourself. I'm afraid the only benefit of your celibacy as it were is unseemly envy of the normal men around us, that know wimmen was put upon the earth for our delight. It's a narrow view you have, Father, that would deny another man his pleasure because you get none for yourself. Although I see by the papers that there's one or two of you lately that's apparently seen the light of day and found the consolation of a woman's arms. Judgin' only by what I read, of course."

"It's good news that you can, Minihan," Fahey said. "That's one of the things I always wondered about you. Whether a man as popular in the press as yourself was aware of the fine reputation you've acquired as a faithful son of Holy Mother Church and a man of many other enterprises as well."

"Now, Father," Minihan said, removing his coat and unbuttoning his shirt, "I would remind you, do not be uncharitable to those who are afflicted by the infidels. Nobody's ever charged me with anything."

"No, they haven't," Fahey said, turning toward the showers, "and Judas had to hang himself, too, there being nobody else around with the wit to see it needed doing and the common decency to do it for him."

"I've betrayed no one," Minihan bellowed at Fahey's naked back, as the priest removed his glasses, put them in the locker, and headed for the showers.

"I know, Daniel, I know," Fahey said, at the entrance to the showers, "that I know. Which is not to say you haven't been afforded the opportunities, on many occasions, what with all those subpoenas and all. I will say this for you, Daniel: You may be a reproach to your family, your Church and your community, but you give the lie to one proverb, and that may be to your credit—obviously there is some honor among thieves. Not much, but some." He went into the showers.

When Fahey reached the last shower, Ted Norman was shaving his swarthy face at the sink, drawing the skin down carefully but strongly from his sideburns, using the razor as he used the instruments in the operating room at the New England Medical Center. He kept his gaze on the mirror. "Hey Vinnie," he said, "I hear that asshole's arrived again."

Fahey threw the damp towel into the plastic barrel and took a fresh one from the stack, along with dry paper slippers and a piece of pink soap. "Ted," he said, "you're on the membership committee. Why can't you remove guys like him the way you'd take any other tumor out of an otherwise healthy body?"

Norman thrust his chin toward the mirror, working the skin around to inspect the completeness of his shave. "Can't do it, Vinnie," he said. "Committee's for letting people in, not throwing people out. We've got the shorts here, you know. Besides, you think it'd be a good idea, Armenian kid like me attacking a fine broth of an Irish lad like Minihan? I'd enjoy it, and you'd enjoy it, but Minihan's not the only one, you know. Where do we stop, will you tell me that?"

"Now that, Ted," Fahey said, mixing the water in the stall

he had selected, "wounds me more than anything Minihan ever said to me. Not because I don't think there's a little of truth in it. Because I'm more and more afraid there is."

Norman satisfied himself that the shave was finished. "Cripes, Vinnie," he said, "there's nothing to be afraid of. We've got this kid named Kamal or something that's one of the residents in surgery, and my God if the little bastard doesn't think God put him on the earth to flash a scalpel around like a samurai warrior. Every time somebody tells him he screwed up, Kamal puts it down to prejudice against Mideast types. Naturally, he's widely admired, and when his requests for references started to come in, the word got around fast enough so that pretty soon even Kamal the Camel, as he is affectionately known, stupid as he is, knew what was happening to him. And *that* was prejudice too, of course."

Norman rinsed his face and rubbed it vigorously with a towel. "I, naturally, being the resident Arab, am his friend and confidant. I don't know what I did to get God so pissed off, but I am Kamal's unofficial guru and dervish. So he came in to me, practically in tears, and wanted me to do something because all this prejudice was going to cost him a staff position at Columbia Presbyterian. It became my job to explain to him that there is no recognizable benefit to being a little prick and prima donna all the time, because it tends to make people angry. And that made me the quisling of the Arabs at the center, because I was siding with the Aryan hordes.

"I didn't say anything about his ability," Norman said, splashing shaving lotion on his face. "I never had a chance to get to that. Fact of the matter is that he's got the makings of a good surgeon. Matter of fact, by the time I get finished with the little bastard in June, he will be a damned good surgeon, or one of us will be dead. But there's no way he would listen to such a speech. He knows what's going on. He is getting the shaft. And because he is so goddamned convinced that he is getting the shaft, he is *going to get the shaft*. Self-fulfilling prophecy. Neat, huh? Why the hell did Allah appoint us the guardians of the jerks in our contingents?"

Fahey was satisfied with the temperature in the shower. He paused at the open door. "That's not what bothers me about Minihan," he said, "the little pisspot. It's not that he's Irish. He isn't Irish. Oh, he's got an Irish name, which I presume he inherited from his father. Although there are reports that his mother wasn't really sure who it was that was responsible for the sad event, and took the easy way out by blaming the disaster on the last drunken longshoreman who paid a quarter to have his way with her down at the pier in Chelsea one night when she got lucky and went home with a grand total of two dollars and seventy-five cents for the night's work and her bloomers down around her ankles. Where they usually were when she was working for her meager living, doing the only thing that God gave her the talent to do. And his name may not even've been Minihan, for all she knew. It could have been some two-boater from over in Melrose, down at the docks for the night to steal what articles he could and buy what affection he couldn't obtain from a respectable woman in a marriage bed."

"He looks Irish, sure enough," Norman said, stepping back from the mirror. He took a comb from the plastic container of combs standing in antiseptic fluid on the glass shelf above the row of sinks, sweeping his hair straight back so that it resembled the crown of a hawk.

"And a glass of ice water looks like a martini," Fahey said. "The humidity condenses on the outside of the glass, on a humid day, just as it does when there's honest Beefeater's for the clear liquid cold inside. But there's a difference in the beverages, Ted, and you can tell it right off, by the mere act of comparing the taste of the water to the taste of the merest sip of the real thing. Hell, you can tell the difference by the smell or the lack of it in the old woman's drink, and the power of it in the man's.

"It's the same with the Irish, Ted," Fahey said. "There's them that're Irish and will always remember it. They don't try to remember it. It takes no effort at all for the real ones. The effort would be in the tryin' to forget it, because for the real Irish, it's in the blood and they could no more forget it than they could demean themselves ever to kiss His Majesty's bright-blue baboon's arse. His icthial callosity, as it were, all swathed in ermine as it may be to hide the embarrassing fact.

"It's the Minihans of this world that've misled the stupid bastards of the sceptre and the crown into believing that the Irish have resigned themselves to the boot heel of oppression. It's the Minihans of this world that've done that, fawning and licking the hand that cuffs them, like spaniels. Imitation Irishmen. Counterfeit Irishmen. Shit-on-shirttail Irish. Minihans. I despise the lot of them. They give a bad name to the rest of us."

"He acts Irish," Norman said, rubbing the flakes of sunburned skin from his forehead. "Damn, I lecture so well to my patients, but give me a day and I'll be out in the sun myself, no hat and no lotion, doing exactly the same damage to myself that I'm always telling them to avoid. He belongs to the Clover Club and all. I see his picture in the paper every year, when they have their annual dinner."

"To prance and dance around like the stage cartoons of Irish that they are. And not content with that, make bigger fools of themselves by gettin' their antics published in the newspapers."

"He's always at the dinners down at Southie for the Evacuation Day," Norman said. He finished rubbing his forehead, rather absently rediscovered the comb in his hand, rinsed it and replaced it in the sterilizing solution. "Bad sign," he said, "forgetting an instrument like that. Hope I didn't leave the retractors in Mrs. Samuelson's duodenum when I closed her up this morning. Every year, when they print the stories of the big political dinner for Saint Patrick's Day."

"Evacuation Day," Fahey said, "and aptly named, too. Evacuation of the bowels of a proud race plagued since the Battle of the Boyne by the presence in the body of human waste such as Minihan. 'The Wild Colonial Boy.' Indeed. Jack Duggan wouldn't've wasted his spit on the likes of Minihan. Cockles and mussels, alive, alive oh, when what we really need is cocks and muscles, alive and bursting with strength, to throw off the yoke of the tyrant. Like the men of the Airborne, proud. And fierce. Men of Kerry, climbing up the cliffs from Dingle to defend the faith."

"I hope your oratory keeps you heated enough so you don't stiffen up before you finally get into that shower, Vinnie," Norman said. "What I should do is connect you to some of my more eccentric brothers who aren't sure Yasir Arafat's PLO is an entirely bad idea. You sound something like them. You want have lunch? I can even have a drink today."

"You're not playing golf?" Fahey said, stepping into the shower, closing the door and raising his voice above the sound of the water.

"Nope," Norman said. He headed toward the locker room, pausing in front of Fahey's shower. "The rain out there may not fall upon the Irish hierarchy, but it sure does hamper this Armenian's golf game."

"Oh," Fahey said, soaping himself. "I forgot. Wednesdays. Doctors. I assume: golf. Well, I can't. Having lunch with the Bishop, as a matter of fact."

Norman looked in at the steam which hid Fahey. "Command performance?" he said. "What'd you do, come out against busing again?"

"Ted," Fahey said in the steam, "I never came out on busing. All I said was that I could understand why people didn't want their kids shipped all over town. As a matter of fact, I am against busing, but that's a different matter, and I never said it publicly. Not a command performance, though. This's just Bishop Doherty, and I can't imagine what he wants. He most likely can't, either. Rather of a fool, actually. Poor fool. Not the Cardinal Archbishop. The Fall River Fishmonger."

"Doherty?" Norman said. "God, is he still around? There was awhile there, when we were all being White Liberals and Doing Good, and I thought we'd never hear the end of him. I thought he was dead, he's been so quiet. Didn't he have a heart attack or something?"

Fahey remained behind the steam. "Minor one," he said. "He recovered. He's tough enough for that, at least, a minor heart attack. Even though there's quite a bit of the Minihan strain in him, too. Must be it crept in a couple generations back. The Dohertys are sort of mongrel Minihans and Paul's the carrier of the weakness for this generation. His brother Jerry's tough enough, I guess. Did some time at Walpole. Man who stands up for his rights."

"Could see where he might," Norman said. "Prison. Good God. How do men stand it?"

"With courage," Fahey bellowed in the steam. "They stand it steadfastly, as they're doing today in H Block, Long Kesh."

"Yeah," Norman said. "Well, okay, Vinnie. I'll see you about lunch the next rainy Wednesday. Have a few laughs, and if Minihan shows up on my shift in the OR, I'll check on the malpractice insurance and see if I can afford to do you a favor."

"Good," Fahey said. "And if you can't afford it, call your brother, the lawyer, and see if he can get you court permission to abate a common nuisance."

"And if he can't?" Norman said, smiling.

"Do the deed anyway," Fahey said. "I'll give you absolution."

15

THE METALLIC BLUE Dodge Aries coupe with the matching blue landau vinyl roof came slowly up St. James Street in the noonday rain, and turned left on Clarendon Street at the John Hancock Tower. There were cars illegally parked on both sides of the street, leaving one lane. Pedestrians, their shoulders hunched against the warm rain, their coat collars turned up, jaywalked across Clarendon, the younger ones breaking into a sprint as though expecting to find shelter in the lee of the wind behind Trinity Church. The Aries stopped at the Stuart Street intersection, where the front of the brick University Club building faces the back of the blue glass Hancock Tower. The driver wiped mist from the windshield and passenger-side window, making broad, haphazard swipes with his handkerchief. The rain fell steadily The light changed to green and the brown-and-white Boston Cab immediately behind the Aries sounded its horn. The driver of the Aries deliberately waited precisely fifteen seconds, the cab horn bleating behind him all the while, and then proceeded across Stuart Street and up the small hill on Clarendon. The driver of the blue Aries commenced his turn into the concrete layer-cake garage on the right just below the crest of the rise, across the street from Jason's nightclub. The taxi lurched around the Aries at Jason's, its horn blowing loudly, as the Aries entered the garage. Once under the roof, the driver opened the window on his side and stuck a black-sleeved arm out to reach for the parking ticket. The articulated gate lifted like a forefinger bending, and the Aries proceeded slowly up the ramp. In the extreme lower left-hand corner of the rear window there was a small red-and-white sticker, with a red picture of the statue of the Minuteman.

The driver of the Aries found a parking place on the second level of the garage, up against the outside wall. He parked the car gingerly between a metallic silver VW Jetta and an old black Cadillac sedan. Over the waist-high wall, the rain slanted away from the garage toward the back of the University Club.

The Aries engine shut down. Paul Doherty opened the driver's side door and got out. He wore a well-fitting black suit, a well-pressed black dickey, and a perfectly fitted Roman collar with a narrow crimson ribbon at the throat. He reached into the car and took out a black narrow snap-brim hat. He placed it at an angle on his freshly-styled gray hair, being careful not to disturb the coiffure. He had been exposed for two and one-half minutes to a sunlamp, and he had kept his hands under it as well. His face had been deep-cleaned and massaged, as had his neck. He smelled of St. Johns Bay Rum and he liked that. He smiled experimentally against the facial muscles, then more broadly as he felt them tighten. He reached into the car again and took out a black raincoat, and put it on. Once more he reached into the car for a black Totes umbrella. He shut the car door and locked it. As he passed the left rear wheel, he kicked the tire. "Junk," he said.

Bishop Paul Doherty emerged from the bright green painted doors of the elevator on the Clarendon Street end of the garage, unsnapped the umbrella, pressed the trigger that opened it, and stepped out into the rain. He carried the umbrella at an acute angle behind his head, warding off the slanting rain. He walked briskly. At the corner of Stuart and Clarendon he turned left, walking close to the front of the University Club for its partial shelter from the rain. He ducked under the carriage lamp on the left-hand side of the double doors and pressed close against the black strips criss-crossing them as he rang the bell on the right-hand side of the door frame. Through the glass he could see the clerk look up from the desk, peer into the gray light outside, and push the unlocking button.

Stepping back slightly, Bishop Doherty opened the door with his right hand, collapsing and furling the umbrella as he stepped onto the red carpet in the foyer. He stepped into the comparative darkness of the lounge. There were people in there in the gloom, looking toward the door. He could see their faces but he could not make them out. No one spoke. There was no one on duty in the checkroom to the right. He put his umbrella on the top shelf. He removed his hat, brushing the beaded drops of water from it, and put it next to the umbrella. He took off his coat and hung it under the hat. He stepped back into the foyer and went to the desk. He asked for Monsignor Fahey.

The clerk was briefly puzzled. He was about nineteen, with longish red hair. Then his expression cleared. "Oh, I'm sorry, Your Eminence," he said. "Monsignor Fahey's very informal. We've all been calling him Vin Fahey for so long. He asked us to, when he became a Monsignor. I guess I just don't think of him as a Monsignor."

"Well," Bishop Doherty said, "as long as he occasionally recollects it himself, I suppose it's all right."

"See," the clerk said, grinning, "he's so *regular*, you know? Just another one of the members."

"No doubt," Bishop Doherty said. "Yes, I can see where such familiarity would engender some sort of offspring. It nearly always has, in my experience with Vin. Limited as it is."

"He was in the service, you know," the clerk said.

"I had heard something about that," Bishop Doherty said. "He might have mentioned it to me himself, come to think of it. It was a long time ago, though. Wasn't it? Chaplain, I believe, like many other priests who were in the service."

"Oh," the clerk said, "not just the service, though. Airborne. Eighty-second Airborne Division. The one that jumped into Normandy on D-Day."

"And got cut to ribbons, as I recall," Bishop Doherty said.

"Sure," the clerk said. "But that wasn't their fault. And the ones that survived were heroes. I don't think a man'd probably ever get over that, you know? Like, being with guys like that, you know, you probably wouldn't ever want to make too much of any title that you got later on. If Vin Fahey was good enough for those guys, the paratroopers, which is what Vin said to us, you'd probably have to think it'd be good enough for anybody else you ever met afterward."

"Sure," Bishop Doherty said. "Well, is Monsignor Fahey here? I'm supposed to meet him for luncheon."

"Oh," the clerk said. "Forgive me, Your Eminence. I got so interested in talking, I guess. . . . Yes, he's right in there, to your left. In the dining room. We use the bar as a dining room for lunch."

"Thank you," Bishop Doherty said. "And don't apologize for our little chat. I enjoyed it."

"You're very kind, Your Eminence," the clerk said.

Bishop Doherty stopped just over the threshold of the lounge as he entered it for the second time. There was light enough on the grand piano immediately to his left, but the rest of the lights in the room were dimmed except for the lights under the bar to his left that illuminated the sinks, and the ones under the glass shelves behind the bar which illuminated the liquor bottles from below. The Bols liqueurs —red, green, blue, dark maroon—were at the end of the shelf closest the door, and looked like colored bottles of water.

His eyes adjusted and he stared down the room in time to see Monsignor Fahey turn his back abruptly and bend over the wheel of yellow cheese striped and dappled with port wine.

Bishop Doherty walked briskly down the center of the room and stood behind Fahey on the red carpet. "Vincent," he said.

Fahey turned around, picking up his drink in his left hand and holding a saucer with cheese and Ritz crackers in his right. "Paul," he said, smiling, "I didn't see you." He gestured with both hands as Bishop Doherty slowly allowed his extended right hand to drop. "Oh, hell," Fahey said, helplessly. "Come on, the table's right over here."

Fahey led the way through the centered tables to the third of the tables arranged in banquettes along the wall of the room. The table was dimly lighted by a sconce fixture above it. Fahey set the saucer and the drink at the place to the left of the table and with his right hand indicated the place to the right. "Sit yourself right down there, Paul," he said. "I was afraid you might've forgotten our little appointment." He glanced at his gold Hamilton watch, which he could not possibly have seen in the gloom.

"If you don't mind," Bishop Doherty said, reaching a chair at the table in the center of the room behind him, "I think I'll just stay on this side of the table. I always feel like I'm out on a date for the junior prom when I sit at one of those things on the inside. Too old for that. I kept you waiting, did I?"

"Oh," Fahey said, "not long. I finished my laps early today and so I hurried on down here. Curiosity, you know? Been a long time since you called for lunch."

"Yes," Bishop Doherty said. He placed the chair at the banquet table and sat down across from Fahey, holding his body erect so that the scant light from the sconce would fall on his face. "Well, sorry I kept you waiting. I stepped in just briefly to hang up my coat when I came in, but it's so dark in here I couldn't see you. And of course I suppose if you'd been looking at the door, the light from the lobby would've dazzled your eyes so you couldn't've seen me. Pity we didn't have our clickers."

The waiter approached. "May I get Father a drink?" he said.

"*Bishop*, Joseph, Bishop. Bishop Paul Doherty, Joseph. I assume you'll have some of the usual sherry, Paul?" Fahey said. "That lousy stuff."

"Oh," Bishop Doherty said, "I think not. It's such a wet day out there, you know, Joseph? Not cold, but still, the dampness does get into your old bones. I'm sure Monsignor Fahey can corroborate my opinion on that. No, today I think I'll just have a Beefeater martini. Olive. Straight up."

The waiter thanked Bishop Doherty for his order. "Clickers?" Fahey said.

"Sure," Bishop Doherty said. "You know, Vincent. Those little metal snapper sort of things that make a clicking noise that sounds something like a cricket? Little kids used to play with them. Adults can use them to locate each other in the dark, or so I heard. At least they did when I was growing up in Saint Gregory's parish. Harmless little gadgets."

"I guess I had a deprived childhood in Sacred Heart," Fahey said. "I don't recall ever having one."

The waiter brought the drink and left.

"Well," Bishop Doherty said, "surely you must have had one in the service."

"The service?" Fahey said.

"Sure," Bishop Doherty said. "That's what reminded me of those little cricket clickers and using them to locate other people in the dark. I haven't thought of them in years. But before I realized you were in here all the time, I had a little chat with the desk clerk, and that reminded me of them. He's a nice lad."

"Phillip is a very polite and well-bred young man," Fahey

said. "He's in my parish, as a matter of fact. Grew up in Most Precious Blood. His mother and father live there."

"Certainly salubrious circumstances for raising a fine young man," Bishop Doherty said. "Auspicious, you might say. Lived with his parents and all."

"What?" Fahey said.

"Oh, nothing," Bishop Doherty said. "I was merely commenting that a boy growing up in Most Precious Blood and living in the parish with his mother and father is a fortunate kid these days. So many broken homes, you know, Catholics or no Catholics."

"I'm glad to hear you say that, Paul," Fahey said. "We're losing control, you know. The evidence is all around us, and the powers that be seem to be blind to it all. It's not the way it used to be."

"Certainly isn't," Bishop Doherty said. "Why, when I was growing up, the worst that ever happened, it seemed, was that the father took to drinking, or ran off, and the mother had to get a job and support the family. Sometimes as many as six or seven of the little nippers. It was all she could do to dress them in rags and keep them in porridge, sometimes, and the only hope she had was a free turkey and some used clothes from the Saint Vincent de Paul Society at Christmas. And maybe a bag of coal from James Michael Curley."

"But they kept those families *together*," Fahey said. "Raised them right. Now, left and right, all you hear about's divorce, divorce. But Phillip's a fine boy. Just finished his second year at the Cross. His parents, fine people, but there's no substitute for the Jebbies and the Jesuit training, I say. They were planning to send him to Stonehill. But, confidentially, I got him into the Cross, and then when the question of money came up, I got him the job here."

"Odd he didn't mention that, Vincent," Bishop Doherty said. "I know he thinks very highly of you."

"Oh," Fahey said, "I told him and his parents at the time, it was to be kept entirely confidential. You know how it is, Paul. Phillip happens to be a very bright kid. Excellent grades at Saint Sebastian's. Good college boards. He was a kid that I could do something for, and I was happy to do it. But then if the word leaks out that you did it for Phillip, pretty soon Mrs. Moriarty who empties the bedpans down at the VA hospital is after you to get a full scholarship for her idiot daughter at some swell joint like Marymount, and you just can't do it. So they get the idea that you're playing favorites."

"Well," Bishop Doherty said, "you can't have that, certainly." He raised his drink. "Happy days." Fahey raised his glass. "*Dominus vobiscum*," he said. "And also with you," Bishop Doherty said. They drank.

"You don't miss the Latin, Paul," Fahey said, as they set the glasses down.

"Oh," Bishop Doherty said, "I couldn't say that. Of course I miss it. But I miss it when I'm saying the Mass in the vernacular, because of course it was in that context that I was trained to say *Dominus vobiscum* and not the Lord be with you. In bars? No. I had an aunt once, at least I think she was an aunt, who used to say God bless whenever she knocked back a drop of the craythur, as she called it, but somehow I never thought of her in terms of her celebrating a Mass when she had herself a belt."

"God has no context, Paul," Fahey said. "God is in all contexts."

"Oh, most assuredly, Vincent," Bishop Doherty said, "but I incline to the notion that He prefers some haunts over others. Such as this place for example. Even God, omniscient as He is, would have been able to make good use of a clicker to find you in here, had He dropped in for a bite to eat on His weekly afternoon off from the tabernacle at Most Precious Blood. And, of course, as Phillip unwittingly reminded me, if God had come in here, scouting you up, and clicking His clicker like crazy, you would've known right off that your Friend was near, and that it was no enemy to fear."

"I . . ." Fahey said, as the waiter reappeared and asked whether they would like another round. "Oh," Fahey said, "no, no, we'll . . . What's the special today?"

"Vincent," Bishop Doherty said, "I'm surprised. One drink each, as seldom as we see each other? Is there something wrong with your small bowel? You know, we are getting along in years, though, come to think of it. Especially you. I hadn't realized how much older you must've been than I, when we were ordained. Why don't you have some milk or something to settle your stomach, and I'll have another drink while we look at the menus. Then when Joseph comes back, we can order."

"No." Fahey said. "Another round, Joseph." The waiter left. "What the hell do you mean, older," he said. "I'm almost two months younger'n you are. You know that."

"I did," Bishop Doherty said. "At least, I thought I did. But then after talking to Phillip, I realized that you must've been a late starter and thoughtfully concealed your much greater experience from us callow youths in the class for fear of hurting our feelings. I approve of that sort of lie, Vincent, the kind that one tells to spare the sensibilities of another and not simply to inflate one's self or advance one's own causes. I guess, all these years, I never really understood you. And, you're right: Young Phillip there is a very intelligent young man. If he hadn't reminded me—heck, caused me to realize it for the first time, as far as that goes—I never would've come to the understanding that you had done so much for all of us. I doubt the boy even has a glimmering of the good he did. But that's the way God works, isn't it? I guess you're right. He is in here, working His plan through the unlikely vessel, the unsuspecting vessel, of Phillip. God's having drinks and lunch with us, right here in the University Club. I didn't know you were at Sainte-Mère-Église."

"Sainte-Mère-Église," Fahey said.

"Yes," Bishop Doherty said. "What does *Mère* mean, Vincent? I've sadly neglected my French, I'm afraid. Have to depend on you Latinists for enlightenment. Does it have something to do with a lady horse?"

"It means *mother*, you ass," Fahey said, too loudly. "What the hell do you think you're doing?"

"Of course," Bishop Doherty said. "*The Church—Église* I think I've got down pretty well—*the Church of Holy Mother You Ass*. Funny name for a French parish. Sounds like one of those inner-city hellholes where they send young rebels with fresh mouths in the sem."

"You son of a bitch," Fahey said. "You're making fun of me. You always do this. You call me up and I invite you to lunch at my private club, and you, you goddamned snob . . ."

"Vincent, Vincent," Bishop Doherty said, "lower your voice. Is this any way to address your ecclesiastical superior? In your private club? Suppose someone like Daniel Minihan heard you? What do you think he'd make of this display on the street? I know he's a member here. I recall considering a membership once, but then I found out that Minihan belonged, and we all know what a gossip he is. In addition to being a horse's ass, of course. Why, you keep this up and he'll have people ridiculing you from Sacred Heart in Weymouth Landing to Notre Dame in Springfield by nightfall. By the time the weekend comes, you'll be a figure of fun from New Bedford to the Canadian border."

Fahey was silent. The waiter brought the second round of drinks. "Just let Vin Fahey here have a moment or two to compose himself, Joseph," Bishop Doherty said to the waiter, "and then we'll have a look at our menus and be all ready to order. I'll beckon you."

"Thank you, Your Eminence," the waiter said.

"Now then, Vincent," Bishop Doherty said, tilting the menu to catch the light available, "why don't you just rest yourself there for a moment, try to catch your breath and all, and then we'll see if perhaps we can conduct ourselves with the dignity appropriate to our vocation.

"I was merely alluding to your Phillip's report of your exploits with Slim Jim Gavin and the Eighty-second Airborne, on the parachute jump behind enemy lines into Normandy at Sainte-Mère-Église. On D-Day, the sixth of June, nineteen-forty-four. You remember, Vin. I of course know only from my reading —my snobbish reading as you might call it—that Brigadier General Gavin, at twenty-nine or thirty, was one of the youngest generals in American military history. And of course that he and his brave commandos carried cricket clickers so that they could signal each other in the dark without alerting German sentries. I knew, naturally, that you served as a chaplain with the Airborne after we graduated from the seminary in the same class, but that was several years after World War Two. At least that's my memory. Until Phillip recounted the swath your unit cut through Europe, I had relied upon that memory. I see now that I was mistaken."

"I was with the Eighty-second," Fahey said. "That's all I told Phillip."

"That may be all you told him, in so many words," Bishop Doherty said, "but that was not all that Phillip clearly took away from your tales of cameraderie and derring-do among the stalwart warriors of the paratroopers. Nor was it all that you meant Phillip to take away from your narratives. I'm sure, for example, that Phillip would be quite astonished to learn that your service with the Airborne was exclusively during peacetime, and that your closest brush with combat service occurred when you resigned your commission just in time's nick, thus missing the Korean conflict. You never left

Fort Bragg. Perfectly named. How do you think your Phillip would react to that information, eh, Vincent? Think he might be a little taken aback by it? That he might possibly conclude, after some reflection, that good old Vin Fahey is a bit of a fake? Think he might? And is he really that bright, that he can't tell from your age that you couldn't've been there?"

"I don't have to take this from you," Fahey said. "I don't have to tolerate this. You've got no power over me. Not anymore. Not since your patron there, old Gargle-throat himself, died and left his favorites like you scattered to the four winds. You've got no more clout with the Fall River Fishmonger'n I have. I don't have to take your crap."

"Yes, Vincent," Bishop Doherty said, "as a matter of fact, you do. For one thing, I'm not the first person who's heard you call the Cardinal Archbishop the Fall River Fishmonger, but if you provoke me, I might be the first to curry a little favor by being the first to report your filial affection to him. Think you could keep the parish school open without a few bucks now and then from the Cardinal Archbishop? What would you do then, Vincent, with no school over which to reign, to show off in each morning? Try to bamboozle the youth of the parish one night a week at Christian Doctrine classes? Hard to do, Vincent. Too much opportunity for them to come in contact with sinister outside forces."

"Ass," Fahey said.

"And in the second place," Bishop Doherty said, "you have to put up with me because I might take it into my head to start chatting with Phillip about how he gained admission to the Cross, and how he got this job, and carelessly let it drop in the course of that conversation that you mentioned to me that it was all your doing. Think that might surprise Phillip's parents? Think that might be a greater weight of deception than they'd be willing to carry around the parish?" Fahey did not say anything. "Well," Bishop Doherty said, "I think so, and my guess is that you think so, too. You know what we used to call you in the sem, Vincent? We used to call you Trimmer, because you had such a fine hand in fitting the truth to your purposes."

The waiter returned. "Joseph, my man," Bishop Doherty said, "I believe we are ready to order."

"I don't want anything," Fahey said. He did not look up.

"Very well, Monsignor," he said. "Your Eminence, the special today is baked stuffed lobster."

"Lobster," Bishop Doherty said. "Excellent. But the crumbs bother me. Might I have one, simply steamed, and removed from the shell, with some melted butter and some lemon wedges?"

"Well, uh, Your Eminence," the waiter said, "we can do that. But it's not on the special, and . . . ."

"Perfectly all right," Bishop Doherty said. "Do one up for me like that. No salad, potato, or anything. Would you like some wine, Vincent? I'm thinking of white, myself."

"I don't want anything," Fahey said. He poured off his second martini.

"Just another drink for Monsignor then," Bishop Doherty said. "I'll have a half-bottle of your Graves. That will be all." The waiter left again.

"I didn't want another drink," Fahey said.

"Don't drink it, then," Bishop Doherty said. "But you're going to stay here until you tell me the entire truth about your relationship with Ticker Greenan and Michael Magro, and no bullshit about housekeepers, either. The entire truth. Not just selected portions of it. And you're going to have something in front of you while I eat and we talk. I am going to take my time eating and you are going to give me every shred of information that you possess. We will sit here all afternoon until you get so looped you can't see, if that proves necessary, until I get what I came for. And if you do stall me that long, I will leave you here like a drunken sot to make your own explanations to the members of your private club who arrive for cocktails and squash after work. Your choice. Make it."

"How do you know about Magro?" Fahey said. He looked up as he said it.

"God works in mysterious ways," Bishop Doherty said. "He has your mind tapped, Trimmer, and He is copying your Bishop in on the tapes. Not that there's that much material to read in the transcripts. Never more than one thought a day, and that one banal. No wonder people complain about your sermons. But, we must make do, Vincent, make the best pots we can from the poor clay the Lord sends us. So, as John Kennedy said, let us begin."

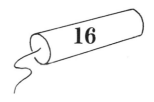

16

By NINE-FIFTEEN, the last stragglers of the midweek traffic jam, brought on by the rain, had escaped from the city. Pete Riordan, his white shirt wilted and his trousers rumpled from the day, removed his booted feet from the top of the desk in his office in Government Center. He leaned forward, resting his elbows on the desk, and rubbed his eyes. He looked at his watch, sighed, and reached for the red telephone on the left side of the desk. He picked it up and began punching numbers. A man answered, his voice eager. "Rampart," he said.

"Rampart," Riordan said, "this is Rocket." His voice was weary.

"Rocket," the man said, "what developments?"

"Nothing new," Riordan said. "It's the same old thing. I keep telling you guys down there: I'm not going to get anywhere chasing a man I can't recognize, whose name I don't know, and whose whereabouts are just as unknown to us now as they were when I went galloping off to California there. I can't get probable cause to arrest somebody until I know what crime's been committed."

"Rocket," the man said, "we do know what crime's been committed. It's gunrunning, to an all-out terrorist organization with definite Marxist connections and a strong and sympathetic underground in place in this country. If they can achieve their objectives in Ulster, they'll attack Dublin the same way, and if they win there, they'll be poised to begin activities in the United States with the complete cooperation and encouragement of Moscow. This is a real potential and serious threat to our national security, Rocket, and you're the only one who's in an immediate position to do anything about it."

"Chuck, for Christ sake," Riordan said.

"Code, Rocket," the man said.

"Code, my ass," Riordan said. "This phone's as secure as anything the Joint Chiefs've got to talk to NORAD, for the luvva Mike. You think with all the scramblers you've got on this thing that any illiterate Mick from Ulster's going to be able to tap it? Be serious, Chuck."

"Those Ulster kids," the man said, "have access to sophisticated KGB training and technology. If the Soviets can do it, we have to assume that the Provos can do it. Whatever it happens to be. Remember, Rocket, this is a top national security assignment you're ordered to perform. I'm ordering you to use the code, as well, and I expect you to do it."

"Suppose I don't?" Riordan said.

"You'll be reassigned," the man said. "You'll go back to your old desk tomorrow and await reassignment. Given your specialty, we can both guess what your next duty will be."

"Something involving a jungle, no doubt," Riordan said.

"Or Beirut," the man said. "Maybe only as a stopover to someplace else. You could wind up doing a lot of traveling, Rocket. You think you'd like that better than following your present orders?"

"Negative, Rampart," Riordan said.

"Roger, Rocket," the man said. "Glad we've got that solved. You knew your obligations when you signed your contract and took your oath. We expect you to live up to them."

"We haven't got anything solved, Rampart," Riordan said. "My God, doesn't anybody listen to what the cop on the beat says is going on? I've been trying to tell you this for weeks."

"What is the precise status of the case now?" the man said.

"I've got a glimmer of a chance of finding him," Riordan said. "I think he's somewhere around Boston. I still don't know what name he's using. I don't know where he's been. If he's doing what we think, we haven't caught him at it. I doubt any of his helpers will be eager to tell us about it. Therefore I have no probable cause to arrest him or them. I can't get a warrant, and I can't arrest him without one."

"And in the meantime, Rocket," the man said, "he continues to operate as a threat to national security."

"Who, if he's arrested and convicted," Riordan said, "will probably only be deported as an undesirable alien, or else released to the custody of the British, assuming they can pin something on him, and we'll have six more just like him coming into the country within a week."

"Correct," the man said. "Is it necessary for me to tell you what to do then, when, as and if you do locate him?"

"Go on, Rampart," Riordan said. "I've known for some time that this was what you had in mind all along. But you're going to have to say it. I'm too old for the jungles, and I'm not interested in the Middle East. But you've got to say it, out loud, because what you guys want done is quite illegal now. And some day, Rampart, somebody's going to check those credentials and find out there ain't no such agency in Justice. Which will get me in the shit for fair. I know what you want. Say it."

"Thank you, Rocket," the man said. "Good night and good luck. This is Rampart off and clear."

Riordan got up and raised the Venetian blind on the window nearest his chair. He satisfied himself that the gridlocked traffic around the Quincy Market, City Hall, the JFK Federal Buildings and the municipal garage to his left had cleared up. The streets were wet and the street lights and occasional automobile lights made them shine. Across the street, the lights were off in the Bell In Hand Tavern, relocated from the old newspaper row on Washington Street to the low brick building next to the parking lot. The Union Oyster House was still open, the red neon sign in its window beneath the ivory wood façade and the brick upper stories glowing red, trolling for stray tourists. The surface of the streets steamed.

Riordan picked up his white phone. He punched out numbers and held the receiver to his left ear. He waited for several rings.

"Did I get you out of the tub?" he said. "Sorry. It's not the clumsiest thing I've done today, but at least the rest of them were things that screwed up other people. . . . No, people I didn't really care about in the first place, before I screwed them up. . . . Yeah, Freudian. Actually, you know, you're probably right. I didn't want anything to do with the bastards in the first place, but they would've fucked me up first chance they got if I didn't let them play pretend with me and bore the ass off me. I knew they'd be fundamentally useless to me, but I had to talk to them so I got even by screwing *them* up. . . . You're awful smart, you know that? I wished I had a college education. . . . Oh, yeah, you're right. I *did* have a college education. I must not've been paying full attention. Well, look, get back in the tub, and if you use my razor, for the luvva Christ put a new blade in it. At least take the old one out. And at very least, if you don't do either one of those things, remind me in the morning so I don't get up and remove half my face with the first slice. . . . No, I don't know why broads' legs ruin men's razors. . . . Yeah, I'm bushed. I'm heading for the barn. Pick anything up? . . . Good. See you."

Riordan lifted his sports coat from the back of his chair, reached across the desk and shut off the white cylindrical

Braun fan that had been blowing on his legs, went to the door, opened it, took one last look around at the cluttered desk, the banker's boxes stacked waist high on the brown vinyl tile floor, the gray metal filing cabinets with the supplementary steel-barred locks down the front, said "Shit," and turned off the lights. In the corridor outside, he shut the door and tested it against the snap lock in the knob. He put on his jacket and buttoned it over the gun. Then he got his key ring out of his jacket pocket and locked the cylindrical lock just below the knob, and the cylindrical lock just over the knob. He used a third key to slam the bolt lock at the top of the door frame, and he selected a fourth key as he crouched to drop the bolt at the bottom of the door into the hole drilled in the vinyl tile and the concrete under it. "There," he muttered, straightening up slowly against the sound of the shrapnel, "safe and secure at beddy-bye, everybody. Take a man who knew his business a good fifty, fifty-five seconds to get through all that protection. Shit."

Swinging his right leg awkwardly, Riordan made his way down the corridors to the back door of the building. There was one short overweight man in his middle fifties in the corridor. He wore a green uniform and he was pushing a green trash canister ahead of him on wheels. It had a broom sticking out of it. Every so often he stopped and took the broom out. He made a few brief sweeps, pushing dirt against the baseboards, then put the broom back into the barrel and pushed it along another five or six feet. Riordan came up behind him, his boot heels clicking, the left cleanly, the right after the sliding sound as he swung it on the pivot in his knee and then put it down again. The man with the broom did not look up.

When Riordan reached him, he said, "I thought you guys only worked days now. Save on energy." The man looked up at him. Riordan noticed the hearing aid in his left ear. The man did not answer him or have any expression on his face. "Oh," Riordan said, feeling silly, "sorry. I didn't know you were . . ." The man stared at him. "Say," Riordan said, pointing with his left index finger to his left ear, "wouldn't that thing work better if you turned it on?" The man stared at him. "Batteries're dead," Riordan said to himself. "Tomorrow," he said very loudly, "go up to Secret Service. They got loads of batteries. Get a special rate on them." He smiled. The man stared at him. "You know," Riordan said, "Secret Service? Guys always with the President, keep him from getting shot? Looks like they're wearing hearing aids? Huh?" The man stared at him. Then he dropped his eyes and swept a few more times before turning his back and pushing the canister another six feet with the broom in it.

"Right," Riordan said. He slipped past the man and reached the back door. He opened it, went outside into the warm evening, shut the gray metal door behind him, tested the lock, and went down three concrete steps. The green Ford sedan was parked under a sign that said U.S. GOVT VEHICLES ONLY. There was an eagle on the sign. There was a blaze orange ticket on the windshield. Riordan took the ticket off the windshield, unlocked the door, threw the ticket onto the floor in the back to join several dozen others, unbuttoned the coat, and got in. He started the engine as he was shutting the door and drove up toward State Street. He took a right on State, ignoring the red light against him and the sign which advised NO TURN ON RED. State was deserted, except for a derelict asleep in his Morgan Memorial overcoat, against the grated subway entrance under the old State House. The unicorn and the lion, newly gilded and painted, were rampant in the floodlights. The plaza in front of the New England Merchants Bank buildings at One Washington Mall had a population of two, a man and a woman who were skipping, hand in hand, out of the revolving doors. "Bay Tower Room,"

Riordan muttered. "Nice clothes, lovely view of the harbor and the airport, dinner for two with lots of wine and cocktails and after-dinner liqueurs: 'We're a little lighter, a buck and a quarter, My Dearest. But who cares when you're having fun and stiffer'n a goat with rigor mortis on the best hooch money can buy?'"

Riordan turned right into the driveway of the condo apartments at 226 Beacon Street, easing the Ford between two cars encroaching on the entrance. He passed through the wrought-iron gate, went down the ramp, rolled down the window, removed the plastic key card from his inside pocket, slipped it into the machine, opened the corrugated steel door into the underground garage, and drove in as the door closed behind him.

Riordan on the third floor of the building closed the apartment door behind him. He threw the dead bolt, took off his jacket and tossed it on the beige couch, and unsnapped the magnum holster from his belt. He unsnapped the keeper strap on the holster and moved the revolver in the leather two or three times. He put the gun on top of the white bookcase along the interior wall. He hitched up his pants and for a moment stared out the picture windows onto the Charles River, broad and black in the night between the lights of Storrow Drive on the Boston side and the lights of MIT and Memorial Drive on the Cambridge side. The only light in the room was from a low white cylindrical floodlight on the floor in the corner beyond the couch. It shone upward toward the ceiling through the foliage of a large ficus in a straw basket, throwing shadows on the white walls and the beige drapes. Riordan stared at the lights. He could hear Freddie singing "Lovin' Arms" in the bathroom. When he looked down the hall, he could see a wedge of light on the floor and the wall, from the partially opened door. There were wisps of steam drifting around the edge of the door.

"Freddie," he said, "I told you before and I tell you again. You can't sing at all."

"Hi, honey," she said. "You home already?"

"No," he said, "this is a singing telegram from your ever-solicitous government, which wishes none of its loyal citizens ever to be lonely ever again."

"You must've driven like a bat out of hell," she said.

"Yeah," he said. "If they pulled me over, I was going to identify myself as one of those crack federal agents, the elite of law enforcement in all the world. In hot pursuit of somebody. Frederika Thomas. Suspicion of singing with felonious intent. Our motto: 'We make the Mounties look sick—they only get their man; we get his fucking brother-in-law and a couple of the guys from his bowling team as well, even if they didn't do anything. We also get our women, by God. Especially if they didn't do anything. Adds spice to their otherwise dull gray lives.'"

"I'll be right out," she said. "Just toweling my hair dry. You had any dinner?"

"No," he said, "and I don't want any, either. I haven't had any loving, either. That I do want. I want a good old drink and some good old loving."

She came out of the bathroom with a towel turbaned around her hair. She wore a pale gold short bathrobe. She was short, about five three. She had well-proportioned legs and she had a good figure, but she was sturdy. "So help me," she said, "you'd better not say it."

"But you do," he said. "I can't help it. Every time I see you, I think of a palomino Shetland pony. From the time I was six until I was close to twenty and finally realized I was far too big to ride her—"

"—And you were certainly right about that, big boy," she

said. "My back's damned near broken. Female superior on all occasions from now on. Don't care how excited you get."

"—I pestered my parents for a palomino Shetland like the Monahans' 'Christmas.' God she was pretty. Small, but beautiful. Willing. Sweet-tempered, lively. Just like you."

"I realize it's supposed to be a compliment," Freddie said, going into the kitchen and switching on the light, "but I really don't feature being compared to a horse. Bourbon and water?"

"No," he said. "Too hot. Thank God for central air conditioning you can regulate yourselves. And damn Jimmy Carter for his goddamned eighty-degree bullshit about Federal Buildings. That asshole have anything to say today? Anything new, I mean."

"No," she said. "Oh hell, I don't know. I got home too late for the six o'clock news and I haven't read the paper yet either. How the hell do I know? What do you want?"

"We got any rum?" he said. "Rum and tonic. Some lime."

"Yassuh, yassuh, massa," she said. "Comin' right up, massa."

"Oops," he said. He walked down the hallway to the kitchen and embraced her from behind. The top of her head barely came over the top of his belt. "Hi, honey," he said, "I'm home. You somewhere around here, honey? Say something, so I can find you."

"You clown," she said, laughing. "At least you could take those damned shitkickers off, so I'd come to your breastbone." He turned her loose. She turned around and stretched up her hands toward his neck. He took her waist in both hands and lifted her to his eye level. She put her arms around his neck and hugged him. He hugged her around the waist. She initiated the kiss, her feet dangling a foot from the floor. After a long minute, he slowly released her, and she slid to the floor.

"We must look like a pair of fools when we go out," she said, laughing. "People must think I'm your mascot or something. 'Huh, big guy like that, think he'd at least get himself a great Dane or something. The hell's he want with that Chihuahua?' 'Very simple, sir,' " she said, deepening her voice, " 'when my little lady here gits tard, an' her little ole dawgies starts to gitting sore there, y'all know? Wal, I jes' picks her raht up by the scruff the neck and I puts her in mah pocket there, and she jes' rides along as comf't'ble as you please, head stickin' out and them bright little eyes a-lookin' the whole world raht over. Thet's why.' "

"You don't sound like you had a bad day," he said.

"Yeah," she said, turning to the counter to prepare the drink. "Shows you how deceitful I can be, because I sure damned right well did."

"Care to tell me what happened?" he said.

"Make a deal with you," she said. "I'll go first, but only on the condition that you come clean when I finish and tell me everything that went haywire on your farm today too."

"I was going to enforce that agreement even if it wasn't made," he said.

"I'm not going in tomorrow," she said. "When I got home from the office, I had a phone call. As a result, I'm going to stay here in the morning and lie on the roof in the sun."

"A phone call," he said, as she handed him a drink.

"Yup," Freddie said. "Funny, but disruptive in a way."

Riordan sat down on the couch. For a while he did not say anything. He swallowed some of the rum and tonic. He cleared his throat. "Look," he said, "I would like to make a request, okay? I can't say my day was much of a success. I am grateful for that, because the day I succeed in this case, that clown Bolling down there at the Seat of Government will probably send me out to destroy the KGB. All I had to do today was put up with a bunch of amateur detectives who're so eager to ingratiate themselves with the Feds that they're falling all over each other telling me things that I read in the paper yesterday. I've got a guy up at the State House who apparently's spent his entire adult life worrying about going to the penitentiary himself, and now he's cozying up to me like I was his long-lost brother. Maybe he helps me, maybe he doesn't, but boy can he talk. And then Bolling called, also chatty.

"Anyway," Riordan said, "I didn't get anything done today, but I'm still kind of tired and I can't stand any sudden shocks. So let's sort of treat this telephone call like we were going into a cold swimming pool, okay? Very gradually, so I don't get cramps in my legs."

"Okay," she said.

"This was, no doubt," he said, "a long-distance telephone call."

"Yes," she said.

"Was it prepaid?" he said.

"No," she said, "it was collect."

"It originated in Manhattan, area two-one-two," he said.

"No," she said, "it originated from Camden, Maine. I don't know what the area code is for Camden. Two-oh-seven?"

"Camden," Riordan said. "It wasn't from Jennifer Thomas, who is vacationing with her father, Attorney Arthur Thomas, of Gatskill, Campbell, Foye and Several Other Guys, Two-fifty-two Park Avenue?"

"It was from Jenny," Freddie said. "She spent one night in the wonders of summer evenings in Manhattan, with her doting father who had scheduled his vacation for the month in order to spend it with his daughter."

"But not in Manhattan," Riordan said.

"That was the original plan, the way I understood it," Freddie said. "But then, what does a foul-mouthed broad like me know about planning, huh? Somebody tells me what the schedule is, I'm gullible and I believe it. Arthur did take his vacation. Jenny did fly down on the shuttle. He did have the limo meet her at LaGuardia. He wasn't able to be there himself, of course, wrapping up some last-minute details and so forth. You know how it is when you're leaving the office for a month. So much to do, and everything. Busy, busy, *busy*.

"Jenny didn't mind that," Freddie said. "Kind of heady, actually, fourteen-year-old girl, gets on the plane in her Calvins with her backpack and her carry-on bag. Thoughtful businessmen suppressing lewd thoughts and helping her with her hanging bag. Gets off the plane, all alone, so mature, there's the limo driver holding up the sign: Miss Thomas. She doesn't know those businessmen understand all about summer visitation. She thinks they think she's a child star, off to shoot another sequence on location.

"Arthur took her to lunch at the Plaza. Chauffeur delivered her luggage to the condo on Sutton Place. Arthur gave her his charge cards at Bloomie's and Saks. Arthur gave her five hundred dollars to spend at Pappagallo and Gucci, because Arthur doesn't have accounts at those stores. Arthur gave her Miss Manning, his secretary's secretary, Gail. Gail is about twenty, but Arthur's secretary, Kathy, has been training her very carefully, and Gail after a year or two is now almost as stylish as Kathy. Arthur doesn't like dowdy secretaries. Arthur went back to the office to wrap up some more last-minute details.

"Gail and Jenny went shopping. Jenny went through about eighteen hundred of Arthur's after-tax income on the charge accounts. 'I didn't spend any of the cash except eight dollars when me and Gail had drinks at the Tavern-on-the-Green,' she told me, quite breathlessly. 'Gail and I,' I said. 'What exactly did you have to drink, Jenny?' 'Same as Gail,' she said, 'white wine spritzer. Gail ordered them. She said they're very refreshing on a hot day after shopping.' "

"Oh boy," Riordan said.

"Well," Freddie said, "now let's be reasonable here. We let her have a glass of wine with dinner with us. If a glass of wine with dinner here isn't going to hurt her, a glass of wine after shopping in New York isn't going to hurt her either."

"No," Riordan said, "but a four-dollar glass of wine at the Tavern-on-the-Green is by sure sweet Jesus going to hurt us, when she comes back here and decides she'd prefer to have her dinner wine served to her by the sommelier in the Ritz dining room every night, perhaps a Médoc with the meat and a Sancerre with the boneless chicken course."

"The chauffeur picked them up at the Tavern," she said. "He handled all the packages, the new bathing suits . . ."

"I just can't wait to see those," he said.

"You just remember," Freddie said, "that I'm a practicing counselor, and I've read all that stuff about how Mummy lets her new boyfriend move into the house and the next thing she knows he's bothering her adolescent daughter by her first marriage. One false move out of you and I'll have the law on ye, Jocko. And then of course there was the Ralph Lauren suit and all manner of other stuff. Chauffeur took care of all of it."

"Who is it that's supposed to have this visitation with her anyway?" Riordan said. "Some time I want to see that custody agreement where it says that Arthur Thomas's chauffeur shall be entitled to the uninterrupted visitations of Jennifer Thomas each summer, until she shall have attained the age of eighteen years. That how she got to Maine? Chauffeur took a wrong turn on FDR Drive? That's kidnapping."

"That's his way, pork chop," Freddie said. "That's Arthur's way of showing affection."

"By not showing any," Riordan said. "Cocksucker."

"Peter," she said, laughing. "I do believe you're getting protective."

"Bullshit," Riordan said. "What did Arthur do that night, have Gail tuck her in and the chauffeur kiss her good night while he cleaned up a few more details at the office?"

"He was very nice," Freddie said. "He came home to shower and change for dinner. His maid ran a bath for Jenny and put some kind of nifty bath salts in it. 'Mummy,' she said, it was heavenly. Just like being in champagne.' "

" 'Mummy,' " he said. " 'Mummy,' for Christ sake? What happened to 'Hey, Fred'? And what is this pervert doing, making her wash with Lawrence Welk in the tub with her?"

"After the bath," Freddie said, "they had white wine on the terrace and watched the skyline for a while."

"Gail and the chauffeur and the maid and Arthur, no doubt," Riordan said. "What'd they do, put on blackface and stage a minstrel skit for the kid?"

"Just Jenny and her father," Freddie said. "Then they got all gussied up. She wore her new white suit and he looked very distinguished in his gray silk, and the limo picked them up and took them to the Four Seasons for a pretheater dinner in the Pool Room. They were going to see *Sugar Babies*."

"Oh my God," he said, "you would think a man who has got that kind of cash to throw around would at least want to contribute an occasional dollar or two for the support of his kid."

"Pete," she said, "we both know who's to blame for that. I am. I didn't want him making another brittle little Gloria Vanderbilt copy out of that kid. But I also wanted out of that marriage, and I wanted out fast. He could've tied me up in court for years, with his money and his connections. He offered me the deal. If he was going to pay, then he was going to have custody. If I wanted custody, then I would have to pay. I took the deal. It was the best one available, and I'm convinced I was right."

"He's bribing her," Riordan said. "He may call it 'polishing,' or 'showing her a side of life' she doesn't see with you, but a kid that age is impressionable. He's trying to buy her. I don't like it a bit."

"You think Jenny can be bought?" Freddie said.

"I don't think she'd go for it if she knew what it was," he said, "but she's still only fourteen. You can turn a kid's head."

"Uh-huh," Freddie said, "okay. Now, this is the part in the story of the Garden of Eden where the snake slithers in to inquire politely whether anyone would like a nice piece of fruit. So listen up.

"They stopped on the way to the Four Seasons, at another co-op building on Fifth Avenue. There Arthur called for Mrs. Felicia Cannon Weatherbee."

"Unlikely name for a snake," Riordan said. "I'm afraid I don't recognize it, right off the bat. Could this be one of those New York socialites?"

"Indeed," Freddie said. "Felicia has had a most unfortunate time with her first marriage. Jay Weatherbee is such a bore, you know. They're legally separated and she's going through with the divorce."

"Represented, no doubt, by Gatskill, Campbell and Nearly Everybody Else."

"Goodness, no," Freddie said. "That would be *tacky*. She has Roy Cohn. She and Arthur didn't meet professionally. They've been friends for simply *years*. Ever since dancing school, for Christ sake. The Knickerbocker Greys parades.

"Arthur, of course, is a carbon copy of Jay. In every respect but one, I guess. Jay tended to be high-strung. He was always disobeying her wishes and going out drinking with his men friends. Why, I understand that one night he just up and refused to escort her to a Beverly Sills appearance at the Lincoln Center, which made her very upset."

"Is there, ah, something fragile about Jay?" Riordan said.

"Queer as green horses," Freddie said. "Jay's got more

boyfriends than Marilyn Monroe could claim in her prime. Arthur is a man who has faults, but there is one thing to be said for him: He is resolutely and exclusively heterosexual. He is also a total stuffed shirt, and Felicia will have no trouble getting him to observe all of the social proprieties. Hell, he thinks he's Teddy Roosevelt even when he's getting laid. When I was married to him, I always expected him to complete the conjugal act by shouting 'Bully' as he dropped off to sleep.

"Felicia joined them for dinner and the theater. This was not at all what Jennifer had had in mind. She thought she was Daddy's date for the evening, and here was this Felicia cropping up like an abscessed tooth.

"They had a lovely dinner," Freddie said. "Then back into the limo and off to the show, and after the show to the Café Carlyle to hear Bobby Short. Then they dropped Felicia off and returned to Arthur's pad, and that's when Jennifer began to suspect that maybe Arthur hadn't had the maid lay in the bath salts especially for Jennifer's visit. Because it was painfully obvious to Jennifer that dropping Felicia off at her residence was a departure from Daddy's usual evening routine with Felicia. One which Felicia did not like a bit.

"Now," Freddie said, "keeping in mind that Jenny ain't stupid, and also keeping in mind that she's been living with a rat-ass detective in the same house with her for going on three years, you can probably guess what happens next."

"She tossed the joint while Daddy was snoring away," Riordan said, "and found feminine undergarments and other evidence suggesting that Daddy did not always sleep alone."

"Crass, crass," Freddie said. "It's a good thing Jenny didn't hear you say that. She would say, 'Dammit, Pete, don't be such an absolute dink.' Or whatever this week's word is.

"No," Freddie said, "she conducted an interrogation. She's learned a lot from you. The apparently harmless question.

The casual aside that the suspect immediately denies, thus proving his guilt. All that stuff. They sat on the terrace and she bubbled like the bath water at Arthur and asked him if they could go to another play the next night, and could they have dinner at Twenty-one the night after that. Which of course flushed him out at once. He had to tell her it'd be hard to do, because they weren't going to be in New York. He had reservations on a flight to Maine at noon the next day. After all, he spends all his time in the city. When he takes his vacation, he wants to go somewhere else. Get away from the things and the people he sees every day. Have some family time. Go to see his mother and father, up in Maine."

"That still doesn't get us to Camden," Riordan said. "I thought his parents had a summer place in Rockland."

"Patience," Freddie said. "Jennifer didn't go for that shit, not in the slightest. For one thing, she does not like her paternal grandparents."

"He makes her call him Grampy," Riordan said.

"Right," Freddie said. "And he tells her how he's going to send her to Vassar. 'But, Mother, he talks like I won't have any choice. It'll be like he was sending me to prison or something. He never asks me what I think. He just sits there and tells me how I'll be meeting all the boys from Yale and Princeton, and I'll get married and raise a nice family, and every summer we'll all come up to Rockland and go swimming and play tennis and do all those things he did when he was a boy. Yuck.'

"So," Freddie said, "Jennifer explained tactfully to Arthur that she was not interested in going to Maine, because she wouldn't have anything to do there. She would much rather stay in New York. That was when Arthur changed the subject to something less dangerous. He chose Felicia. He asked Jenny what she thought of Felicia.

"Jennifer was tactful," Freddie said. "Jennifer said she

really didn't know Felicia very well, but that she seemed nice enough. Arthur pressed her."

"Always a risky maneuver," Riordan said. "You keep at Jennifer long enough asking her what she thinks, she is liable to tell you."

"He did, and she did," Freddie said.

"What'd she say?" Riordan said.

"She came right out and asked him if he was shacked up with Felicia. Which shocked him so much that he admitted she occasionally stayed overnight at his place. Jenny asked him if he intended to marry Felicia. He said it was very possible, which is as close as Arthur ever gets to committing himself to a course of action that he has every intention of following—he always hedges his bets. Then she hit him with the old one-two. Was Felicia perhaps going to accompany her and Daddy to Maine? Yes, as a matter of fact, Felicia was going to Maine with them. Where was Felicia going to stay? Grampy, you see, is very straitlaced, and does not approve of sexual intercourse, or even the appearance of it, between persons who are not married to each other. Felicia was going to meet some friends of theirs on a sailboat in Camden, and spend two or three weeks cruising the Maine coast. They might even sail to Nantucket. Hard to say. Jennifer asked Arthur if they meant Felicia and the people who were already on the boat. Yes, it did. Did it also mean Arthur? Well, ah, yes.

"Keep in mind also," Freddie said, "that Jennifer has a mean streak to go with her suspicious mind. She nailed him. She jumped out of her chair, squealing with delight, the little minx, flung her arms around her darling daddy, and gushed all over him. Oh, that would be wonderful. Three weeks of sailing. She'd never been on a big boat like that. That would be excellent. Who were the other people going to be? Would she like them? Would they like her? Did any of them have kids her age? Any of them boys, maybe, a year or two older?

Would she have her own cabin? She was so grateful that he wasn't leaving her with Grampy in Rockland. He knew she was bored at Grampy's."

"I think I know what comes next," Riordan said.

"Right you are," Freddie said.

"That poor kid," Riordan said. "Jesus, what a shit he is. Get the kid and dump her so he can go off frolicking with his girlfriend. I must become a pillar of the community one of these days. Those bastards can get away with anything. Kicking a kid in the guts like that."

"Oh, come on, Pete," Freddie said. "This isn't Little Nell we're talking about here. She had the dirk in Daddy, but she wasn't satisfied with stabbing him—she was going to twist it a few times. Jennifer has a very healthy sense of cruelty, you know. She knew very well he was going to dump her with Grampy and Grammy and go gallivanting off with Felicia. She couldn't stop him, but she sure could make him feel like a piece of shit for doing it. And she did.

"Yesterday morning," Freddie said, "Jennifer got up pretending to be hurt and sad, and made Arthur squirm some more. Finally he said he wouldn't go with Felicia. He would stay in Rockland with her and Grampy and Grammy and Grammy's blue hair. He admitted he'd been thoughtless. Maybe even somewhat selfish.

"More ammunition for Jenny. She put on this great display of courage and forced gaiety. Oh, no, she didn't want to spoil his plans like that. He worked hard all year. He deserved to have his vacation too. She'd be perfectly happy with Grampy and Grammy in Rockland. Grampy could tell her about when he was growing up, and she could go to the auctions with Grammy. And see the museums, again. And maybe they would take her to the church clambake, or one of those seafood festivals. It'd be keen. And then when he got through sailing with Felicia, they would still have a whole week and maybe he could rent a car or borrow one of Grampy's and they could drive up to Quebec, just the two of them."

"Spoiled it for him," Riordan said.

"Damn betcha," Freddie said. "Pissed all over his little strategy, and then made him eat it. They flew up to Maine and she was just ever so nice to Felicia, and that night they had lobster at Grampy and Grammy's and she gushed all over that, too, making everybody see that she was being a brave little trooper. Except for Grampy and Grammy, of course, who're too fucking stupid to see what's being done right at their own dinner table. Arthur and Felicia had separate rooms, and Jenny gave Arthur an especially big hug and she kissed Felicia good night.

"This morning they all got in the car, with Arthur driving, and they went to Camden to meet the boat, and Jennifer looked just the slightest bit sad. Just enough so everybody could tell she knew she was being left behind, even old Bonehead Grampy. She bit her lip some when Arthur and Felicia got on the boat, and she helped cast off the lines.

" 'And then, Fred,' she said to me, 'I stood on the dock with my hands folded in front of me and I put my head down so nobody could see I was crying, and when Grampy told me to wave goodbye, I just shook my head and kept looking at the ground. It was really beautiful. Grammy had to take Grampy by the sleeve and shush the old jerk. You know how she whispers louder'n most people talk, because he's hard of hearing? "Stop it, Herbert," she said, "can't you see the child's crying?" I almost burst out laughing. Then we all went off for a nice lunch, and right in the middle of the clam chowder I started to look worried. And Grampy asked what was the matter, and I just shook my head and leaned over to Grammy and told her I had to go to the drugstore right off, because I didn't bring any, and then I jumped up from the table and ran out of the restaurant, and she was calming him down, and I did go to the drugstore. I called the airport and the first flight I can get out of this fucking hole—well, that one slipped out,

Fred—is at one o'clock tomorrow. Can you pick me up, and maybe take me to lunch? I could use some fresh air.'

"So," Freddie said, "I asked her how she's going to get to the airport, and she said she already took care of that with her imaginary bag of tennis gear that Grampy didn't know she hadn't brought and Daddy wasn't around to contradict her about. She told Grampy that the airline lost it in New York, but said it'd be at the airport tomorrow by twelve-thirty. So could he drive her down. He said he would. I told her I'd have a ticket waiting for her at the airport. She told me she already had her ticket. Bought it at the travel agency in town right after she made her reservation."

"How'd she pay for it?" Riordan said.

"Remember the five hundred cash that Arthur gave her?" Freddie said.

Riordan started to laugh. He doubled over on the couch. He pounded the cushions with his fists. Tears came to his eyes. The noise he made got Freddie started. When they stopped, they were gasping.

"You know," Riordan said, "for a bad day, I think you had a pretty good one, and I appreciate you sharing it with me."

"Now," she said, "your turn. Another drink, maybe?"

"Yes to the drink, no to the turn," he said. "I'll tell you about Seats Lobianco and his Baker Street Irregulars some other time. And it's bad enough talking to Bolling, let alone talking about him at home."

"Can you join us for lunch?" she said.

"No," he said, "I can't. I've got to see Bishop Doherty for lunch, and Seats in the afternoon, and then I've got to go crawling around in a low dive in Dorchester, at least until midnight."

"No Felicia-type, though," Freddie said.

"Christ, no," Riordan said. "I couldn't stand the torture from Jennifer."

17

PAUL DOHERTY was sitting on the patio with Mrs. Blake and Mrs. Tobin, under a yellow beach umbrella with green ivy vines painted on the underside. He wore golf clothes that fitted well, and a white straw hat with a plaid band tipped over his left eye. The ladies wore their usual uniforms.

"You look so fit, Paul," Mrs. Blake said. "Just like Bing Crosby used to. For a while there you did not look at all well. You were thin and gaunt. Your clothes just hung on you." She waved her left hand and raised her lemonade glass to her lips.

"We were all worried about you," Mrs. Tobin said. She had had her hair streaked ash-blond at the beauty parlor. She had freckles on her pug nose.

"Oh, come now, Peg," Doherty said, "who was worried? I scarcely ever see anyone but you ladies here at the club. The men all play on the weekends, when I tend to be rather busy. I never use the pool. I haven't been to any of the dinners and buffets this summer."

"A good many have commented on that," Mrs. Blake said.

"Have they now," Doherty said. "Who? And what have they said, may I ask?"

"Well," Mrs. Blake said, "offhand, I can't think of any names. But I know there's been talk that you never come to any of the functions. People do tend to talk, you know."

152

"Indeed I do," Doherty said. "I noticed that some time ago." He put his left hand over her right hand. "Nevertheless, Agnes, I don't like people to fret. So if you find somebody worrying my absence like a dog with an old bone, you just tell them that you asked me why I never show up at the functions and I told you that I don't attend because I don't like 'em. Simple as that."

Mrs. Blake and Mrs. Tobin both began to giggle. "It's true," Doherty said. "I really and truly dislike all kinds of functions. It's an aversion I developed when Cardinal Cushing was still among us."

"That dear man," the ladies said together.

"Yes," Doherty said. "Well, it may surprise you to learn that Cardinal Cushing also hated functions. And needless to say there was scarcely a day went by that he wasn't invited to a baker's dozen of them. So as he grew older and craftier, he would avoid having people beg him to come by agreeing that he would come. And then when the appointed day arrived, of course, he had five or six of them to choose among. He picked the one that seemed least likely to annoy him, or most likely to get him on the evening news. Then he summoned up his palace guard, of whom I was a ranking member, to pinch-hit for him at ones he planned to skip. He liked them well enough when he got to them and started talking and showing off, but he hated going. He told me he made me a Bishop so that I could cover even more of the obligations he accepted willy-nilly for himself. He assured me the promotion had nothing whatsoever to do with my ability, piety, saintliness or the fine example that I set for the young of the flock. It was purely and simply that people who would be enraged at being stood up by a Cardinal and forced to make do with a mere Monsignor would be much easier to placate if they got a Bishop, at least."

"Oh, no," Mrs. Blake said. "He couldn't've meant that."

"Well," Doherty said, "I will grant you that he spoke half in jest, but no more than half."

"But everyone revered him so," Mrs. Tobin said.

"Which greatly amused him, in private," Doherty said. "Oh, he reveled in it in public, the old lion out among his cubs in the late afternoon of his illustrious life, basking in the sunlight, letting out a few amiable roars, just to keep his hand in, taking the nuns to the ballgame, snapping at the less respectful members of the tribe, keeping good order in the jungle. Oh, he enjoyed it, no question about that, but he had a full-sized ego at least, and that was to be expected. But when he got home, he seemed to think he had to laugh at himself, and so he did. It was an attractive trait.

"Anyway," Doherty said, "that's why I don't come in for lobster Newburg and chicken wings, on Friday evenings. Or for the scrambled eggs in the steam-table pans at the Sunday brunches. As for the dances, well, I've supervised my last dance, whether as principal of the high school or as the Bishop visiting to see how fine the young folks are in some prosperous parish. I did those chores when I was young, and now I think it's only fair to let the younger fellows reap the full enjoyment of those experiences."

Riordan, in a blue-and-white cord suit, white shirt, no tie, came onto the patio. Doherty saw him before his eyes had adjusted again to the sunlight, and called him over to the table. "Agnes Blake, Peg Tobin," he said, "meet my friend, Peter Riordan." Each of the ladies said she was pleased to make Riordan's acquaintance. "And Riordan it is," Agnes said. "Well, the top of the morning to you. Is it the Riordans from Wicklow we have here?"

"And the balance of the day to yourself, madam," Riordan said, bowing slightly. "As to your question, ma'am, there's a good deal of doubt about that. I've heard Knock and I've heard Kenmare, and indeed it would be hard to name a county or a town in the south that hasn't been mentioned as a birthplace of one brand of Riordan or another. My own guess is that the first of the male Riordans was a disgraceful scoundrel, probably a tinker or a hog thief, or some other sort of low person, and that after he had had his way with one or more of the village maidens, he found it prudent to move on."

"It's a family trait to this day, I understand," Doherty said.

"It is that," Riordan said. "You'll find Riordans in Fall River, Riordans in Chicopee, Riordans in Lawrence and Riordans in Lowell and Worcester. We're not the best judges of our surroundings, but we could call a fair muster from the provinces, if the need arose."

"And what is it that you do, Peter Riordan?" Peg said.

"Ah, well," Riordan said, "now that's difficult to answer, you know. I do a number of things. Some of them're quite respectable, but then there're others that I'd just as soon not discuss."

"Paul," Agnes said, "is that what you're doing with this young man?"

"Indeed it is, Agnes," Doherty said. "Peter here is a good-hearted lad, and he shows a lot of promise. But the truth of it be known, he has not applied himself diligently to his catechism, and finds himself now at this relatively advanced age one of the slowest of my students in the confraternity of Christian doctrine classes. So, to save him the further embarrassment of having to cramp his long legs into the pew with the twelve-year-olds, I've agreed to tutor him privately in these more comfortable surroundings, in the hope that a few drinks and some serious discussion will enable him to pass his requirements for the sacrament of Confirmation. So, if you'll excuse us?"

They took a table at the far end of the terrace, away from the ladies. The waiter appeared at once. "Something to drink,

Peter?" Doherty said. Riordan looked at his watch. "After noon," he said. "Yeah, all right. Heineken, please."

"That didn't bother you the other day," Doherty said, "whether the sun was over the yardarm."

"I was injured the other day," Riordan said. "I'm not injured today."

"Vodka and tonic," Doherty said. The waiter went away, nodding.

"How the hell do you stand it, Paul?" Riordan said.

"Stand what?" Doherty said.

"Those damned bloody women," Riordan said. "How the hell do you stand it? There must be thousands of them, hundreds in this parish alone. Good God, you're an intelligent man. And there you sit, chewing the Irish bubblegum with a couple of airheaded, tittering matrons drinking lemonade."

"Their husbands're worse," Doherty said, "if that's any consolation."

"I'm sure they are," Riordan said. "I don't doubt it for an instant. But I don't need the consolation because I don't have to associate with them. You do hang around with them. How the hell do you stand it?"

"It comes with practice," Doherty said. "You learn how to do it, very early in the game. The first thing is that while you have to hang around with them, they are not your friends. Your friends see Doherty, warts and all. Agnes and Peg see Bishop, the last name of which in this case is Doherty. You're strictly in the same category with the trick pony at the circus. You're something to watch, a display piece for them. They pride themselves that they really know the Bishop, and they probably do, but they don't know Doherty and they don't want Doherty to act like he might really know them. What tips you off is when one of them gets in some kind of trouble and comes to you for help. Counseling, advice, verbal therapy—you can call it by any name you want—as soon as one of them comes in just about beside herself because she's discovered that her husband's running around, or the husband comes in because he finally faced up to the fact that his wife starts in on the sauce as soon as he leaves for work in the morning, the days of idle chatter and stupid banter are gone forever. When the crisis is over, no matter how it's resolved, they shun you. Because, you see, they are also playing roles: respectable middle-class people, devout and damned near perfect. Once they let their guard down and you know them for the scared, imperfect, maybe stupid people that we all are, they stay away from you. They have their masks on too, and when those masks're stripped away, the play is over."

"It must be awful rough to go on with it, year after year, though," Riordan said.

"Not rough so much as sad," Doherty said. "Good God, I don't think less of a man because he got in trouble and didn't know what to do. I don't think a woman has anything to be ashamed of when she's at her wits' end and at very least needs somebody to talk to. I've got some problems in my own family that've baffled every attempt that I've come up with to solve them. I don't know what the hell to do about the Digger, as his pals call him. I've known him all his life. He scares me, and now his kids're getting old enough so they scare me. It seems as though I ought to be able to do something to make him behave himself, but I've been trying now for over thirty years, and I haven't come up with a way to solve it. It's really too bad that my parishioners come away from seeking the help that they desperately need, and which I'm all too often unable to give, with the feeling that they've done something dirty and ought to be ashamed to face me. But I haven't come up with anything yet. Maybe I should be ashamed of that."

The waiter brought the drinks and withdrew.

"Look at us," Doherty said. "I've known you since you were a kid and I was sent in here to make sure Monsignor

LaBelle didn't sell the parish for a shopping center while he was in one of his periods of senile dementia. You were just a kid then, almost twenty-five years ago. I probably know you as well as anyone on the earth today, including your parents. I had a luxury they lacked, because I had some critical distance from you. I didn't have any real emotional investment of my own in watching you grow up. I could take you as you were, and if you had a shorter fuse than the ideal kid would have, well, that was just the way that young Peter Riordan was. Might've bothered your parents, but it didn't bother me.

"Your father," Doherty said, "I'm telling tales out of school, but the hell with it, your father was absolutely wild when he found out what you had in mind as a means to avoid being drafted into the infantry."

"I seem to recall his mentioning something about that to me," Riordan said.

"Yeah," Doherty said, "I'll bet you do. He lingered after one of those blasted parish council meetings, until we were alone. 'The Marines,' he yelled at me, 'the Marines? The little fool is going to duck the draft by enlisting in the Marines? The Marines are his idea of a way out of the infantry? Can't you do something about this?' I said, 'No. And for that matter, neither can you.' 'He could get himself killed doing this,' your father said to me. 'He certainly could,' I said."

"He never knew about the Recon part," Riordan said. "He got lathered up enough just thinking I was busting ashore off LSTs, like they did in World War Two. If he'd known I was spending most of my time in the woods, alone, he would've gone straight up in the air."

"Well," Doherty said, "why did you do it? He was right, you know. He could've gotten you deferred. All the doctors he knew? Easy. Hell, you could've gotten yourself deferred. Just gone right on to graduate school, and waited it out. Why didn't you do that?"

"I dunno," Riordan said. "Partly to goose him, I suppose. He was always feeling my forehead, even when he had to reach up to do it. Taking my pulse. Worrying when I played football."

"You were his only son," Doherty said.

"Yeah," Riordan said, "I know that. But I was also pretty well along the way to becoming my only man. Besides, I was young and nutty when I set the whole thing in motion. I read too many books, I guess, believed all that shit about courage and all that crap, the man who tests himself against the enemy. The ultimate peril, faced and faced down. Friend of mine married a girl in college that was so light she would've floated clear off the ground if she didn't have lead weights in her shoes. Here is this guy with an absolutely indecent genius for quantum physics, and he goes out and marries this bubblehead. Maybe he didn't know that she had Timken roller bearings on her heels. Maybe he didn't know that whole armies had marched over her. Maybe he knew and didn't care. Two years later, divorced. Asked him why he did it. Shrugged his shoulders. 'I dunno,' he said. 'Seemed like a good idea at the time.' Same thing with me and the Marines. 'Nothing else to do right now, think I'll go and become a jungle fighter. Better'n hanging around down at the gas station.'"

"Which at the time I could pretty well surmise," Doherty said. "We were old friends then. We still are. But we still keep things from each other, and we always will. For a complete inventory of the other guy, you have to draw a lot of inferences."

"Draw any from your talk with Father Fahey?" Riordan said.

"Peter," Doherty said, "I will tell you honestly, I have never had so much damned fun in my life. Well, maybe as much fun, a long time ago. But not lately."

"I could tell that," Riordan said. "You look a hell of a lot better since you started this Father Brown gig with me. That's one of my inferences."

"Don't doubt it for an instant," Doherty said. "What I did was whip it out of him. See, if you've known Trimmer for a long time, as I have, you will dislike him but you will also respect him. Trimmer knows that he is not a man of blinding intellect. That's why he's so damned aggressive. He starts out trying to throw the other guy off balance. Like the fastball pitcher who's wilder'n a March hare while he's warming up, so the hitters come up there worrying about whether they'll need baskets to take their heads home after the game. If you let him buffalo you at the start of any discussion, he will win by the end.

"Once he gets the advantage," Doherty said, "he holds it with partial truths. He knows he's not fast enough to win an argument with someone who's smarter, so he distorts the subject. If you say a panda bear is actually part of the raccoon family, and he is committed to the position that it is a part of the bear family, you will never get to the issue. He will spend the rest of the discussion asking you if you seriously mean to say that there is such a thing as a three-hundred-pound Chinese raccoon. Anybody listening will of course conclude that you are crazy and that Monsignor Fahey has the common-sensible best of you, you fool. Even though you happen to be right.

"The way to stop that," Doherty said, "is to embarrass him before you ever get to the thing you want to talk about. Get him on the defensive. If you can get the bastard rattled, he's nowhere near as cute as he is when he's got the upper hand. Just by chance I found out that he'd been lying to the kid that's at the desk at the club. Seems Trimmer was the warrior priest who single-handedly liberated Normandy on D-Day, or so he led the kid to believe. So I blew him out of the water with that one, and allowed as how I'd make a fool of him with the kid, who lives in his parish, and pretty soon everybody in town would be laughing at him. Then I whacked him with Greenan and Magro, and much as he hated it, I think he told me enough of the truth so we can guess the rest. I think he regurgitated most of it."

"Another round?" Riordan said, finishing his beer.

"By all means," Doherty said, finishing his vodka. The waiter, peeking around the door to the lounge, caught Doherty's circular motion for a second round.

"The housekeeper's nephew story about Magro is bullshit," Doherty said. "Like most of the stuff that Trimmer tells people, it's true. But it's bullshit. Magro is the housekeeper's nephew, and she apparently is on her last legs. But she doesn't give a curse about springing her nephew from Walpole. She thinks he's a no good killer and a scandal to her sister that gave him birth, and she blames all of this on her sister's selection of a husband. There was bad blood in the Magro family, she's convinced, and it's all the father's fault. But Magro *is* her nephew, and unless Trimmer's learned to tell lies better than he ever did before, that is really all he told Greenan. Greenan, of course, is solid bone from earlobe to earlobe, and he'd give his right testicle as well as his left for the chance to ingratiate himself with the good Monsignor who holds sway over much of his district."

"That's what Seats told me," Riordan said. "Seats said Greenan'll do anything a common ordinary voter asks him to do. Says Greenan'd jump in the cesspool in a white suit if a priest asked him."

"That's no compliment to the clergy," Doherty said. "Greenan'd jump into the sewer naked in front the sodality, if he thought it'd get him a vote. But he's still just a dupe on this one.

"Piecing things together," Doherty said, "and it's no easy

task, the cornerstone of this little adventure, as far as Fahey's concerned, is a fellow who goes by the name of Scanlan."

"Scanlan have a first name?" Riordan said.

"Probably," Doherty said, "but Fahey swears he doesn't know what it is. Says he's only met the guy once."

"Believe him?" Riordan said.

"Yeah," Doherty said, "I think I do, actually. I don't think the guy's name probably is Scanlan, and I don't think Fahey believes it is either, but I do believe that Scanlan is the only name that Fahey's got for the guy."

"Fahey would get himself out on a limb like this for a guy that he knows is giving him a phony name?" Riordan said. "He really is stupid."

"Sure," Doherty said, "and he has another weakness too: he loves conspiracies. Inside stuff. Top secret. Eyes only. Burn before reading. The surest way in the world to get Fahey's undying loyalty is to let him think he's working undercover on some plot, and the people that he's talking to are engaged in some clandestine work. He was that way when we were all jockeying for position in the Church, and he's that way now, when all that stuff is dead and gone. For us. So he's found something else."

"Which would be?" Riordan said.

"I'm guessing, Peter," Doherty said. "I think it's a pretty firm deduction, but that's all it is. I think Fahey's gotten himself hooked up with the Provos. It's the sort of thing he'd do. Right in character. Or the lack of it."

"Does he admit it?" Riordan said.

"Not in so many words, no," Doherty said, "but yes, he admits it. I put it to him, right between the eyes. Asked him if he was running guns for the IRA. He never answered me directly. Just gave me one of those Up the Rebels harangues. Went all the way back to the Battle of the Boyne. He would've reviewed the career of Brian Boru, if I hadn't shut him off."

"Does he really believe all that shit?" Riordan said. "Do any of them really believe all that shit?"

"Sure," Doherty said. "It's exciting. Why the hell do you think he misleads kids about his heroic deeds in the Airborne, huh? Excitement. He lives vicariously. You think he feels like a conqueror, dominating the first graders at the parish school? Oh, he does the best he can, but his thirst is for glory on the field of battle."

"Huh," Riordan said, "probably turn tail and run when the first shot was fired. I love people like that, full of big talk and no experience. There's nothing quite like firsthand acquaintance with hostiles to take care of that problem."

"No," Doherty said. "No, you're mistaken. Fahey wouldn't run. He's not bright enough for that. He'd think he was Patton. Charmed life and all that foolishness. Invulnerable to bullets. He'd stand up straight, his cross in one hand and his carbine in the other, and lead on his troops in the name of the Lord."

"He'd get his ass blown off in short order," Riordan said.

"Of course," Doherty said. "That's how you can tell for sure he never was in combat—he's still walking around in our midst. He's pretty old now for active service, and besides, he'd miss his swimming and his comfortable life, but he's not about to relinquish that dream of his. So, this Scanlan, whatever his real name is, is Vinnie's free ticket to the land of his own private enchantment. Fahey not only suspects that the real name isn't Scanlan—he prefers it that way."

"Get a description out of him?" Riordan said.

"Not a very good one," Doherty said. "He was evasive. He kept asking me why I was so interested in this thing, being as how I am not a patriot. By which I took it to mean that he doesn't think I am a partisan of the IRA. Which I am not. And I in turn had to be evasive with him, because I was not about to tell him that I was trying to figure out why he was cooperating in some enterprise that seemed pretty likely to get my no-good brother knocked off. Best I could wring out of Vinnie was that the guy's fairly short, five seven or so, but very strong and very dangerous. Vinnie wanted me to think that Scanlan's on the run from the British, which as a matter of fact he probably is, and that he got into this country using a forged passport."

"As indeed, he probably did," Riordan said. "He could hide out for months if he got into the right neighborhoods in Cambridge or Southie or Dorchester. What's he doing, raising money?"

"I think that's already been done," Doherty said. "I'm not sure Vinnie really knows, but from what he said, I think the money is in hand. The problem now is locating the goods that they want to buy with the money."

"Guns," Riordan said. "Shipped over there in furniture boxes and packages of bedsheets and towels to blind aunts and dead cousins in the peaceable Irish Republic, and smuggled north across the border three nights later. The damned fools."

"What they want Magro for," Doherty said, "at least what Vinnie thinks they want Magro for, is that he is the guy with the contact who can get the weapons. Is there such a thing as an AR-fifteen?"

"Sure," Riordan said. "Looks just like the M-sixteen that the army used in Vietnam, which was a piece of thirty-caliber junk. The AR was the pilot model, seven-point-sixty-two millimeter, lightweight, full-automatic for combat, reliable, accurate, the whole bit. Naturally the army didn't like it, so they crapped around with it until they got the M-sixteen. Those Micks may be crazy, Paul, but nobody ever said they didn't have good taste in firepower."

"Could somebody like Magro get them?" Doherty said.

"Sure," Riordan said. "Just about anybody can get one. All you need in this Commonwealth's a firearms ID card. Go into a gun store, show the card, ask to see one, buy it."

"A machine gun?" Doherty said.

"Semi-auto, in the stores," Riordan said. "Hunting weapon. Probably wouldn't take a good gunsmith more'n an hour to figure how to make it full-automatic, and if he was casting the parts to modify one, he could cast enough to modify a hundred of them in a day or so. Wouldn't really matter if he couldn't. Machine guns aren't much good anyway, the kind of work the IRA prefers. All everybody does is spray the buildings and the landscape with scarce bullets. You got a semi-auto, you aim on each target, and you can still fire damned fast even pulling the trigger every shot."

"Well," Doherty said, "if anyone can buy them, why do they need Magro? All they need's some respectable citizen who hates England. Let him go out and buy as many as they want, legally."

"Couple hundred of them?" Riordan said.

"Couple dozen, couple hundred," Doherty said. "What difference would it make?"

"Records," Riordan said. "The state laws're pretty tough. And the federal laws're even tougher. Every gun sale's logged. Those logs're regularly inspected. Same legitimate credentials start showing up in store after store, some guy's stockpiling AR-fifteens, going to make a lot of people curious. Nobody can use two hundred rifles all by his lonesome. Chances are, he's planning to sell them to somebody, or outfit a private army. Can't do that. Got to have a dealer's license to sell guns in quantity. Got to have a dealer's license to buy guns in quantity. Got to have permits to shift guns across state lines. You want to export guns, you got more paperwork to do than the Post Office loses in a month.

"That's why the IRA hooked up with the PLO—those Palestinians've got Kalashnikov assault rifles, which is an even better weapon, and the Soviet Union doesn't make it nearly as difficult for the PLO to get Russian guns as the good old USA does with American guns. There've been stories that the PLOs've got the Israeli machine guns too, the Uzis, but I tend to doubt that. They would've had to capture those, and they haven't had much luck capturing Jews or their equipment. Still, the AR's a fine weapon. Perfect for your informal little bushwhacking. No terrorist organization in its right mind would turn down a few crates of those little gadgets, Russian guns or not.

"No," Riordan said, "if you want ARs in quantity like I expect they probably do, there is only one way to get them, and that is: steal them. Get into a warehouse, get into a few sporting goods stores, that kind of thing. Hijack a truck. That's what Magro specializes in. He's good at cutting chain-link fences and getting doors open, and he's been around long enough so he knows where they store the stuff that people want. He's good enough so he never got caught at it, either. It was only when he branched out into shooting a guy that the cops grabbed him and put him away. Magro's a thief, and he's a capable one. Doesn't matter to him what he steals, especially if being willing to steal something that somebody really wants will get him sprung from a murder rap eight years early."

"And put him on the loose to take care of a little private business on the way through," Doherty said.

"You don't think your brother's involved in this?" Riordan said.

"Nope," Doherty said, "I don't. For once I think Jerry's skirts are clean, at least from this escapade. He's probably doing something else, equally bad, but I don't really think, from talking to Fahey, that Jerry's got anything to do with this IRA thing at all. If he is, Fahey isn't clever enough to keep it from me, and Fahey never said a word about him or even somebody that sort of sounded like him."

"Son of a bitch," Riordan said. "That's kind of upsetting."

"I don't follow you, Pete," Doherty said.

"Oh, no offense, Paul," Riordan said. "I didn't mean I was sorry your brother doesn't seem to be tangled up in this. I'm glad if he isn't. It's just that I've been convinced for quite a while that he was, and I don't like making mistakes like that. I dragged you into this mess and got you thoroughly worried for absolutely no good reason. I'm sorry."

"Pete," Doherty said, "you're not going to duck out on me now, are you? No good reason?"

"I don't follow," Riordan said.

"Is there any doubt in your mind that Magro will go after Jerry if he gets out to steal those guns?" Doherty said.

"No," Riordan said. "No, not in the slightest. Far as I know, that's what he'll do." He stood up suddenly, skidding the chair back from the table.

"Where're you going?" Doherty said.

"I'm not going anywhere, dammit," Riordan said. "I just locked my damned knee, is all. That damned scrap metal gets in between the joints when I move in just the wrong way, and it locks on me." He shook his leg awkwardly.

"Spike does that," Doherty said, laughing. "He did that very same thing the night he peed on the Holy Water font."

"I know it looks silly," Riordan said, "but it works. That's all I ask. There." He sat down again.

"You ought to get that fixed," Doherty said.

"There's nothing anybody can do about it without dismantling my whole damned leg and putting me in traction for about six months," Riordan said. "I can't do that, for the luvva Mike. I haven't got time."

"I've got a good surgeon that's a friend of mine," Doherty said. "Ted Norman, at the New England Medical Center. He's a thoracic specialist, but I'm sure he could find an orthopedic man for you. When it looked as though I might need a bypass, after the attack, Ted was the man I went to see to set things up for me. He's very good. Known him for years.

Another fan of Vinnie Fahey's. I must call Ted about this little
meeting that I had with Vinnie. Tell him about Vinnie
routing the Germans."

"Some other time," Riordan said, grimacing slightly as he
stretched his leg out. "I'm busy right now. I may need this leg.
You find anything out about this Emmett guy from Fahey?"

"Not much I didn't know already," Doherty said. "Once
Vinnie mentioned him, it all started to come back to me.
Emmett's the power behind the University Club swimming
team. Vinnie's a great swimmer. Emmett, according to
Fahey, is as crazy as Fahey is on the IRA stuff. He may be
carrying Magro's water in a bucket to the Council, but he's
not crooked and he's not intentionally setting out to get Jerry
killed. I don't think. He's just another dreamer trying to bring
back the race of kings. The ones that lived in sod huts, and
worshiped mud. I don't think he's much to worry about. He'll
do it if Fahey asks him, and Fahey has asked him. Don't
misunderstand me, now. I embarrassed Vinnie, and I humil-
iated him, but I didn't change his mind one single iota. He's
just as determined to get Magro out today as he was yesterday.
And he still doesn't know why I'm interested. The question's
probably never crossed his mind."

"Okay," Riordan said, "let's think about it. First thing is,
we're not under any immediate pressure. Magro can't get out
this week because the Council has to meet again just to decide
whether they should hold a hearing on his petition for
commutation. They can't do that before next Thursday. The
earliest the hearing could be would be a week, more likely
two, after that. So it's at least three weeks before Magro could
get out under any circumstances, and the Governor'd probably stall around for at least another week before he signed
anything if the Council did decide to let Magro out. Make it a
month. Magro is the guy you want to stop from killing your
brother, and if what I get this afternoon and tonight checks

out with what you've got, Magro and this character Scanlan are the people who interest me. Not your brother. Therefore we're not under any real time pressure."

"I don't know as I agree with that," Doherty said.

"Well," Riordan said, "I don't mean we can just sit around and dawdle and wait for something bad to happen. What I mean is, we don't have to do anything right off the bat. End up making a mistake because we hurried. If Ken Walker's little gambit to screw up Magro's recommendation from the corrections department works the way he hopes it will, and we won't know that until the inmates come in—or don't come in—from their furloughs this weekend, it could be six months or so that Magro's got to wait before he even gets so much as another nip at the apple. We've got time enough to be sure."

"In the meantime," Doherty said, "what're you going to do?"

"Paul," Riordan said, "all I can tell you for sure is what I'm going to do today. This afternoon. Seats Lobianco must've spent half an hour on the phone with me yesterday. He's been playing sleuth. He wants me to see a guy named Mattie at the State House this afternoon. I'm going to do that. From what Seats hinted, I've got an idea I'm going to have to go out tonight. For what, I don't know. Until I've done those things, I don't have any idea what I'm going to do next."

"What about me?" Doherty said. "I'm on a hot roll here. It's like playing golf and sinking every forty-foot putt you try."

"What about you?" Riordan said. "Isn't much more you can do, I can think of."

"What about Jerry?" Doherty said.

"What about him?" Riordan said. "You say he's not in it, and yours is the best information I've come up with so far. If, as and when Magro looks like he's maybe getting out, we can decide then what to do. We've got plenty of time."

"No," Doherty said.

"No?" Riordan said.

"I don't like it," Doherty said. "Put yourself in my place. The man is my brother. He's no good, but he remains my brother. I don't want him killed. And I'm a priest, too. If any man has an obligation to his brother, a priest does."

"You want to tell him," Riordan said.

"I want to tell him," Doherty said. "I want to tell him tonight. I want to meet him as he closes up the Bright Red and go home with him and tell him. Tonight."

"Jesus," Riordan said. "You know what he'll do, don't you? Brother or no brother, Paul, the Digger is a decisive man. You convince him that your information's good, and you know what he'll do. You really want that?"

"I think a man has a right to defend himself," Doherty said. "I'm on firm scriptural ground there. Turning the other cheek is one thing. Getting ambushed's quite another. Jerry has a family to support. He's not much of a husband and he stinks as a father, but that family is his responsibility no matter how little attention he pays to them. He won't even be able to do that, dead, and I don't want to pick up his burdens for him. I told you that. So I've got some rights in this matter too, personal rights. Mine."

"There's self-defense and there's self-defense, Paul," Riordan said. "The Digger was a boss con. Unusual for a man serving a short stretch. Those gentlemen're mostly lifers. If Digger was an equal, he was an equal with some guys that're still in there and haven't got a thing to lose. They know him. You think of self-defense as shooting back at a guy that's shooting at you. The Digger may have a more generous definition. He can make arrangements from outside that'll permanently screw up Monsignor Fahey, Councillor Emmett and maybe even the guy who calls himself Scanlan, but I don't think that's self-defense. Not in the usual meaning of the word. I think it's jailhouse murder. Useful murder, maybe. Save everybody a hell of a lot of annoyance if Magro got dead 'fore he ever got out. But murder just the same. Magro's no threat to the Digger, long as he's in. I think you're jumping the gun, Paul."

"Do you, now," Doherty said.

"Actually," Riordan said, "no. But I had to say so. I can't endorse it, but I can't see much difference between Magro planning to kill Digger and Digger planning to kill Magro. The one who gets it done first is a murderer, and the other guy's a corpse. Other than that, there isn't much to choose between them. The only advantage that either of them's got, in my estimation, is that the Digger has you for a brother. He didn't earn that edge, but he's got it."

"Mind you, now," Doherty said, "I don't propose to suggest to Jerry that he kill Magro on sight. Or that he have somebody else kill Magro while he's still in prison. I don't intend to do anything like that."

"Paul, Paul," Riordan said, "this is old Peter, remember? You won't have to give him any tactical suggestions. You think Jesse James's mother had to tell him how to rob the trains, once he found out there was payroll gold on them? Split a few hairs if you want, but let's not go too far here."

"You're telling me not to do this," Doherty said. "That's maybe the best reason I could give you, Phantom, for starting your own family. You don't know anything about the sense of responsibility that a man feels. As little as I know, you know less."

"Wrong on both counts, Paul," Riordan said. "I am not telling you *not* to do this. That is your decision, none of mine. And for reasons that I won't go into, I am not the man who walks alone. That was a lie. I haven't been for over three years now. I've got a woman and her daughter lives with us and I don't know what the hell I'm going to do about that, because it's getting very complicated." He laughed. "I must be getting old and mellow. I wasn't ready for all of this. Just sneaked up on me. But don't kid yourself. I'd kill for either one of those two, and I've got a strong notion that I never have to worry about my back when they're lined up behind me. So, yeah, I know. I know what you mean."

"I'm happy for you, Pete," Doherty said. "How on earth does she stand it, knowing what you do? That you could get killed any minute."

"She never mentions it," Riordan said. "And as a matter of fact, the chances're very damned small. It's some poor cop in a cruiser that gets it, stopping a speeder on the highway and getting a bellyfull of buckshot when he asks for license, registration. Not guys like me. The only reason we carry guns is to discourage guys that we arrest from using their guns. I haven't killed a man since Nam."

"So," Doherty said, "you understand. I'm going to tell him."

"Yeah," Riordan said, "but two, make it three, requests."

"Shoot," Doherty said. He grinned.

"First," Riordan said, "tell me where I can get in touch with you later on this afternoon, after I see Seats. He may have something that could change things. Or maybe this guy Mattie will. I doubt it, but they might."

"Around three-thirty," Doherty said, "I've got to call the auto body shop in Brighton to see if my car's ready. If it is, I'll go in to the rental people and drop off that bucket of bolts I've been driving since the Electra went in. My God, how I've suffered with that thing."

"The Avis?" Riordan said.

"You knew it?" Doherty said.

"Had to be yours," Riordan said. "Can't picture you in a Cad. You're not a menopausal suburban matron, so you weren't driving a Volvo. I saw the little red-and-white sticker on the back window, I came in today. What'd you do, smash up the battleship?"

"No," Doherty said, "I just decided to keep it. They don't make those big solid cars anymore, and I don't want one of the tinny little new ones. All that was wrong with mine was minor dents and scratches, so I decided to have it repaired. Supposed to be ready today. If it is, I'll pick it up, come home, have some of Mrs. Herlihy's awful food, get a little rest, and go out to Dorchester tonight in time to meet Jerry when he closes up. If it isn't, I'll just stay at the rectory and get some work done, then go out. One way or the other, I'll be home around dinner."

"Okay," Riordan said. "Second: Since neither one of us knows what time he's going to get home tomorrow morning, why don't we plan to meet here for lunch again tomorrow? Compare notes. Can't tell what we might pick up."

"Good idea," Doherty said.

"Third thing," Riordan said. "Is there any chance of a club sandwich and another beer?"

"Very good chance," Doherty said. "I'll order two of each."

18

RIORDAN PARKED the green Ford on Chestnut Street, to the west of the State House, under a sign that warned of substantial penalties for leaving vehicles unattended without Beacon Hill residential stickers. He walked up the hill and under the canopy between the two buildings of the State House. He went in through the back door and clicked his way down the corridor to Lobianco's office. There was shouting in the private office. It was just after three o'clock.

Alice had put aside her *Rich Man, Poor Man* and had gone back to Rona Jaffe. She looked up expectantly. "I'm late," Riordan said.

"It's all right," she said, "sit down and enjoy the fun."

"What's going on?" he said.

"The other Reardon's in there, Ways and Means Reardon. They're having a fight."

"Oh," Riordan said, "well, look, all right? I don't mean to be a pain in the ass about this, but I did have an appointment which Seats insisted that I make, and I was on kind of a crowded schedule even before that. Think maybe you could buzz him?"

"Uh-uh," she said, shaking her head. "You want to go barging in there, you go barging in there. He's got the other guy in there with him, and the other guy's not used to having

174

people break in on his meetings. Doesn't matter whether they were scheduled or not. You want to do it, you do it. You can probably get away with it. I can't. I have to work in this place. I've been here for thirty years, and if I didn't learn anything else in all that time in this building, I learned you don't go around pissing off the Chairman of the House Ways and Means Committee. Not if you're sensible."

"Okay," Riordan said. He stepped to the door, opened it, and went in.

"—lie to me, you rotten wop son of a bitch," Seats's visitor was saying. He was a short man, about a hundred and eighty pounds, dressed in a three-piece blue suit. He wore a pink-and-black necktie. He was gesturing at Lobianco, shaking his forefinger at him. "You know that little bastard Donald did that to my lights on purpose. He did it this week and he did it last week, and he did it two other times since the first of the year, and you probably put him up to it. You got any idea what I got to make people go through, get the insurance, pay for those lights every time that little cocksucker breaks them? They don't believe it's street vandalism anymore. You take care of this, Seats, and I mean it, or I'm gonna have your ass six ways to Sunday."

"Hi, Pete," Seats said.

The short fat man spun around in the chair and stood up. His face was red and jowly. "Who the fuck're you?" he said.

"Riordan," Riordan said.

"Not in this building, you're not," Reardon said. "I'm the Reardon in this fucking building. Now get the fuck out of here while I finish getting this bullshit settled with Seats."

"I told you how to settle it, Jackie," Seats said gently. "Duke the kid a five or ten. Treat him like something besides a hill of shit. You got to learn, you can't treat these guys like they were something your cat did onna rug. They don't like it. They don't give a shit who you are. They've been here longer'n you have. They'll be here after you're gone. They're not impressed with you."

Reardon whirled on Seats. "Shut up, Seats," he said. He turned to Riordan again. "I told you, you fuckin' hippie, you get the hell out of here until I'm finished with this dago bastard that's getting my new car wrecked for me every chance he gets."

"And I told you," Riordan said, "I've got an appointment. Ask Seats."

"I don't have to ask Seats anything," Reardon said. "I don't give a shit about anybody's appointments. I come before appointments in this building. Anybody's appointments. I waited around long enough for this day to come, and now I got it and it's mine. Now you get the fuck out of here or I'll call the Capitol police and have you thrown out."

"Really," Riordan said. He walked toward Reardon, who stood his ground, panting. "Out you go, Mister Chairman," he said. "Go study your manners someplace."

"You lay a hand on me," Reardon said, "and I'll have you arrested."

Lobianco sat behind the desk, grinning behind his hand.

"Up you come," Riordan said, seizing Reardon on the shoulders and clamping down.

"You get your fuckin' hands offa me," Reardon yelled. "This is a fuckin' assault and battery. I'll have you in court by nightfall. You bastard, you don't let me go, I'll have you killed."

"Aha," Riordan said, "threatening a federal officer in the course of his official duties. That should give you a certain amount of entertainment down in Post Office Square. Care to come down right now? Come on, I'll give you a hand. Two of them." He turned Reardon around, grabbed him under the arms, picked him up two feet off the floor, and said, "Alice, did the rubbish man come yet?"

"What?" she called back.

"Never mind, Alice," Riordan said, "just open the door if you would." The door to the outer office opened. Riordan carried the Chairman through the door and raised him another foot off the floor. The Chairman waved his arms helplessly. Diane and the other clerk-typists crowded to their door to watch. Two elevator operators, passing in the corridor, stopped to watch. "Ever see a slam-dunk in the National Basketball Association, Mister Chairman?" Riordan said.

"No," Reardon said.

"No?" Riordan said. "I'm surprised. How about a touchdown spike in the NFL, the pro football. Ever see one of those? Lot in common."

"No," Reardon said. "Just put me down. Let's forget about it."

Riordan held him up there. "Yeah," he said, "you're probably right. No use in prolonging our little chat, is there, where I'm running late and you're such a hell of an important guy and all. Just let bygones be bygones."

"Yeah," Reardon said, weakly.

Riordan sighed. "Yeah, I guess you're right. Okay." He released the Chairman from three feet in the air. The Chairman landed on his left buttock. He sat there on the floor, rubbing it, looking up at Riordan. "For your complaint to the cops, in case you change your mind," Riordan said, "it's Agent Peter Riordan, U.S. Inspector General's Office. The other cops all know where to find me. And, of course, if they do, mine'll also know where to find you, for a little Q and A in the federal court. Have a pleasant day." He went back into Seats's office. He sat down in front of Seats's desk. "What a fucking zoo this place is, Seats," he said. "How the hell've you stayed sane, all these years?"

Seats was laughing openly now. "Who the fuck says I did?" he said. "There's a lot of people that'll tell you that I'm crazier'n a goddamned coot, have been for years. Tell you that's the only way I could've stood it. And there's others'll tell you, I came in crazy and made everybody else hoopy. What do I know? They could be right. I'll tell you something, though: as crazy as everybody is in this joint, if I'd've gone around this place yesterday telling people they could see Ways and Means Reardon sitting on his ass in his blue suit on the floor of my outer office at three-fifteen today, I think they would've had the guys in the white suits coming in for me this morning."

"He's an asshole," Riordan said.

"Of course he's an asshole," Seats said. "Everybody also knows that. Difference is, everybody in here's afraid of him. He screams and he hollers and nobody wants to take a chance on pissing him off, so he gets away with it. I'd love to be in his office in about fifteen minutes from now, when those elevator guys get through telling the reporters about Ways and Means sitting on his ass outside my office, though."

"What'll he do?" Riordan said.

"Do?" Seats said. "Deny it, of course. He can't make a thing out of it. Then he'd have to explain what he was doing in here that got him thrown out. He'd look even sillier than he did when he was rolling around on the floor. People'll be laughing at him enough as it is. I tell you, Pete, you done good work for the rank and file in this coop today, taking that asshole down a peg."

"Good," Riordan said, "how about the return on my investment?"

"Return?" Seats said. "You charge for the entertainment now? Not that I'd blame you if you did. I been saying for years we should charge admission to see what goes on in here."

"No, no," Riordan said. "What you wanted to see me about? Those phone calls yesterday? You had something for me?"

"Yeah," Seats said. "Okay, lemme give you, little background here. Guy I put on this thing's named Mattie Dyson. Lieutenant in the Cap Police. Nice guy. Done pretty well for himself, all these years and everything. Got himself a little investment on the side. Runs a bar down off Broadway in Southie. Knows fuckin' everything. So I called up Mattie, like I always do when I want some information that I know I'm not gonna be able to get by myself, right? I mean, after all, I am a greaser, if you listen to people like Ways and Means. Nobody tells me anything about the IRA and them guys. The hell'd I know about something like that? Might as well ask me the Hadassah or what them Kennedys were serving for Sunday dinner. I don't know.

"So," Seats said, "what I do is, I call Mattie. And I ask him. So I do that, and I can tell right off, Mattie don't want to tell me nothing. Oh, he says it's because he don't know nothing about what I'm asking him and all that, but he's not comfortable with it so I know he is lying to me and he just don't want to talk to me about this guy Magro and what the fuck everybody is running around like hell for, trying to get him out. So I say to him, I say, 'Mattie, you know something? I know something. I know there is nothing going on down that neck of the woods you don't know nothing about, and I want to know what it is that I don't know anything about. Because there is a guy that I said I would help that wants to know about it. And if you're gonna give me this, that you don't know, I am gonna find I am losing the sound portion of my program next month when that kid Derry McEvoy is coming up for that clerkship in the District Court down there and the guys onna Council start talking to me to see if maybe there's one we get for nothing from the Governor because we gave him this one for nothing. Am I right, Mattie? You seen my little radio. I'm gonna be just like that. No voices on any channel. Just the flashing lights. Got that?'

"Well," Seats said, "I guess he got it. Because he calls me back and he says if somebody happened to be interested in what was going on with this Magro thing, he might try going down to the Kildare off of Broadway and look around. But Mattie would advise him to watch his ass, because there is a lot of rough customers in there and they don't like strangers. 'And if I was your friend, if he is one,' Mattie said, 'I would tell him that I hear tell there is a guy name of Brennan that is in there a lot of the time and he can make every cop in two counties, maybe three, inside of fifteen minutes watching. This Brennan could be anywhere. He kind of prowls around and he makes sure nobody takes them little white canisters that people put money in on the bars. He works down the trolley and he's an American and everything, but he has got this hobby and he don't like people interfering with it. He's got those canisters in my bar, for Christ sake. You think I'm gonna tell him, take them out? No fuckin' way.'

" 'You tell your friend also,' Mattie said, 'that I understand there is a guy named Scanlan that's traveling around here and there these days, and I hear his name maybe isn't Scanlan. I never seen the guy, but he is apparently a hard case to handle. He has got some kind of an eye that was hurt. I heard he always wears a leather scalley cap, and a coat, which maybe he has got something under it he don't want seen all the time, no matter how warm it gets. And he is not very big but he can make a lot of noise when it suits him. I would be careful if I was out looking around where Brennan might be, and especially now because the chances are that if Brennan is in the neighborhood, Scanlan is somewhere around in there with him, waiting in the dark.' "

"I think I've already met Brennan," Riordan said.

"Yeah," Seats said. "Mattie had that impression. He said to me, 'You better tell this pal of yours, I hear tell Brennan thinks there's a Fed in town and he thinks he spotted him one night

down the Bright Red. Tell him also, when I say Brennan and
Scanlan, I don't mean *just* Brennan and Scanlan. Those guys
travel in packs.' "

"This I knew," Riordan said. "Well, okay, Seats, much
obliged. Let's go see him."

"Go see who?" Seats said.

"This guy Mattie," Riordan said.

"Nice try, Riordan," Seats said. "You think Mattie's gonna
get caught dead sitting around you? Somebody might see you.
You're hot, Pete. You're way too hot for a Southie barkeep to
be hanging around you. You oughta know that."

"I do, I do," Riordan said. "Still, you can't blame a guy for
pressing his luck."

"Here it's all right," Seats said. "Down there, I dunno as I'd
try it."

"Guess I got to," Riordan said, standing up.

Seats extended his hand. "Well," he said, "if I don't see you
again, best of luck. And if I do, I'll give you some tickets."

"Thanks," Riordan said. "Thanks very fuckin' much."

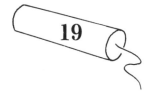

19

FREDDIE AND JENNY came home from shopping in the late afternoon, lugging packages, and found Riordan, wearing only his pants, lying on his back on the living room rug and snoring. The gun was on the bookcase. His jacket, shirt and tie were thrown on the couch. His boots and socks lay on the floor next to it. His feet were gnarled and bony, and there was a yellowish cast to his toenails. There was a pattern of four white scars, each about a quarter-inch wide, which curved up from his beltline at the right of his navel around his rib cage and stopped under his right shoulder blade. There was a thick white welt on his left bicep, puffy along its perimeters.

"My God, Ma," Jenny said, "he certainly is one scraggly-assed son of a bitch."

"Yeah," Freddie said. "Keep your voice down. You know how those animals are when you wake them up. They're either mad and they want to bite somebody, or else they feel frisky and they want to play. I'm not sure the floor beams can take it."

They sneaked around him and he continued to burble peacefully, sounding like an old diesel engine running in good repair—some clatter from the valves but nothing alarming.

"Actually," Jenny said in the kitchen, "it is kind of peaceful, having him grumbling away in there, isn't it?"

"Well," Freddie said, opening the refrigerator and removing a can of iced tea, "I try to look at it this way—he's less trouble than a big dog, because he takes himself out for his own walks. And as far as being a watchdog is concerned, he is far superior."

"He does look sort of dangerous, doesn't he?" Jenny said. "I never think of him that way. He's just old Pete around here."

"Yeah," Freddie said, "but he didn't get all those scars at the Country Club dances."

"Did he ever tell you about how he got them?" Jenny said.

"Once," Freddie said. "We'd just started sleeping together, and we'd been out all day with some friends on a boat up at Marblehead and gotten absolutely shitfaced. We were sleeping on their sunporch, and there was a full moon, and we'd had some wine with dinner and some drinks afterward. We'd all been sailing in our bathing suits, and it was our first sun of the season, so we were all red and sore and those scars really stood out, even in the moonlight, and I asked him about them. He told me. The ones on his side were from a pitchfork. American Tools for Peace. He'd killed this guerrilla by jumping out of a tree on him and garroting him."

"Garroting?" Jenny said.

"Yeah," Freddie said. "He had two wooden handles and a piece of heavy barbed wire between them. He jumped out of the tree onto the man's back, wrapped the wire around his throat, and strangled him. It was quiet. It was the way he killed people who were setting up ambushes for the regular South Vietnamese patrols. Before he finished killing the guy, the man's younger brother sneaked through the bushes and tried to stab him with the pitchfork."

"What'd he do?" Jenny said.

"He said he managed to get the guerrilla between him and the kid, so the kid finished the job on his own brother with the next lunge, and then Pete threw the corpse aside, got the pitchfork away from the kid and stabbed him through the chest with it. He said the kid was about twelve, thirteen, but if the kid thought that was old enough for mortal combat, who was Pete to argue with him?

"That one on the left arm," Freddie said, "wasn't exactly a mere flesh wound. It got in deeply enough, the bullet, so that it had to be dug out. 'Fortunately,' he said, 'I'm right-handed.'"

"God," Jenny said, "did he have any morphine or anything?"

"Had it but wouldn't take it," Freddie said. "Said you don't get all sleepy on painkillers when you're out in the woods with real killers. He couldn't go back into the aid station, and he couldn't leave the bullet in, so he stayed out and took the bullet out. He's got a couple more marks in places where you can't see them, too. There was one slug that missed his manhood by about a quarter of an inch, and you've seen how strange that knee looks, all bent out of shape. He's really all banged up."

"I wonder how many people he's killed," Jenny said.

"Honey lamb," Freddie said, "not even I have ever gotten him drunk enough to get that information from him. I guess he thought I had a proprietary interest that entitled me to know how he came by all his physical blemishes, but there he drew the line. I got kittenish with him one night in front of a roaring fire at a little inn up in Manchester, Vermont, the weekend when you went away with Kathy to the horse show."

"That drip," Jenny said.

"Drip," Freddie said. "There's one I haven't heard in some time."

"Well, she is," Jenny said.

"You didn't think so then," Freddie said.

"Well, she is," Jenny said.

"Anyway," Freddie said, "we were the last ones still up in

the bar. The owner'd gone to bed. The fire was burning down. I was feeling romantic, so I came up with my best make-out line: 'Pete, how many men've you killed?' "

"Jesus, Ma," Jenny said, "what an opening. Does that turn you on or something?"

Freddie drank tea. "If anybody else asked me," she said, "I'd say no. But I'm trying to raise you right, so I'll give it to you honestly. Yes, a little bit, I think it does. I'd never admit it to anybody else, but I think initially one of the things that turned me on to Pete was that he was obviously a very dangerous man. Your father is safe. He is proper and he is distinguished and he never uses the wrong fork. You can take him anywhere. He will dress up for you. He loves to dress up. He will never fly off the handle, give the finger to Mrs. Van Floot, tell the client's chief executive officer to go fuck himself, or complain that the soup's cold when it's supposed to be. There's a lot to be said for that kind of man. But not by me. I thought he was dull. Smart, but dull. He thought I was unruly. We were both pretty intelligent people, and we were both right. Right about, not right for, each other. Pete is a pirate. He just happens to work for the government. But it's not too difficult for me to fantasize that he's Cole Younger and I'm Belle Starr. It's silly, but it's not difficult and it is kind of fun.

"Anyway," she said, "he wouldn't tell me. He didn't say he couldn't remember. He just said he wouldn't talk about it. I pressed him. He didn't get mad. He said finally that he would answer my question that once, but only on the condition that I never ask it again. I was too relaxed to notice that he hadn't offered me a responsive answer, and I took it. 'I've killed a total of men exceeding by one the total of men who've tried to kill me,' he said. And that was it. So the best answer I can give you, Jenny, is that I don't know how many men he's killed, but it must be quite a few."

On the living room rug, Riordan abruptly stopped snoring.

"My God," Jenny said, "he's dead."

"No," Freddie said, laughing, "he always does that just before he wakes up. The resurrection of Lazarus will occur in about thirty seconds."

Riordan sat up on the floor and yawned. "Hi, Pete," Freddie said. "Nice nap?"

He reflected on the question. Then he nodded, scratching. "Yeah," he said, "nice nap."

"You looked like you were dead, Pete," Jenny said, "and you sounded like you ought to be."

Riordan stood up slowly, the knee grinding as he did so. "No," he said. "Appreciate the concern, but not dead yet." He shambled unsteadily out of the living room, paused at the kitchen and kissed Freddie on the lips. "Your breath stinks," she said. "Good," he said. He patted Jenny on the head. "Nice lunch, ladies?" he said.

"Very," Jenny said. "The Haymow in Cambridge."

"Gack," Riordan said. "Ferns. Harvards. Interior decorators. Toy food. Bean sprouts. Tofu. Vietnam food for the intellectually chic. People who read the *Kenyon Review.* Rather have lunch at a drive-in enema center. Next time you get visitation, you stay home and I'll go to New York and let Arthur take me to the Four Seasons. I'd be properly grateful. Chat with his honeys, everything. You don't know when you're well off, young lady. Ungrateful generation, all of you."

"Har, har, har," Jenny said.

"Nice little end-around up in Maine there, from what Freddie tells me," Riordan said, scratching his belly again. "They'll be calling you 'Gray Ghost' up in that establishment if you don't look out. Very neat."

"You don't approve?" Jenny said, grinning.

"Not entirely," Riordan said. "I would've short-sheeted the beds and put dry ice in the hot water bottles or something before I left. Maybe set an incendiary device in the garage or something. But not bad for a beginner, not bad."

"You are going to change, aren't you, Pete?" Freddie said. "Speaking of enema centers, you do kind of stink."

"Pay close attention, now," he said, and started for the bathroom.

"Oh, Pete," Jenny said, "I'm going down to do a wash. Collect all your overalls and throw them in, if you want. I have to take two loads anyway."

"Good," he said. "I've been saving some stuff."

"You got to go out tonight, Pete?" Freddie said.

"Yup," he said as he entered the bathroom. "Another carefree, footloose, glamorous pub crawl in the Athens of America, all in the service of our Uncle Sam." He shut the door.

Riordan came out less than three minutes later. He was wearing a tee-shirt he had taken from the hamper, and the gray twill pants with the green suspenders. He was knotting and unknotting the tan twill shirt. "Pete," Freddie said, "those were supposed to go to the cleaners."

"Yup," he said. He held up the shirt. It was suitably rumpled, and still stained under the armpits. "Fine," he said. He came into the kitchen. He opened the drawer next to the sink and took out a pair of pinking shears. "Only in this menagerie," he said, "would the pinking shears be kept with the butter knife and the forks."

"But I can always find them there," Freddie said.

"Good thing for me you don't have to store your hammers and nails in the bed in order to keep track of them," he said.

"What would you care?" Jenny said. "You sleep on the floor anyway."

"When I can make a place in the middle of your school books and field hockey sticks, for Christ sake," Riordan said. He laid the shirt out flat on the kitchen counter. He used the pinking shears to cut out three quarters of the circle next to the left sleeve seam on the torso of the shirt.

"Hey," Jenny said, "I gave you that shirt for Christmas."

"Yup," Riordan said.

"That goddamned shirt cost me almost forty dollars," Jenny said. "Forty dollars of my own money, once I paid the postage and the extra for one big enough to cover you, you big oaf. That's a nice shirt."

"Very nice shirt," Riordan said. He held the shirt up and examined the cut. "Okay," he said. He spread the shirt down on the counter. He made a horizontal incision on the left, about two inches long, at the middle of the rib cage. He made another the same length behind the torso seam, in the same location.

"You'll ruin it," Jenny said.

"Naw," Riordan said. "That's why I'm using pinking shears. Won't fray. I'm through using it for this, stitch it up again. Good as new."

"Won't be as good as new," she said. "It'll have all mends in it."

"Everything's got a lot of mends in it," Riordan said. He held the shirt up again. "That's how you tell whether something's good. Not if it breaks or gets damaged. Everything does that. The good stuff you can fix afterward and use it some more."

"It'll look funny," Jenny said.

"Not to me," Riordan said. "I got lots of shirts like this. I never felt funny in them."

"Lots of them, huh?" Jenny said. "How come you don't wear one of them, if you already destroyed some other shirts? Why wreck mine?"

"Others're all clean and fresh," Riordan said, starting for the living room. "Don't want to waste a clean shirt on this operation. Nice dirty shirt, that's what I need. Feel more comfortable in it."

"Waste?" Jenny said. "You don't call what you just did wasting an expensive shirt that I gave you for Christmas? Ruining it like that?"

Riordan reached the bookcase. He crouched and pulled from the middle shelf a black leather holster with a triple harness. It was dusty. He used the shirt to wipe it off. "Jenny," he said, putting on the shirt, "everything's a waste, you look at it that way. Hell, at least these past two or three weeks of my life've been a waste, when I was working."

"Really, Pete?" Freddie said.

"Yeah," Riordan said. He fitted the top holster harness through the circle he had cut in the arm socket of the shirt, leaving the holster outside the shirt. He buckled the harness over his shoulder, under the shirt. "I didn't have much on this group when I started, and most of what I had was wrong when I got it, or so it seems now. And then most of what I've gotten since is pretty damned near useless. The IRA's out there all right, and they're doing exactly what those guys down in Washington think they're doing, which is running guns back to the Old Sod. But good Christ, these guys've been at it now at least since Cromwell. They may be communists and they may be crazy, but the fellas ain't stupid. They don't leave any more evidence than the gentle wind drops, blowing across the Lakes of Killarney. Guys down at Tenth and Constitution there in Washington're all over me like Paddy's best Sunday go-to-Mass suit. I don't think they ever heard of probable cause to suspect that a crime's been committed and a given person or persons committed it. Politicians, running the cops and play-acting like they were cops themselves. Just won't listen to me. On what I've got, I couldn't get a warrant for a free Big Mac and fries."

He separated the incisions he had made at the chest line of the shirt and threaded the straps from the top and bottom of the holster under it, sliding the top loop over his left shoulder, buckling the bottom strap tightly just below his right nipple.

He expanded his chest, expelled his breath, rode the chest strap down slightly on his rib cage, and began to button the shirt, the holster riding empty outside the body of the shirt, under his arm.

"See, the Provos, Fred, are pros. They are dealing with other assassins over there. They are used to it. They come over here and they deal with the American Irish. Not pros, most of us, unless you mean golf for two-dollar Nassau. And bullshitting, of course. The people the IRA uses? They're a bunch of well-nourished American kids with strong teeth and good clothes and plenty of milk and good food. Some of those kids are old enough to be adults, but they never made it. They're playing 'Kevin Barry' on the barroom piano, and raising money for the IRA bandits by doing it. So, when I go after the rebels, the best I can hope to get for information is a bunch of people who know all the words to 'Kevin Barry' and not a damned thing in this world about police work and investigations. Or the real IRA, as far as that goes. I can't do it all myself, and I've got no one, as usual, to help me. Kind of discouraging. Makes you kind of want to let the bastards kill each other over in Connaught. Washington says I can't. My own fault, for tripping over that guy in Listowel that was wanted here, when I was there just for a general look around. Now they think I can flush those boyos out of the bushes whenever they snap their fingers. Poor judgment on my part. Next time I'll stand the fugitive a round of the Guinness, and good luck to ye, lad. Up the Rebels."

Riordan sat down on the couch. He pulled on his dirty socks, then his boots. He stood up and started for the kitchen. "Believe I'll have a drink," he said.

"I didn't think you ever drank when you were working," Jenny said.

"This is part of the work, my lass, I assure you," Riordan said. He poured a double shot of bourbon and put two ice cubes in it. He added an equal amount of water. "If you think I'm going to wander into a strange Southie bar at eight o'clock at night, with no whisky on my breath, knowing the IRA is probably in there, you are crazy. A Brooklyn Jew drinking tea and lecturing on the benefits of promiscuous mutual masturbation for the vaginal congestion suffered by the Little Sisters of the Poor'd have a longer life expectancy. No need making your life harder'n it needs to be."

He walked back into the living room, set the drink on the shelf, took the gun and the belt holster from the top of the bookcase, removed the gun from the holster, opened the cylinder and ejected the bullets. He removed an open box of shells from the bookcase, opened it, and dumped the bullets in. He took a cleaning kit from the middle shelf and brought the gun and the kit to the coffee table. From the magazine rack, he removed a newspaper. He spread it out and began to clean and oil the gun.

"I don't like to watch this," Jenny said. "That thing makes me sick."

"Yup," Riordan said, "me too. Trouble is, I tried and failed to get a Dairy Queen franchise in Poughkeepsie, many years ago, so now instead of carrying pre-mix soft ice cream to the freezers, I have to carry this. God's punishment on me. I bear it nobly, I think. It's also handy, if somebody else decides to try to make me sick."

"That cleaning fluid stinks," Jenny said.

"Don't stink as bad as cordite," Riordan said. "Don't hurt your nose as much as when you don't use it, and you shoot, and you've got some tiny little obstruction in that barrel which makes all your nasty plans for the other guy blow up right in your own face. No, indeed." He dried the weapon and oiled it sparingly. He put it down on the papers and had some more of his drink. He stared out the window and watched the edge of the sunset declining into the river.

"I wish you'd do something else, Pete," Jenny said. "I love you, but I wish you'd do something else." He did not say anything.

"Jenny," Freddie said suddenly but not angrily, "I think that'll do it. If the sight of the farm machinery bothers you so you can't keep your mouth shut, take your mouth to your room." Jenny looked at her, startled. Freddie was smiling at her. Jenny nodded, and walked toward her bedroom. Riordan continued to stare out the window.

"You gonna be around long, honey?" Freddie said. "I thought I might take a bath."

"A while," he said. "A while. I'll sing out if I leave before you're marinated."

"See you in the morning," she said, as he got up and went toward the bookcase. He glanced at her, altered his direction, met her in the hallway to the kitchen, bent over and kissed her.

She went down the hall to the bathroom. He returned to the bookcase and took out a new box of shells. He took it to the coffee table, opened it, and began to load the gun.

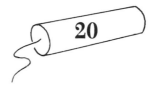

20

WEST BROADWAY and Broadway in South Boston are one wide street with a hitch in it at the Dorchester Street intersection. They lie roughly south-southeast, west-northwest, terminated by the intersection at the bridge over the Fort Port Channel, rank and sluggish at the western end, terminated at the southern end by Pleasure Bay. The buildings along the Broadways crowd the edges of the sidewalks and in many instances share common side walls. They are two- and three-story affairs, mostly residential. The wooden buildings are faced with clapboards painted light green, faded red, bright light blue or ivory. White trim is popular. The better ones at the corners have clapboard on the side walls. Some even have it on the back. The lesser buildings have the clapboards on the front, but the sides are done in tarpaper, textured and patterned in pitiable imitation of brick. Most of the buildings have six apartments, three on each side of the center doors which open onto narrow concrete steps. There are ornate iron bay windows for many of the front and side room apartments. There are no trees to speak of along Broadway. Except for the street lights, the only decorations are the Pepsi signs over the doors to the variety stores and lunchrooms and the Narragansett, Busch and Schlitz signs lighted over the secretive doors of the saloons.

Riordan drove the green Ford down Broadway at a reasonable rate of speed, giving no indication that he was looking over the men, women and children who sat on the doorsteps, lounged against the lampposts or pushed single bags of groceries along the sidewalks in wheeled wire baskets. The people, who were watching him, gave no evidence of doing so. Only the teenagers showed much sign of life, the boys in their summer wiffles, tee-shirts, jeans and sneakers moving in the deepening twilight heat with spastic exaggeration that they took for swagger, the girls in tight jeans and tank tops rewarding the boys with spells of convulsive laughter that required them to bend over double, and then, when they had finished laughing, to swat the jokers of the moment on the upper left arms.

At intervals along Broadway, older teenagers convened in automobiles, double and triple parking, leaning against fenders, sharing bottles of Budweiser and Busch. The drivers usually remained in their cars, some of them caressing the foreheads of their girlfriends, who lay on their backs on the front seats and hung their feet out the passenger windows, dangling their strapless wooden-soled fuck-me shoes over the pavement. The older kids were not quite as practiced as their parents in the art of watching without seeming to watch; they stared with hungry anger as the green Ford went by. Several mouthed "fuckin' cop" to each other, and one kid, waving a king-size can of Bud, darted from between the clustered rows of cars waving the beer and shouting: "*Nigger lover, Nigger lover.*" He threw the can after Riordan's car, the beer spiraling out of the top as the can arched through the evening, landing twenty yards behind the moving rear bumper. In the mirror, as he paused for the next light, Riordan saw an old man get up from the steps across the street from where the can hit, walk out and pick it up, shaking his head. He moved slowly back toward his seat, raising the can to his mouth and drinking from it.

Three blocks west of the Dorchester Street intersection, Riordan slowed even more. The street was clear, and he made a sweeping U-turn, nosing the Ford into a parking place at the end of the block, pulling it back just far enough from the Oakleigh intersection to leave the route clear while preventing anyone else from parking in front of him. He studied the intersection. There were a utility pole with a fire box and a street lamp on the corner opposite his car. There was a newspaper vending machine on the opposite corner. There were no trash barrels to his right on either side of Oakleigh. The lights in the first-floor apartment next to the passenger side of his car were dim, and he could see a television flickering in the gloom. Lace curtains slowly billowed languidly from the open window, furled themselves in the light breeze, and were swept in again. He supposed that the bottom edges must be dirty from the grime on the sills.

Riordan, first struggling into the gray tweed jacket, opened the driver's door and got out of the Ford. He locked it with his left hand, while simultaneously slipping his right hand inside the jacket to adjust the holster slightly on his torso. He could leave the jacket unbuttoned when he wore the shoulder holster. It was not as comfortable as the belt holster for driving or sitting at the desk, but it was easier to hide and faster to use.

Riordan turned away from the car. There was a man hidden in the shadows on the opposite corner of West Broadway. His feet and lower legs were visible in the light from the street lamp on the corner opposite him on Oakleigh Street. He wore a cap pulled over his face. Riordan could not make out the color.

Riordan crossed Broadway at a slight diagonal, reaching the south-southwesterly side in the middle of the block. He stepped between an old Plymouth and a recent Ford that had been hit on the left rear quarter panel; the cars were parked very closely, and Riordan had to help his locking knee through with his hand. Once on the sidewalk, he picked the route in the middle, allowing the light from the street lamp on the corner of Cottage Gate Street to hit him full. Beyond the light, on the other side of Cottage Gate, the Kildare Tap occupied a one-story building.

The Kildare had a white hollow sign, illuminated from within, furnished by Schlitz. The corner of the building at the point of the intersection had been chopped off, so that the door invited trade from both streets. The entrance was slightly recessed on a low concrete rise. The Schlitz sign was suspended from a steel frame mounted on the roof above the door. The Schlitz logo was large and brilliant. The name of the tavern was painted in black block letters, large and plain, below the ornate beer trademark. There was a long narrow window, the sill at chest level, about six feet long, set in the Cottage Gate side wall. There was another window, the same size and height from the ground, set in the brick wall fronting on West Broadway. Over the door frame there was a large electric lantern, made to resemble the gas lights of England, but it was enclosed in mottled golden glass that made everything dim except for the patch of light thrown on the entryway from the bottom, and the white Schlitz logo affixed to the front. There was a Budweiser neon sign in the West Broadway window, and there was a Miller neon sign in the Cottage Gate window.

Riordan checked traffic. There was none. He crossed Cottage Gate, his right hand in his right-hand pocket. Just before he reached the curbing, he took out his handkerchief. A quarter fell from it onto the pavement. Holding the handkerchief in his hand, he bent to search for the quarter, turning to avoid throwing a shadow on the gutter by standing between it and the street lamp on the corner. He spotted the quarter, bent over, picked it up, straightened up, put the coin back in his pocket, and without changing his position, blew his nose. The man who had stood at the corner of Oakleigh and West Broadway was gone. The street was empty, although the parking places were full. The apartments fronting on West Broadway were also quiet, except for the occasional curtains rustling out over windowsills and fluttering back inside.

Riordan turned again and walked up to the door of the Kildare, putting his handkerchief back in his pocket. He opened the door and went inside. The door closed behind him on a pneumatic piston. To his left, under the West Broadway window, there were four Formica tables, with tan tops, each with two chairs. There were two men talking quietly over beers at the farthest. The inside wall running toward the rear from the West Broadway wall was long enough for nine tables adequate to seat four men eating or six men drinking. There were two men at each of the first five tables, with two cribbage games in progress. Two tables were vacant. The last four-man table in the corner at the rear was occupied by at least two men, perhaps three. Riordan could not see them very well, because they sat under a high buttressed shelf which held a large color television set. The picture showed leopards or cheetahs chasing gazelles across a broad plain sodded in tall brown grass. The gazelles tried very hard to escape and some of them did, so that the leopards or cheetahs had to skid to a halt, or fall over and look foolish. The sound was off on the set.

There was a U-shaped bar in the center of the room, with red vinyl upholstered stools around the outside perimeter. It had a thick, raised, rounded rim in front. The bar was dark wood. There were eight plain white canisters on it. There was an island in the center bay where the liquor was displayed on tiered translucent white shelves, lighted from below. There were three tiers that extended about ten feet in the center of the bar area. They were very crowded. There were draft beer and ale taps, two banks on each side. There was a mesh rubber mat, about eighteen inches long and a foot wide, in front of each tap. Between the taps, on each side of the bar, there was a gray National Cash Register. Above the bar there was a veneer coping the same shape on the ceiling. There were seven dim white lights under it, aimed upward against the white ceiling, three on each side and one over the middle of the narrow end of the bar at the door. At the rear of the bar there were two small serving windows, one on each side. There was a blackboard between them—it had been wiped but not washed of the day's menu's chalk dust. There was one man leaning back against the wall on the last seat at the bar on Riordan's right. The nine four-man tables along the Cottage Gate wall were unoccupied.

Riordan walked down the right side of the bar and took a stool in the middle. He rested his hands on the bar. After a while the bartender, a thin man in his late fifties with very thin gray hair combed straight back, emerged from the room behind the television pedestal opening into the corridor to the back room. He wore a white shirt that did not fit him. He was doing up the zipper of his dark pants. He ducked under the bar at the end on the other side and reappeared through a kneehole, inside the island enclosure. He took a rag from the counter and leaned on it with his right hand while he watched one of the cheetahs. Riordan's view of the television was blocked. "You see that, Jimmy?" the bartender said. "Jesus, that fucker can run." One of the men at the table said something in a low voice. "Fuckin'A right, you are," the bartender said. "Only problem that fucker's got's the fact he's not all black and he walks on his hands too. Way he can jump, run, if he looked something like a man he'd play inna fuckin' NBA any day."

The man at the end of the bar pulled himself away from the wall. "Hey, Patrick," he said, "ya dumb son of a bitch."

The bartender did not look at him. "Yeah, numb-nuts? Whaddaya you want?"

"I don't want nothin', asswipe," the customer said. "Oh, I could maybe use another fuckin' beer before the fuckin' sun comes up. But hey, you got another customer here. He ain't had nothing yet, you stand there like a big dumb cocksucker, watchin' television."

"Eat shit, numb-nuts," the bartender said.

"Hey, mister," the customer said to Riordan, "you sure you wanna stay in this here fuckin' hole?" Riordan turned and looked at him. "See what we got to go through here, the fuckin' treatment we fuckin' get, tryin' get this fuckin' asshole here, pour us a fuckin' beer? See? I don't wanna make you feel bad, mister, but you sure picked a fuckin' winner of a fuckin' bar, you pick this fuckin' place and this fuckin' asshole runnin' it. I was you, I'd go someplace else. This fuckin' guy wouldn't give the fuckin' Pope a fuckin' drink."

"Hey, numb-nuts," the bartender said, "the next time you're talkin', your pal the Pope, you can tell him for me if he comes back around this town he should make plans to drop around and I will personally buy him as many drinks he wants. Onna house. That don't apply you, though. You're still supposed to pay cash, and I'm telling you, you better pay me cash tomorrow when the eagle shits, you're not gonna have no fuckin' credit anymore like the boss says I'm not supposed to give you and I risk my job, I give you every week. You gotta get a better job, numb-nuts. You ain't making enough dough pushin' broom down the carbarn, pay for your drinks. That's why you're always going tab."

"See?" the customer said to Riordan. "The fuckin' asshole, he'd rather get mad at a guy that's got a little temporary trouble'n sell booze to a guy that can probably pay for it, can't you? Huh?"

The bartender turned slowly away from the television and

faced the customer. "Okay, numb-nuts," he said, "that's enough outta you. I told you and told you, and the boss was even gonna throw you out, permanent eighty-six, you didn't stop doin' this. Just because a new guy comes in here that don't know you for the fuckin' moochin' bum you are, don't mean we're gonna stand still here and let you get away with it."

"The hell're you yellin' at me for, Patrick," the customer said. "I didn't do nothing. You didn't do nothin' either, which I'm not supposed to do and you are, on account of you being the bartender, shitbum."

"Just shut up for a while now, numb-nuts," the bartender said. He came around the rear of the island and walked up the right-hand side to Riordan's seat. "Didn't see you," he said. "Getcha drink?"

"Yeah," Riordan said. "Bally ale draft."

The bartender rinsed a beer glass, tipped it under the ale spigot, and began to draw the brew. "Hey, mister," the customer said to Riordan, "you better watch that fuckhead there. Give ya all foam, you don't watch him. Looks like somebody give you a fuckin' glass Mrs. Murphy's fuckin' best laundry detergent, after she used it, you're not careful with that prick."

The bartender clicked his tongue in his teeth and shook his head slightly as he finished drawing. He set the glass on the rubber mat to let it drain, then placed it on the bar in front of Riordan. "Fuckin' guy," he said, "you wouldn't believe it. Quietest little shrimp in the world. Every night, rain or shine, gets through work the carbarn, gets in here by six or so, don't say a word until he's had at least seven, eight beers. Then you couldn't shut up him if you hadda fuckin' baseball bat. Wife. It's his wife. He don't go home till she's in bed. He goes to work 'fore she gets up. Kids're all grown up, moved Dorchester. Weekends she goes see them, he stays home. During the week, she stays home, and he comes here. I'd do the same thing. Thirty-five cents."

Riordan took a crumpled five out of his left-hand pocket and handed it to the bartender. The bartender rang up, made change in the register and counted out bills and coins. "Hey mister," the customer said to Riordan, "don't let the cocksucker put it down onna counter now. Take it in your fuckin' hand." The bartender placed the bills and change in the puddle of ale that had seeped out under the rubber mat in front of Riordan. "See, I told you," the customer said. "He always does that. Puts the money right inna fuckin' beer. Pick it up and put it in your pocket, you walk outta here down street and you'll look like you fuckin' pissed your fuckin' pants. He always does that. Figures you'll either drink it or give it to him the tip."

"If he gets enough drinks, does he shut up?" Riordan said. "Pass out or something? Go home?"

"He didn't used to go home till eleven-thirty," the bartender said. "Now, now it's fuckin' midnight. She always watched the late fuckin' news, and went to bed. That Iran thing, when they start having that hostage thing on every night, we usually close eleven-thirty, you know? During the week. We got a one o'clock, but it's all regulars. They come in after dinner, they have a few pops, by eleven-thirty they're ready, go home. No customers, close up. His wife got all interested in that hostage thing. Up every night till midnight. Every fuckin' night I have to keep open till midnight now, she finally goes to bed and he can go home. That's what's screwed up his drinking budget, that extra half-hour. I tell you, mac, you think the rest America is gonna be glad them fuckin' hostages finally get out after all this time instead of that fuckin' asshole Carter doin' what he should've done right the beginning, give 'em a real Jew commando raid, 'stead of fuckin' around all this time, I am gonna be the happiest fuckin' bartender in Southie because that's gonna mean that Clement'll be able to go home again as soon as Johnny Carson comes on, and that means I'll be able to go home and see some of Johnny Carson too, or maybe even the old fuckin' movie, I don't care.

"Clement," the bartender said, "Clement never passed out in his life, not that I saw or heard about. Drunk? Yeah, I guess Clement gets drunk, but once that fucker's drunk, which he is every night of the week, he don't get no drunker. It's like he needs a certain amount, get his motor going, and then he just sits there and keeps the tank full all the rest the night until that fuckin' goddamned woman finally goes to bed."

"Why don't you throw him out, eleven-thirty, and just go ahead and close up?" Riordan said. "I'll have another ale."

The bartender took the glass, inspected it, and began to refill it.

"Hey, mister," Clement said, "should've made him give you a clean glass. See those fuckin' cheap bastards savin' money on you again? Soapy water. They won't even give a man a clean glass, they're fuckin' savin' onna fuckin' soapy water."

The bartender put the glass in front of Riordan on the mat, then on the bar at his seat. He gestured toward the money. "Okay to take this out?"

"Sure," Riordan said. "While you're at it, take out one of whatever it is he's drinking. But he drinks it down there. Not here."

The bartender grinned. "Narrie," he said. "Okay." He rang up thirty-five cents. "Do I tell him or do you?"

"You tell him," Riordan said. "I'm buyin' the guy a fuckin' beer. I don't want no philosophy from him with it."

"Hey, numb-nuts," the bartender said loudly, "man's buyin' you a round. Same thing, though. No Courvoisee-fuckin'-air for you on him, Clement. And you gotta stay the hell you are and keep your big fuckin' mouth shut. He's buyin' a beer. He don't want a fuckin' friend for life."

"Hey," Clement said, "thanks, mister. Decent of you." The bartender poured the Narragansett and slid it faultlessly the length of the bar. It stopped in front of Clement. He drained his previous beer and began to relish the new one.

"See?" the bartender said. "See what a little fuckin' thing looks like fuckin' heaven to you, when your own goddamned front door opens right straight into fuckin' hell? Jesus, what a fuckin' life that man's had. Parents born two streets down, next door to each other. That cunt he married grew up four houses down. Never had no education, speak of. Knocks her up, quits school, goes to work, the carbarn, four kids. He's doin' the same fuckin' thing now he's doing when he's twenty, except he sure ain't banging her no more. Only one of those kids worth shit and he enlists in the fuckin' army so he gets helicopter training and gets shot down over Vietnam. Christ. You wanna know something, we been lucky. I can't go home because I gotta work, but if I could go fuckin' home, I could go home, you know? I could do it. I wouldn't have to sit around no bar. My daughter stays up and makes a little dinner, we watch TV, it's all right. My wife's dead, good woman, she had cancer the pancreas, you know? Terrible. Long time. But my daughter takes pretty good care me. She's a good kid. Works over Filene's, in the ladies' luggage. Just got a promotion. I pity that Clement."

The street door opened and a small, wiry man came in. He was wearing a gray scalley cap. He glanced at Riordan from under the cap, turned left and headed directly to the table under the television pedestal at the rear. Riordan saw him sit down at the remaining chair on the outside. He could by then see a third man in the gloom under the television shelf. He leaned toward the man in the cap. Riordan could not hear what they were saying.

"I didn't see you around before," the bartender said to Riordan. There was an edge to his voice.

"No," Riordan said. He finished the second ale and hunched his shoulders against his elbows, resting against the bar. With his right hand he felt the gun under his coat, and shifted it slightly to bring the butt farther forward. He nudged the empty glass toward the bartender. "Fill 'er up, okay?"

The bartender took the glass and began drawing ale. "You work around here?" the bartender said.

"Sometimes," Riordan said.

The bartender drained the glass and placed it before Riordan. He took money and paused over the register. "You wanna send Clement another one?"

"Christ, yes," Riordan said. "Guy's quiet now. Maybe he was happier when he was thirsty and loud. Poor bastard."

The bartender drew another Narragansett with his right hand while he shut the register drawer with his left. He slid the beer down the bar to where Clement sat hunched over the previous gift, staring into the corner under the television set where the four men were talking. Clement did not look up.

"Whaddaya do?" the bartender said.

"Various things," Riordan said. "You know. Little of this, little of that. Whatever's available at the time, man can make a living at it."

"Yeah," the bartender said. "Sure, but I mean, like right now. What're doing right now? Because I didn't see you before."

"Drinkin' ale," Riordan said. "Never drank ale in here before is probably the reason, you didn't see me."

"Yeah," the bartender said. He straightened up. "Uh," he said, "uh, look, all right? You seem like a pretty nice guy and everything. I, ah, we . . . this's a pretty small neighborhood, you know? The people live down here, you know? Most of them, they always lived here. They all know each other, you know? And they, they had a lot of guys down here, the past few years. The busing thing, you know? And they didn't like it. What happened to them. Shit, I mean even Clement hates fuckin' niggers, and I bet Clement didn't know ten niggers his whole life, and his kids're all grown up except the one that's dead. He hasn't got no kids in school. And you couldn't meet a nicer guy that didn't want no trouble, you know? Than Clement. But even Clement hates them niggers, just from him living here and them coming in here, just from that. Kids. I bet he never even seen one of them nigger kids. Goes to work before they come in, he don't get home, they're gone. Even works, there's a couple black guys inna plant where he works, the carbarn, and they been there for years, and Clement knows them and he gets along all right with them. He says that's just Todd and Frank there, and they ain't niggers. But he hates niggers, just the same. You see what I mean, right?"

"I haven't got anything to do with no busin'," Riordan said. "Don't worry about that."

"No," the bartender said. He thought for a while. "Well, I mean, whaddaya do, then? 'Cause you don't live around here, or I would've seen you."

The small man in the gray scalley cap stood up and glanced sharply across the bar at Riordan. Then he walked quickly down the aisle on the other side of the bar. When he reached the end, he stopped and stared briefly at Riordan. Riordan ignored him. The man went to the door, opened it and went out.

"Well," Riordan said, holding the glass off the counter, halfway to his mouth, "like I said, various things. Tonight for example, I am looking for a guy."

"Is he down here?" the bartender said. "Does he live down here?"

"That's what I heard," Riordan said. "I'm not sure it's true. That's just what I heard."

"Does he come in here?" the bartender said.

"I heard that," Riordan said. He drained the glass. "Fill 'er up, huh?"

The bartender began to fill the glass again. Riordan belched. "Jesus," he said, "that stuff makes you all fulla gas. Smell like skunk piss. Probably fart polka dot tomorrow." He belched again. "Love it, though."

The bartender put the drained glass in front of Riordan. "Well, shit," he said, "the guy comes in here, maybe I can help you. I'm here every night. I'd know if he was in here."

Riordan shook his head, puffing his cheeks as he belched again. "No," he said, when he had finished. "Personal matter."

"Personal matter," the bartender said.

"Yeah," Riordan said. "You know how it is: personal matter. This is a guy that I want to see about a personal matter. Don't want, embarrass him, spread his fuckin' business all over town. How'd you like that, somebody wanted to see you, lookin' for you on a personal matter, and the first thing he does is, he's walkin' around and havin' beers in your own neighborhood, tellin' people he wants to see you on this personal thing, huh? Howd'ya like that, huh? Wouldn't." He belched again. "Shit," he said, "damned stuff. Didn't drink enough of it, that's why I'm having all this trouble." He drank half of the fresh glass. "Ahh," he said, putting the glass down, "better." He rubbed his stomach. "You wouldn't like it. You'd get mad, guy runnin' around all over the place like that, tellin' your private business, people."

"Well," the bartender said, "you could tell me his name, couldn't you? That wouldn't do no harm. Couldn't bother nobody. I might know the guy. I see him, he's one the guys comes in here all the time, I could tell him, you wanna see him, have him call you up, meet you someplace. No harm in that."

Riordan sat straight on the stool and belched. He shook his head vigorously, puffing his cheeks. "Uh-uh," he said, when he was finished, "I don't think he'd do that. I don't think I wanna depend on him to do that. I gotta take a piss. Goddammit, now I gotta take a piss. Draw me another one there, and leave this one." He stood off the stool, barely wavering. "Where 'sa pisspot?"

"Over there in back," the bartender said, gesturing with his right thumb over his right shoulder. "Door right next the television. Behind it."

"Thanks," Riordan said. He displayed some difficulty getting under way, and had to grip the bar for balance. He looked at the bartender, somewhat sheepishly. "Didn't have no supper," he said. "Oughta know better. Didn't have no supper and now I got so much ale in me, I don't want any." He bumped the stools as he passed them.

"Hey, Patrick," one of the men yelled at the dark table, "you gonna spend all night over there fallin' in love with that big drunk, or can we get another round here?" The bartender, watching Riordan lurch around the bar, knocking into one or two of the chairs at the table along the inside wall, refocused his gaze on the darkened table. He went around to the other side of the bar and began to draw Narragansetts.

Riordan reached the darkened table as Patrick started drawing the third beer. "Hey," he said into the darkness, grinning slightly and weaving a little, "one you guys call me big drunk?"

"Yeah," said the man in the dark in the corner. "Wanna make something out of it?"

Riordan held up his hands and wove back half a step. "Nope, nope," he said. He laughed. "Just asking. Man likes to know, who his friends are. Can't argue with you. I'm sure big, and I guess I'm kind of drunk. Say, that Patrick there, he always this much talk? Guy talks more'n my wife." He wiped his nostrils with the back of his left hand, and snuffled.

"You're not insulting Patrick, are ya?" the voice said. "Patrick's a friend of ours."

"No, no," Riordan said, "just asking." He put his hands in his pockets. "Well, have to excuse myself, I guess. *Excuuse* me. You like that Steve Martin, huh? Funny guy." None of the men said anything. "See him on television, alla time." There was no reply. "Well, okay. Don't want interfere your private party. Just tryin', be friendly. Go take a piss."

Riordan nearly fell against the door and staggered into the narrow hall to the back room. There was a small room with no door. The walls to the left were flaked with green-painted plaster. There was a trough urinal to the left of the entrance, with rust stains on the inlet valve. There was a sink stained with dirty soap, dried on. The flush did not have a seat. There was a fresh pink deodorant cake in a wire basket on the inner side of the upper rim. The light was a sixty-watt bulb. Riordan stood before the flush and banged his shoulder on the wall to the right as he unzipped his pants. He began to urinate copiously and noisily. He could hear the men talking in low voices on the other side of the partition next to the urinal, but he could not hear what they were saying. When he had voided about half the contents of his bladder, he flushed the toilet. As the rushing water began, he exerted tension on his bladder sphincter and shut off the flow from there. When the flush started to quiet down, he relaxed his muscles, so that he resumed urinating. When he thought he had about a quarter of his ballast left, he repeated the procedure with the flush, and when that was ending, finished relieving himself. He forced a large belch. Then resuming his weaving, he left the toilet, opened the door to the bar, and stood on the threshold, fumbling with his fly and grinning to himself. He managed to close his pants, and stepped all the way into the bar.

"Jayzuss," the voice said in the corner darkness, "you're a real pisser, aren't you?" There was something in the tone that was supposed to pass for admiration.

Riordan turned slightly and looked into the gloom. "I been some other places before here tonight," he said. "Lookin' for a fuckin' guy, don't seem to be around."

"You a cop?" the voice said.

Riordan put on a drunk's version of a crafty expression. "Cop?" he said. "Cop? Why, think it might help? Been chasing this guy all over hell and gone, past week'n a half. Can't find him. Cop helps, I'll be cop. Sure. I'm a cop."

"You really a cop?" the voice said.

"Sort of, a cop," Riordan said. "Yeah. Sort of a cop. That's what I am. Rules. I go out and . . . the rules. That's what."

"Sort of a cop, is it now?" the voice said. The other two men at the table smiled at the voice. "Sort of a cop. You mean, a private eye? One of them jamokes?"

"Yeah," Riordan said, his face showing consideration of the idea. "Private eye."

"Got a license?" the voice said.

"License," Riordan said reflectively, "oh, sure. License. I got a license."

"Private eye license, I mean," the voice said.

"Private eye license," Riordan said. "Sure. I got privates eyes' licenses. Yeah."

"Let's see it," the voice said.

At the front of the bar, two men in gray sweaters came in. Riordan saw them from the corner of his left eye, but gave no sign. He saw Patrick incline his head to his left. The men walked down behind Riordan's stool and took a table behind it.

Riordan shook his head. "Uh-uh," he said. "Secret. Secret license. Can't show it, anybody. 'Gainst the law."

"Let's see where it says on it you can't show it to anybody," the voice said.

Riordan broke into a big grin. He extended his right forefinger and shook it at the voice. "Uh-uh," he said, "you're tryin', *trick* me. Too smart for you."

"Got a gun?" the voice said.

"Sure," Riordan said, "got a gun. *Big* gun."

"You can show us that, can't you," the man next to Riordan's left elbow at the aisle said. He had iron-gray hair, a big belly, and thick, tanned forearms. The left one was tattooed with a fouled anchor. "Uh-uh," Riordan said. "Secret gun. Very secret. Lookin' for somebody. Can't show gun."

"Well," the man said, "maybe we can help you. Who're you looking for?"

"Secret too," Riordan said triumphantly. "Secret party."

"Okay," the man said, "nice talking to you, big fella. Go have your beer with Clement there. Everything'll be all right in the morning, 'cept for maybe your belly."

"Yup," Riordan said. He wove around the bar to his stool. There were four full glasses in front of it, in addition to the half-glass he had left. "Hey," he said, "Patrick. Where'd all these brews come from, huh?"

The bartender came around to Riordan's side of the bar as he clambered onto the seat. The two new customers were behind him now. "Your new friends over there," Patrick said. "Told me they decided after you went in the head, they'd been too rough on you."

"Gee," Riordan said. He raised his voice. "Hey, fellas," he said, "thanks, thanks a lot." He waved.

"Thing of it is," Patrick said, "they insisted, but the way you're goin', if I was you I don't think I'd drink them things. No supper and everything, you know? You're gettin' pretty stiff. You got to drive somewhere or something, you know?" Riordan heard the two gray-sweatered men behind him stirring in their chairs. "Nah," he said, waving his left hand and picking up the half-glass first. He drained it. He put it down and picked up the first of the four full glasses. He drained that. He put it down. "Insult guy like that, buy you drinks. Can't do that. Finish these. Go home. Honest. Perfectly fine." He belched. He leaned forward over the bar and beckoned Patrick closer. "Say," he said, whispering, "confidentially, you ever hear a guy named Scanlan around this neighborhood? Just asking, huh? Don't tell anybody."

"Scanlan the guy you're looking for?" the bartender said.

Riordan nodded. "Scanlan," he said. "Dunno his first name, where he lives. Gettin' sick of this, runnin' around night after night, Cambridge, Charlestown, Somerville, lookin' for Scanlan. Wanna go home."

Patrick straightened up. "Never heard of no Scanlan in this neighborhood," he said, in a normal tone of voice.

"Shh, shh," Riordan said. "Maybe he lives here, you just don't know him. Could be." The gray-haired man got up from the end of the corner table across the bar.

"Hey, Patrick, see you for a minute," he said. Then he stared at Clement across the bar. From the corner of his eye, Riordan could see Clement put down half a glass of beer and slide off the stool. Patrick crossed behind the island in the bar.

Clement walked rapidly up the aisle. Riordan heard the two chairs scrape again behind him. Clement brushed behind Riordan's back, then stopped at his left shoulder and put his right hand on it. "Hey, mister," he said.

Riordan hunched over the bar. He nudged the ale glasses away from him, up to the edges of the rubber mat. He turned his head to Clement. "Yeah, old pal?"

"Listen," Clement said, wetting his lips, "I gotta go home now, all right?"

"Home?" Riordan said. He fumbled at his cuff and peeked at the Rolex without showing it. " 'S only little after ten-thirty. Patrick told me, you never leave 'fore midnight, these days.

Got lots of time. Guys buying drinks'n everything. Nice place. Stay awhile."

"*No*," Clement said, "listen. Why'ncha go home now, all right? Like me. Go home, sleep it off. Be all right in the morning."

Riordan saw the gray-haired man straighten up. Patrick ducked under the bar and went into the back room, the door swinging shut behind him. The gray-haired man nodded. Riordan heard the chairs scrape fast behind him. He saw Clement's face change before he fled. The heel of a hand snapped down against the base of Riordan's skull. His face slammed down against the bar, his nose striking the rounded rim. As he hit, another hand grabbed him by his left shoulder and began to spin him toward the door.

Riordan ignored the blood streaming from his nose onto his shirt and coat. He let the momentum of the turning stool go into the leverage of his right leg, the knee locked, as he brought the heavy boot up from the floor into the crotch of the man who had grabbed him. As the kick landed, he brought his left fist back over his right shoulder, swung it back in a flat arc and caught the left side of the jaw of the man who had rabbit-punched him. The hinge of the jaw broke loudly. The puncher was stunned. He reeled off to his own right, into the tables. The man on the floor was screaming and holding his testicles. Riordan bent down, grabbed him by the gray sweater, hoisted him up, held him with his left hand and used the flat of his right fist to break the right hinge of the grabber's jaw. The man screamed again. Riordan dropped him to the floor. He took the rabbit-puncher out of the tangle of tables and chairs, stood him erect, spun him around so that he was back-to, yanked his hands down from his jaw, brought them behind the man in a double lock, and jacked them upward together until the elbows shattered. The rabbit-puncher screamed for the first time. Riordan threw him on the floor. He turned toward the door. The grabber was lying on the floor, whimpering. He held his hands up before his face. Riordan raised his left leg about eighteen inches and stomped down on the man's knee, breaking most of it. The man gave a garbled scream through his shattered jaw.

"Souvenir, shitbag," Riordan said. "Something to tell your fuckin' grandchildren. What a tough guy you were, the night you and your buddy got wrecked tryin' to roll one stupid drunk. Tell 'em what you got isn't quite as good as the one the drunk had, but it was all they had available at the store. You'll still know when it's gonna rain, though. Shitbirds." Riordan looked around. Except for the three of them, the bar was empty.

He reached over the bar and found a clean dry towel. He dipped one end of it in the soapy water and washed the blood off his hands. He dried his hands on the other end. He reached into his breast pocket and took out a Ray-Ban case. He opened it and took out clear aviator glasses with oversize lenses and frames. He put the case back into his pocket. He reached inside his jacket and drew the magnum. He checked the load, and snapped the cylinder shut. He carried the gun in his right hand. He looked at his watch. It was 10:46.

Riordan opened the outside door slowly, letting his left arm hang slack in the opening. After a few seconds, he dragged his body around the edge of the door. Carrying his right arm stiffly against his side, with the gun against his pant leg, he limped slowly out into the street, his head down, his left leg dragging slightly. When he reached the illumination from the street light, he paused as though out of breath. He raised his head back, displaying the blood, and used his left hand to massage the neck and the base of the skull. He staggered now and then, weaving also, sometimes quite abruptly, although he looked as though he was walking slowly. There was no one in sight when he reached West Broadway. Dangling his right arm in his own shadow, so that it would seem useless, he crossed on the southerly side of the intersection to the other side of West Broadway. He kept well away from the parked cars and doorways. He lurched back and forth. The curtains billowed out of the windows, and the light from television screens flickered against the curtains from the inside.

He was three cars behind his own when the passenger-side door of a dark sedan opened fast at the curb. The man in the gray scalley cap dove out of the door, in the act of turning and firing a single-shot sawed-off shotgun at Riordan. The range was too great for a sawed-off to do much damage. Some of the pellets spattered off the shooting glasses, but ? lan paid no attention to them or the ones that dug into his forehead and neck. He brought the magnum up precisely in his right hand, clamped his right wrist in his left hand, and fired one round that hit the man dead center on the sternum. He was not a very big man—the shot knocked him into the gutter, under the right front wheel of the car.

Crouching, Riordan moved quickly between two parked cars and into the street. Lights were coming on in the apartments now. As he trotted down the street, outside the cars, he saw a muzzle flash above the trunk of his car, on the sidewalk side. He stopped in his tracks and counted to fifteen. He stood up just as the gray-haired man stuck his head up over the trunk of the car, the automatic gleaming in his hand. Riordan shot him in the face. A large red spray erupted from the back of his head, and he fell into Oakleigh Street, on his back.

Riordan bent over and ran forward again. He was behind his own car when he saw a man in a brown leather scalley cap, barely visible in the area beyond the aura of the Oakleigh street lamp, pressing himself against the house at the corner next to Riordan's car. Riordan stood up. *"Scanlan,"* he roared, "the great hero won't use his own name. What is your name, you coward?" Scanlan made his position a little better, fired once with a 9mm. Walther PPK, hit Riordan in the musculature of the left side of the neck, and left his feet at the impact of the first bullet from the magnum. Riordan fired again as Scanlan's body extended with the shock, the second bullet entering the torso one inch to the right of the one that exploded Scanlan's left lung.

Riordan could hear the sirens now, and then he could see the flashing blue lights. He stood there next to the car, using his left hand to explore the neck wound, not to see whether it was serious, but whether the bullet had passed through. He needed both hands, and he was feeling lightheaded. He holstered the gun and sat down in the yoga position in the street next to his car, under the light. He was still pawing the wound when the police came to him.

He rode sitting upright in the ambulance, pressing a compress to his neck, to Boston City Hospital. He had preserved possession of his gun with his credentials. The oxygen which the attendant had given him brought him back to life.

"Oh," the cop said, leafing through the forms on the clipboard, "most people of course don't know this, but it helps the medical examiner if you know what kind of bullets you were using, you know? So he can rule out whether anybody else did any of the shooting."

"Somebody else fuckin' damned right did a little shooting," Riordan said. "The three of those bastards that I shot. I don't know what they were using. Cheap shit, though."

"Yessir," the cop said, "but what'd you use? Standard government issue, maybe? If that's what it was, we can find out easy enough for the report."

"No," Riordan said, "hundred-and-ten grain slug. Twenty-point-four grains Hodgkin one-ten powder. Fifteen-hundred-fifty feet-per-second, muzzle velocity."

"Jesus Christ," the cop said, "that's the killer load."

"That's one of them," Riordan said. "That's the one you fire from a revolver."

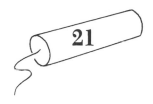

21

SHORTLY BEFORE 12:45 in the morning, Paul Doherty took the East Milton Square exit northbound off the Southeast Expressway. He waited in front of the fire station for the light to change, then drove up Granite Avenue toward Dorchester. He reached Gallivan Boulevard, stopped at the lights, and drove up through the business district on Dorchester Avenue until he reached the satellite parking lot for the J. J. Donlan Funeral Home one block up from the boulevard. He turned right into the dark and deserted lot and drove to the back row, under the overhanging branches of the maple trees that grew on the other side of the stockade fence. He backed the blue Aries into a space against the fence and shut off the lights and ignition. The engine ran on, shaking the car with its dieseling. "Junk," Doherty said.

There was nothing in the parking lot between Paul Doherty and the curb of Dorchester Avenue. There was one Oldsmobile parked at the curb on the other side of the street. It was a metallic chocolate Ninety-eight luxury sedan, and it was new. It partially blocked Paul Doherty's view of the main entrance to the Bright Red Tap and Gentlemen's Bar. The door was flanked with plate-glass windows which were heavily tinted smoke-gray. The plastic relief picture of the Budweiser Clydesdales, hung against the window on the left, was legible, and the Schlitz display sign against the window on the right was legible, but everything more than six inches behind the glass was indistinct. Paul Doherty could see human figures moving around in the dim light inside the bar, but he could not identify them. At one o'clock, the door opened and two men emerged into the warm, still evening. They stood and talked for a moment, and then separated and left in opposite directions, on foot. There was no observable activity in the bar for a few minutes. Then the lights that shone through the window on the left were extinguished. The light that illuminated the sign on the front went out. The door opened again and a figure emerged partway. The lights that shone through the window on the right went out. The beer advertisements remained illuminated. Paul Doherty could see one dim light over the bar as the door opened wider and the figure came out.

Digger Doherty triple-locked the front door of the Bright Red and armed the burglar alarm so that the warning light glowed red over the keyboard. He put his keys in his pocket and stepped onto the sidewalk, into the light from the street lamp. He hitched up his green chino pants around his heavy belly and stuffed his white cotton shirt more deeply into the waistband. He patted his stomach while he looked up and down the street. He nodded at nothing in particular. He walked across the sidewalk and around the back of the Oldsmobile. He stopped at the driver's side door and took from his pocket the same key ring he had used to lock the door of the saloon. He unlocked the car, got in, and reached under the dash to disarm the automobile burglar alarm. His left leg stuck out the open door and he had considerable difficulty compressing his belly enough against the steering wheel to permit him to reach the alarm lock. He got the key into it just as the siren began to sound, and shut it off before it had reached full blast. He straightened up in the seat and glanced into the Donlan parking lot as he shut the car door. He saw the

Aries in the lot, but he could not see whether it was occupied.

He closed his car door and started the engine of the Oldsmobile, settling his hams into the deep, loose, crushed-velvet seat cushions as the engine caught and purred, running his tongue over his teeth to root out the remains of the pastrami sandwich he had only nominally chewed before swallowing it as his dinner, gazing speculatively at the blue Aries in the Donlan parking lot. He kept his left hand on the steering wheel, where it would be visible in the light. He slid his right hand off the bottom part of the steering wheel and felt under the seat. By touch he located a cigar box. He pulled it out onto the floor mat under his thighs and opened it without looking down. He reached into the box and took out a 9mm. Luger. He slid the Luger under the cushion of the passenger seat, closed the cigar box, and slid it back under the seat. He turned on the headlights, shifted his gaze from the Aries, and put the Oldsmobile in gear.

Digger Doherty headed south on Dorchester Avenue toward the Gallivan Boulevard intersection. There were no other cars on Dorchester Avenue behind him. He watched in the rear-view mirror and saw the headlights on the car that came out of the Donlan lot and turned left on Dorchester Avenue behind him. He did not have a green arrow for the right turn on Gallivan Boulevard, but there was no traffic approaching the intersection in either direction, and he made the turn without using his blinker. He shut off his headlights as he completed the turn. He did not straighten the wheels of the car, but pulled into the parking lot behind the branch of the Shawmut Bank beyond the intersection on the right, stopping just short of the chain that blocked through traffic. He put the car into reverse and backed up into the side street opposite the entrance, blocking a driveway which was shaded from the street lamp by three large maple trees. He kept the engine running.

The Digger saw the blue Aries reach the intersection as the light turned green on Dorchester Avenue. It turned right on Gallivan Boulevard, without hesitating. The Digger put the Oldsmobile in drive and pulled out of the side street. At the corner of Gallivan Boulevard he paused, the headlights still off, and peered up the boulevard. The Aries was passing under the railroad bridge and heading up the hill. The Digger waited until it disappeared. Then he turned left on Gallivan Boulevard, ran the light at Dorchester Avenue again, turning left. He repassed the Bright Red and headed north four blocks. He took a left on a side street and varied his speed on several more intersecting and parallel streets, always proceeding in a generally westerly direction, until he reached the middle of the block on Moraine Street in Saint Gregory's parish, where he lived.

He did not pull out. He parked and shut off the lights. It was a neighborhood of cramped colonial three-bedroom homes, crowded together on small lots on a steep hill. His was three doors north of the intersection where he had stopped. He took the Luger out from under the cushion of the passenger seat and put it in his pocket. He got out of the car and shut the door. He locked it. Then he unlocked it. He reached in and set the alarm. He closed and relocked the door.

Preferring the shadows, the Digger stayed close to the low retaining walls that kept the tiny front lawns in place when the rains and the melting snows of winter threatened to erode them down the hill into Dorchester Lower Mills. Two doors from his house, on the other side of the street, he spotted the blue Aries, parked with its lights out. He could see one occupant, the driver. He crouched as much as he could and walked quietly across Moraine Street, approaching the Aries diagonally from the right rear, so that he would be in the blind spot of the rear-view mirror. When he got to the car he moved very quickly to the front passenger window and pointed the Luger at the driver as he grabbed with his left hand for the door handle. The door was unlocked. He snapped it open, keeping the pistol leveled at the driver, and said, "Aw right, you cocksucker, open that door and get out real slow and keep your fuckin' hands where I can see them."

Paul Doherty grinned in the illumination from the dome light. " 'Evening, baby brother," he said. "Small case of the jitters tonight? Is our conscience bothering us? Do we feel the need of absolution, or is the handgun the only thing that will make us feel secure?"

"What the fuck're you doing here?" Jerry Doherty said. "Whose car is this?"

"Make a deal with you, Jerry," Paul said. "You put the gun away and get in and sit down and shut the door, I will answer your questions. I assure you that I have no intention of shooting you. From what I hear, you've got some reason to be apprehensive about such a thing happening, but it won't be at my hands, honest."

The Digger got into the Aries and shut the door, turning off the dome light. "All right," he said, "what're you doing driving this shitbox, and why're you tailing me? You should be home in bed."

"Couldn't sleep," Paul said. "My car's being repainted, and it wasn't ready today. Yesterday. I'm not used to your hours, Jerry. So I came out to see you in this. You wouldn't want me tossing and turning out there by myself in Weston, would you, when the Lord is telling me to go and see my little brother? Ye gods, but you're fat. You get fatter every time I see you. I'm going to have the devil's own time explaining to Mister Avis what happened to the passenger seat to squash it all down as you're doing. He'll think I had an anvil in here."

"You oughta drink warm milk and crumble up some bread in it, you can't sleep," Jerry said. "Lots safer'n driving around in the dark scaring the shit out of people that might shoot you because they figure you're getting set to shoot them. Besides, I may be fat, but I haven't had no heart attack yet, and if that's the way the Dohertys get thin, I'm gonna be fat a hell of a long time, is what I'm gonna be.

"Now," the Digger said, "whaddaya want to see me about, you got to come hiding around like you was some guy, had it a mind to knock me off? You ever hear the telephone, you call a guy up and tell him, you would like to see him and have a meeting with him and talk to him, that kind of thing? And would he meet you someplace so you can sit down and have this talk you want to have? You ever hear of guys doing that? I have heard of guys doing that. I know lots of guys, do that. Sometimes one of those guys will call me up and he will say, 'Digger, I would like to have a talk with you about this thing and the other thing there, and how's about you and me, we sort of get together down the Saratoga there or someplace, and we will have a couple drinks and maybe a pizza and we will see what each other has got to say for himself.' I do that. I do that all the time."

"Jerry," Paul said, "after all, I am, we are brothers, you know. Do I have to ask for an appointment?"

"Well, actually, yeah," Jerry said. "Yeah, the same as I would think it would be the right thing to do, if I was the one that wanted to see you, that I would call you up first and tell you that I had something I wanted to talk about with you and when would be a good time to sit down. Yeah, I think you should call me up first and tell me, so I wouldn't come out of work in the middle of the night which is when I work and there you are in this car that you know I will not recognize and so forth. Lemme ask you this, all right? You wanted to see the Cardinal there about something, would you just show up some night and make him think you were setting him up? Or would you call him first?"

"Jerry," Paul said, "let's face facts here. If I called you up and told you I wanted to see you, you would either refuse to take the call, if you found out who wanted to talk to you, or if you took it without knowing, you would hang up on me the minute you found out who it was. The best I can hope for, calling you up, is that you just made a lot of money doing something that has probably captured the attention of every cop, state, federal and local, in New England, and you are feeling so pleased with yourself that you will take the time to be courteous enough to take the phone and tell me that you don't want to talk to me, and say goodbye before you hang up. Now, let's be practical, shall we, Jerry? If I want to get some information to you, the only way I can do it is to sneak up on you."

"That is exactly right, big brother," Jerry said. "And you know why that is?"

"Because you don't like me," Paul said. "I can endure that burden."

"Fuck you," the Digger said. He twisted slightly in the seat, leaving the Luger on the floormat. He spread his hands.

"I don't like that language," Paul said.

"Go fuck yourself," Jerry said. "You started this and you're this determined to talk to me, for once you're gonna listen to what I got to say. You think I don't like you? I guess I don't. You know why I don't like you? You remember back about eight, nine, ten years ago, I had to go and see you when I got inna scrape that I hadda . . . I owed some guys some money and I was either gonna pay it or they were gonna do something to me, and I couldn't get it nowhere else so I hadda ask you?"

"I gave you that money," Paul said. "It was a lot of money, too."

"I know you did and I know it was," Jerry said. "It was your new-car money, which I notice you got the new car a couple years later anyway. You remember the deal you made me make with you about that money? I hadda promise I would never ask you nothing again, right?"

"Right," Paul said. "The deal was, that was the last time."

"Right," Jerry said, "and I made that deal and I kept it, didn't I?"

"Yes," Paul said, "I'll give you credit, Jerry. You made the deal and you kept it. Of course, I'd expect nothing else from Digger Doherty, from all the things I hear, and—"

"Shut up, fuckface," Jerry said. "You got any idea how you made me feel that day? That day and lots of other times I couldn't even count? You got any idea? No, of course not. You high and mighty son of a bitch, you think I don't hear some of the stuff you say to people about me? You're wrong. I do. You made me crawl around on my belly like I was some kind of shit that time. Lots of times. You tell people I don't treat my kids right. I get in trouble with a broad, which I have done, and there is my Bishop brother out having dinner with some fuckin' rabbi and the Attorney General and all them grand fellas giving awards to each other all the time, and when they bring around the brandy, the cigars, old Paul Doherty's always right there, tell a few crowd-pleasers what an asshole he's got for a crooked thief of a brother. And everybody has a good laugh for himself, and the U.S. Attorney or whoever it happens to be goes and tells a few his cops, and pretty soon they're telling it onna street to the hard guys what an asshole my own brother says I am.

"It makes you feel good, don't it, Paul?" Jerry said. "It makes you feel good just like this little stunt you pulled here tonight. Get you all tingly and excited, big brother? Like you're beating your meat with some soapsuds on it, gettin' your cookies without anybody knowin'? Tailing me like that. You knew I'd think you were either a cop or a guy out to hit me. You knew that. That's why, you came around the corner there, you didn't even slow down. You knew I wouldn't know what was going on, and I'd be worried. You knew I'd come back here the way I did with a gun in my hand, so you could make fun of me. You like doing that to me, you cocksucker. Gives you another good story you can tell the Police Commissioner, next time you see him down Pier Four at some goddamned reception where everybody's buying the politicians and eatin' the oysters and getting their names in the paper. They're all good guys, aren't they, Paul? Your pals. Big shots. Not like your asshole brother. And pretty soon I got Petrucelli in my place when it's crowded and he's giving me the business, front of everybody, which I got to take from him on account he is a cop and he can pull my license if he wants, how I was gonna shoot my own brother and the next thing I will probably do is light one off at my shadow. That gives guys confidence, Paul, that don't like me and maybe would like to set me up the way you were pretending like an asshole to do tonight. You're fuckin' around in things you don't understand, and it ain't funny, shithead darling brother. It ain't funny at all, from where I sit."

"Jerry," Paul said, "look, honestly, I didn't mean to . . ."

The Digger held up his hand. "Never mind the bullshit, Paul," he said. "You came out to jerk my chain tonight, and you could've got yourself shot doing it, but I guess the Lord really does like you. He won't even let *me* hurt you, even when you practically make me do it without even knowing. Just say what's on your mind and get the fuck out of here before I get pissed off at you enough to do what I'd really like to do anyway."

"There's a guy named Magro that you know in Walpole and he's trying to get out," Paul said. "There's a halfway decent chance he'll make it." He paused. "I'm sorry I've embarrassed you, and I wasn't trying to get you going tonight. I just thought you ought to know."

"I did know," Jerry said. "Petrucelli and his bellboy were in my joint about on Monday night, and that cocksucker, he never comes in unless there's something going on, so the next day I started asking around: What is going on that I got the wop cop in my place giving me the business? And I find out. So I get the word in to Mikie-mike, that I hear he is taking a shot at getting out and I want to know, is he still being a big asshole and thinking that I put him in? Because if that is what he thinks, he should know he will be a lot safer if he did not get out. And I get the word back that he has got that straightened out in his mind and he has got no beef with me and he is hoping if he gets out maybe we can have a glass of beer.

"See, Paul?" the Digger said. "I know Magro a long time. I know he is not a bishop. I know he has done some bad things. He knows I have done some bad things. But he is not a bad guy, and I am not a bad guy, and we know this. He also knows if he tries to do something bad to me, I will try to do something bad to him. He didn't have to say anything, and if that is what he had in mind, that is what he would have said: he would not have said anything. You guys that're always coming around and fucking around in things that you don't understand, this is where you're always making your mistake. All you got to do is ask the guy, is he planning something? That's all. He will tell you. Now you excuse me," he said, picking up the gun and opening the car door, "I am going to go back and get my car, and bring it up and put it in my driveway, and I am going into my own house and go to bed. Like I was planning to do a lot earlier. And you get the fuck out of here and go home and say your prayers."

"Jerry," Paul said as the door opened, "I only meant . . ."

The Digger was all the way out of the car. He bent down and looked in. "Go home, Paul," he said. "Go home and stay home. At least stay away from me. I'm not your fuckin' hobby anymore, Paul, your goddamned family Wild West show that you use to get your chuckles. I'm just a middle-aged saloon-keeper with some bad habits that I understand and you don't. Now just fuck off." He shut the door.

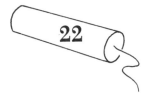

22

WHEN JENNY came out of her bedroom in the middle of the morning, Riordan was sitting on a three-legged wooden stool in the kitchen area, his back to the corridor that led to the bedrooms. There were newspapers spread out on the floor under him. He had a white towel around his neck, and another towel spread over his shoulders. He wore fresh tan pants and a tee-shirt. His hair was wet and shiny. She saw her mother step behind him with scissors and a comb, and cock her head critically. Jenny watched him reach out toward the counter where there was a tall mug of orange juice and a fifth of Smirnoff vodka. He poured vodka into the orange juice and stirred the mixture with his index finger.

"I think it's pretty even," Freddie said. She wore a white bathrobe.

"Jesus, Pete," Jenny said, "does it hurt so much to get your hair cut you have to start in on the booze for breakfast? Cripes, this good grooming thing's a real sacrifice for you isn't it?"

Freddie wheeled around, her hands with the tools at her sides. Her eyes were red and bloodshot. Her face was contorted. "All right, Sleeping Beauty," she said, "now that the dwarfs got you up before you slept off all the poison, get your ass out here and catch up on the late-breaking news."

"Mother," Jenny said, staring, "all I said was . . ."

Setting the glass down on the counter, Riordan raised his right hand and beckoned her into the kitchen. She hurried past her mother and looked him in the face. "Jesus Christ," she said. "Holy shit. What the hell happened to you?"

There were fourteen butterfly bandages on his face, six of them around his eyes and his hairline, so that he appeared to be wearing a white patchwork mask. There was one midway up the right side of his nose. There were three on his left cheek and one on his right cheek. There was one on his right jawline and there were two on his right ear. The towel around the back of his neck had prevented her from seeing the heavy gauze bandage wrapped in layers around his throat, from the collarbones to the bottoms of his earlobes. The mustache was gone; there were four three-stitch sutures on his upper lip, and three three-stitch sutures on his lower lip. There was a white plastic guard taped over the bridge of his nose. His face was mottled maroon and bilious yellow around the nose, and the flesh was swollen under the bandages and stitches. Below the gauze collar on his throat, his chest had been visibly shaven. There were butterfly bandages in lumps under his tee-shirt. "I told you," he said in a hoarse whisper, "never ask me about my business."

Jenny looked at her mother. "What *happened* to him?" she said.

"The damned fool got shot," Freddie said. "That right, Red Ryder? That safe to say? You got shot?"

"That right, Little Beaver," Riordan said in a deep voice. "I got shot, Jenny. Like a damned fool, I went out and got myself shot."

"And then," Freddie said, "in case there was any doubt remaining in anybody's mind about whether he was a damned fool, getting himself all shot up like that, he refused to stay in the hospital where he belonged and where he should be right this very moment, and he came home looking like he'd been in a scrape with a chainsaw just so he could wake me up at three in the morning and scare the shit out of me. You really are an asshole, you know that, Riordan? Listen up, daughter, and avoid the mistakes your poor mother's made: all men are assholes. Right, Riordan? Say *yes, dear*, and make it nice and humble."

"Yes, dear," Riordan said. "Fortunately, some of them're poor shots. Have you got that hair so it's pretty much the same length over the left ear as they made it over the right ear?"

"Patience, patience," she said.

"Who shot you?" Jenny said. "Why?"

"Three guys shot at me," Riordan said. "One missed. One used a sawed-off shotgun which would clean out a small room nicely but isn't much good out-of-doors and we were on the street at the time. Although I will say that he did succeed in ruining that fine Christmas shirt. And what he didn't make holes in, I bled all over. They cut it off me at the hospital, and I didn't really see much sense in bringing home the rags so you could start bitching all over again. Anyway, and the third guy used an automatic, but he tried for a head shot and just nicked me in the neck."

"What did you do?" Jenny said.

"Yeah, Riordan," Freddie said, "tell the little lady what you did."

"I shot back," Riordan said.

"He killed them," Freddie said.

"Three of them?" Jenny said.

"Three of them," Freddie said. "And before he did that, just to warm up, he beat the shit out of a couple guys who jumped him and broke his nose for him. Little barroom brawl before the gunfight at the O.K. Corral. See what fine taste I have in roommates, Jennifer? Nothing but a common thug."

"A public servant, I will have you know, woman," Riordan

said. "I was wounded in the line of duty, the best traditions of an officer sworn to uphold the Constitution and the laws of the United States. Blah. Blah. Blah. I'll probably get a reprimand for wasting the taxpayers' money on special ammunition. Which reminds me: Can I use your car? In all the excitement, I sort of forgot mine, and I have got to meet Bishop Doherty for lunch."

"Lunch?" Jenny said. "You're going out looking like that? How'd they miss your eyes?"

"They didn't miss my eyes," Riordan said. "I had on shooting glasses. Not bulletproof, but pelletproof. I'm not going out for a beauty pageant. I never do that. I'm not qualified for it. I told the guy that I would meet him, and I am going to meet him. You can get the story from your mother."

Freddie came around and stood in front of him. "I'll let you take the car," she said. "You have to bring it back. Yourself. With no new marks on it or you. Is that a deal?"

"Yes," he said.

"Because," she said, "I think I am probably going to lose my job. Which means I won't be able to afford a new car, and I am really going to need a man."

"Gee," Riordan said, "I didn't know I ranked that high. It's nice to feel needed."

"Yeah," she said. "Well, you do and you are. So come back in one piece, all right? No more fights for at least two weeks."

"I promise," he said. "I will not let the Bishop beat me up."

"No," she said, "don't. Ask him instead, to say a Mass for me, thanking God that you're all right, okay?"

"Ask him to say two," Jenny said.

"Gee again," Riordan said. "I must remember to get shot more often. Hurts like hell when they take those pliers to your pelt, get the pellets dug out, but you sure do feel appreciated afterward."

o   o   o

Junior sat on the floor of the front porch of the Nipmunk Country Club, his back against the white pillar that held up the left corner of the roof over the entrance. He was smoking. Howard sat about five feet away from him, on the top step. Cody sat opposite Junior, his back against the pillar on the right. Insects hummed in the midday heat. Junior blew a smoke ring.

"They should let us swim on days like this," Howard said. "Walter—I was in the pro shop when it started to get so hot this morning—and even he was saying that they should let us swim on days like this. Look—" he waved his hand at the two Volvos in the parking lot—"there isn't even anybody here except Mrs. Blake and Mrs. Tobin, and they're not playing today either. There's nobody here. There's nobody even using the pool. They should at least let us use it when there's nobody else even using it. Even Walter was saying that."

"Bullshit," Junior said.

"No bullshit," Howard said. "We're right here. All Mrs. Blake and Mrs. Tobin want to do is drink their lemonade and eat their fruit salad. They don't want to play."

"They're probably afraid," Cody said. "They're probably afraid they'll get you and when you get out around seven you'll try to get them to look at your little prick."

"Leave him alone, Cody," Junior said. "It's too hot. They never let the caddies use the pool, any place, Howard. Walter was just saying that because they don't let Walter use the pool either, unless one of the men guests invites him or something, or it's in the morning before they open up. They don't do that anywhere. We're just niggers. Might make the water dirty or something."

"It's not fair," Howard said. "Nobody's even using it."

"They're probably afraid," Cody said. "They let one of us

use it, they'll have to let all of us use it, and then you'll get in there and try to beat off in the water with everybody looking at you."

"You shut up, Cody," Howard said, turning toward him. "You say something like that, I'm gonna kick the shit out of you."

"Yeah, Cody," Junior said. He tossed the cigarette into the shrubbery next to the porch. "Leave Howard alone. He's not doing anything to you. Just shut up, will ya? Or go home or something."

"He can't go home," Howard said. "His mummy's out selling her ass and his daddy's in his second childhood, chasing whores all over Boston. Little Cody hasn't got no place to go. That's what my father told me. He just gets dumped here every day all summer long until school starts again, and then she doesn't even have to dump him 'cause the bus comes by and picks him up along with all the other kids. Just like the garbage truck picks up the trash. The other trash."

Cody landed on the back of Howard's neck just as Riordan turned the green Fiat into the driveway. The two boys rolled down the wooden stairs, punching at each other, and landed on the pavement of the parking lot as Riordan stopped the car, got out, pulled a blue blazer from the seat and hurriedly put it on over the gun as he trotted toward them. Cody had landed on top and was pounding Howard's head on the pavement, while Howard yelled. Riordan grabbed Cody by the back of the neck and lifted him into the air, still swinging, and crying. Cody's lip was split. Howard's head showed blood and dirt matted in the hair in back under his cap when he sat up. "Jesus Christ," Riordan said, "what is it about me? Last night I walk into a fight and get the shit kicked out of me, and I get myself repaired and go off today thinking I'm gonna have a nice quiet lunch for myself at the country club and there's another fight going on. You guys want to grow up to look like me? That what it is? I think I'm going to go inside and tell the Bishop about you. He oughta know whom to speak to."

"Eat shit, mister," Howard said from the ground, crying. "Bishop Doherty's not coming today."

"He's not?" Riordan said. "Why?"

"I dunno," Howard said, sobbing. "I was in the pro shop and some woman called up and Walter talked to her and when he hung up, we were talking about letting the caddies use the pool on hot days like this when there's practically nobody here, and he said we couldn't even count on Bishop Doherty anymore. So I know he isn't coming either. He was supposed to play this morning."

"Oh my," Riordan said, releasing his hold on Cody. "Oh my, oh my, oh my." He turned away from the boys and started back to the Fiat.

"Hey, mister," Howard said. His face was still streaked with tears, but he had recovered from his crying. "What happened to you? Get in a fight with a garbage disposal or something?"

Riordan didn't answer.

The wooden doors of the Rectory of the Church of the Holy Sepulchre were open behind the screen doors. Riordan parked the Fiat in the driveway and climbed the steps. He knocked once, timidly. There was no answer. He opened the screen door and stepped in, closing it behind him. The fat honeybees circled the flowers along the stucco walls, and there were birds dancing on the lawn in the spray from the sprinkler system. He said, softly, "Mrs. Herlihy?" There was no answer.

Riordan cleared his throat loudly and walked down the hallway toward the study. The door was open. He made as little noise as possible. When he reached the study door, he rapped once on the frame. The bulldog, Spike, walked into his field of vision and stared at him. Then it turned away and walked out of his view. "Mrs. Herlihy?" Riordan said.

She answered in a dull voice. "Who is it?"

Riordan went into the study. She was sitting in one of the red leather chairs, absently scratching the dog's right ear. The dog contemplated Riordan as it sat down next to her. "Pete Riordan," he said. She looked at him as though she had thought it would be sufficient if the dog took care of such obligations for both of them. "Oh," she said, "yes. You."

"I," Riordan said, "I was supposed . . . we were supposed to meet for lunch at the club," he said. "Yes," she said. She returned her gaze to the fireplace. "He wasn't there," Riordan said. "They told me someone called this morning and said he wasn't coming." "Yes," she said, "I did." "I was worried," Riordan said. "I was afraid he might be sick or something."

"No," she said, "he isn't sick."

"No," Riordan said. "Well, is there, is there some trouble in the family or something? That I could maybe be of some help to him?"

"I suppose there's some trouble," she said. "In his family, I mean. That brother of his. There's generally some kind of trouble with him. Always has been."

"Well," Riordan said, "is that, is that where he is?"

"No," she said, staring into the fireplace and leaving the bulldog to make eye contact with Riordan. "No, he's not there. He's not anywhere. He's dead. He's with God. I guess. That's what he always said would happen. With God. Not here, though. Not here. Dead."

"Dead," Riordan said.

"Dead," she said. "He wasn't here this morning. He went out last night, late. He didn't tell me where he was going. He didn't even say good night. I was in my room. I heard him, the door shut. The car start. He was going to see his brother. That was what it always was, when he went out like that. He never said good night to me when he went to do that. Never told me. Knew what I would say. His brother was too much for him. I told him that. After his attack. Too much for him. Before, too. Always worried. Worried about his brother. Worried sick.

"I heard him come in," she said. "Switched on my light. It was after two-thirty. Heard him in the kitchen, getting something. Liquor. Left bottle out. Bourbon. Never drank that. I put on my robe, came downstairs. Peeked in here. He was sitting right in the place where I am now. Spike was sitting there. Father was crying. He was drinking and he was crying and talking to himself and drinking. I went back upstairs. This morning, not here. Knew he had golf. He didn't come down. Went up, knocked on his door. No answer. Called to him. Opened the door. He wasn't here."

"Where was he?" Riordan said. "Where did he go?"

"God," she said. "Said that's where he would go. Sooner, later. Suppose he did. Not here. Just what was left of him."

"His body was here?" Riordan said.

"Umm," she said. "In the bed. What was left of him. He shouldn't've been drinking. Doctor told him, told me. I told him. You. Your fault. And this business you and he had, whatever it was. Shouldn't've been doing that. He knew that."

"He seemed fine," Riordan said.

"Wasn't," she said. "Your fault, got him all excited like that. Made him think he was a young man again. He believed you. Wanted to believe you. Monsignor Fahey said that, this morning. Saw Father this week. Father bothered him. Acted strange. Monsignor Fahey said he was worried at the time. Said he should've said something to somebody. Maybe the Cardinal. Cardinal always had a way with him."

"Fahey?" Riordan said.

"Monsignor Fahey," she said. "Most Precious Blood. Only

friend he had. My sister's in that parish, she and her husband. I mentioned him once to Father. Father was in the seminary with him. He was a hero, you know. Father spoke very highly of him, what a trim figure he cut. I had to call somebody. Father didn't have many friends. Arrangements, you know. I couldn't make them."

"I didn't know," Riordan said.

"No," she said. "Lots of things you didn't know." She put her hands over her eyes. "You can go away now," she said. "You're finished here. Father's dead, and I'm all alone now. There's nothing more for you to do. I just hope you realize what you're doing."

Riordan did not say anything for a while. Then he said: "Yes. Most days, at least. Most days I think I know."

A Note on the Type

This book was set in Highland, a computer version of Caledonia designed by W. A. Dwiggins. It belongs to the family of printing types called *modern face* by printers—a term used to mark the change in style of type letters that occurred about 1800. It borders on the general design of Scotch Modern, but it is more freely drawn than that letter.

This book was composed by Science Press, Ephrata, Pennsylvania. It was printed and bound by R. R. Donnelley, Harrisonburg, Virginia.